I hope you enjoy!

Phoenix

Dixun Cui

Thank you to Allyn, Alex, Bernard, Eric, Rahulan, Steph, Shiv, Ilya, Angela C, Ryan, Catherine, Angela Y, Ian, Enshia for helping out

Special thanks to Brandon Liu for making the cover

Inspired by a 4chan greentext

Foreword

by Bigbelly Shaq

"Dearly beloved, we are gathered here today to get through this thing called life."

The first time I heard the quote, I didn't know any Prince songs. I didn't know who he was or what he did, aside from the fact that he was performing the Super Bowl halftime show.

But still, in the downpour of the Miami sky, those words stuck out to me in a way that I would never forget. And it was never the following statement, a statement about the afterlife, that I remembered. It was always the part about life. The part about how we were together in this battle against existence. If life is something that is so easily granted to all of us, then why is it such a struggle?

In a finite life, there only are so many journeys that one can undertake. A limited number of worlds one can experience. Lives one can meet. And with this finite nature of life, it's so easy to try to latch onto meaning, latch on to purpose. Perhaps this is what forms the basis of life. The struggle against the panic of death, in contrast with the desire to experience life.

And in a world with many flaws, it's hard to find faith, it's hard to look deep within oneself and find satisfaction, find a reason to hold on to dreams, to freely explore the world like one would like to. A broken justice system, that allows those in power to stay in power, while destroying the lives of those who do everything right, but make one small mistake. The uncaring lack of forgiveness that plagues all those who live, and still those who die.

A single story can never reveal everything. To some, it may not reveal anything. But in Dixun Cui's classic novel *Phoenix*, he shows exactly that. What does one story, one journey mean in the grand cosmos of our galaxy and in the eons of time that the stars have been around?

It's the journeys we remember, not the destinations. And to be happy and to find excitement is to live within the mirage of a joyous and plentiful journey. To forget about the pressures, the harms that live in the world around us. To trap oneself in a story, to be mesmerized by the factors at play. To let go of every other struggle, in order to feel the freedom that sprouts from a tale.

So sit back, relax, and hold on to this ride. You never know where it will take you.

With best regards,
Bigbelly Shaq

All events depicted in the novel are fictional. Some settings are based on real names but descriptions in the novel have no relation to actual settings. Events are also purely fictional and are not meant to be an accurate depiction of existence.

"If there is hope, it lies in the proles"
-Winston, 1984

0

I lay under the bridge, as I watched the young couple stroll along the pathway in the park. The lights and the stars illuminated them, as the man caressed the woman in his arms, giving her a kiss, as her blonde hair glimmered behind her.

"They were beautiful," I thought to myself. It felt as if in that moment I was free. Like I could drift away, never looking back, knowing that everything would turn out fine.

I reached over to what remained of my biscuits. Stale, but not bad. I ate them one by one, thinking about the couple I had seen. Were they married? How did they meet? I thought about the idea of being in love again. Did it happen to everybody? Maybe they were just lucky. Who knew?

I could hear their faint laughs as their silhouettes vanished into the distance, away from my sight. I finished the last of my biscuits and dusted the crumbs off my sweater. I rolled over, taking one last look at the stars. They were brighter than I had ever seen.

Dixun Cui

AUTUMN

1

I glanced out the window of our car, looking at the incredible palette of orange, brown, and yellow that masqueraded the branches and trunks of the trees alongside the road. The leaves were falling again, which meant that autumn was coming, but more importantly, it mean that I could see Angie again. I couldn't bear the excitement as I rode in the car on the way home. Though school had already started weeks ago, Angie was finally returning from an exchange program in Europe. We hadn't seen each other for months; she was getting home tonight; I couldn't wait to see her again.

"Mom, how much longer until we're home?" I asked, unable to bear the excitement.

"Half an hour or so," she replied, equally amazed by the vivid colours of the autumn leaves.

I turned the knob on the radio up, upon hearing a Fleetwood Mac song. It reminded me of the long drives I would take with my father back when he worked in a factory down in Jersey City. He would drive us down every other weekend to his small apartment that he shared with his co-workers. We would eat dinner with them, and my father would take me to an amusement park or a museum, happily buying me gifts and souvenirs. He would cherish the smile on my face whenever I got a new toy or later, a cool shirt. We would have fun, laugh together, and make memories that I would never forget.

I smiled thinking about those easier times. Things were different now, and we struggled, and although my father wasn't always in the picture, we still had our times. Though we couldn't afford lavish gifts anymore, mother and I still had the public park to go to, as well as the barbeques hosted by our church group.

We pulled into our driveway and I leapt out of the car, racing up the stairs to check my phone. Angie had called twice within the last hour. I quickly opened my phone and called her back.

"Angie?"

"Marcus!"

"When are you getting back?"

"My flight gets here at 4pm."

"Ok I'll head there with your parents to pick you up."

"See you then! Love you Marcus!"

"Love you too," I replied.

I always liked Angie's parents. They were supportive of us from the start and they were always flexible with what we did, so long as it didn't negatively affect our schoolwork. I had only seen them four or five times during the two years that we'd been dating, but their company had been nice every time we met.

I knew they would be open to taking me to the airport, and I figured I would ask them at church tomorrow morning. Feeling tired and not particularly hungry, I decided to unpack my backpack, and get ready for bed, looking forward to the moment I had been counting down the days until.

2

I walked into my church with my mother, and we made our way towards the right side of the room where we usually sat. Father couldn't make it again, being too sick from his drinking. We sat next to our neighbours, Mr. and Mrs. Wellington and their two kids, both younger than me.

"How has school been for you?" asked Mr. Wellington.

"Same as the usual. My teachers are alright, but it feels great being in my last year."

"That's good to hear. But don't go celebrating yet, you don't want to flunk out this close to the finish line."

I replied with a small chuckle. Our church was a small one, fitting around 200 people for mass, but it was a tight-knit community. We all knew each other, held gatherings together, and a lot of the kids went to school together.

The Wellingtons were particularly helpful to us when we were struggling a few years back when father lost his job when his plant closed. They covered our groceries, and were able to put my mother in contact with the job she's working in. I honestly don't know where we would be now, given my father's struggles, if we didn't have the support of the people of our church.

I glanced at my watch. Mass was starting in five minutes and I still hadn't seen Angie's parents. Just as I turned away from the entrance at the back and faced the stage up in front, Angie's father called to me.

"Marcus! Did Angie tell you about her flight?"

"Yes, sir, I'm really looking forward to seeing her again. It's been quite a while," I replied, gauging his reaction, worrying that I had been too direct.

"I'm sure you do. Do you want to come to the airport with us?"

"I would absolutely love to," I said, amazed that he had asked me.

"Alright kid, I'll come pick you up at 2 o'clock."

They went over and sat in the empty spaces in the back, as the pastor cleared his throat and began our prayer, signalling the beginning of mass. I still couldn't believe it. After an entire summer, I would finally be seeing my girlfriend later today.

3

We arrived at the JFK airport at 3:45, as Angie's father parked his car, and we walked out to the waiting area. We had stopped for burgers on the way to the airport, something that I now had so rarely that it felt like a delicacy to me. Angie's flight was on time, and she would be coming out to meet us soon.

"Thanks again for bringing me here, Mr. Williams."

"No worries Marcus. I'm sure Angie will be really glad to see you."

He paused for a moment.

"By the way, did she ever tell you how glad she was when you were chosen as captain for the team?"

I had never known before that she bothered with what I was doing with the soccer team. But I guess it wasn't a bad thing.

"No, I don't think so. But thanks."

At that moment, the announcement for her flight went off, and the sliding doors opened.

She walked out towards us in the front of the crowd. She was tanned, wearing a grey sweatshirt and sweatpants. She was never the most beautiful girl in the school, but she was pretty. She had short brown hair that reached just short of her shoulders, the way she always liked it.

She ran towards us almost losing her suitcase along the way.

"Mom! Dad! Marcus!"

She leapt into her mother's arms before hugging her father and coming towards me, giving me a kiss.

"Marcus it's so great to see you!"

"Come on Angie, we've got a surprise waiting for you in the car. And I think Marcus has something too," her mother said.

"What is it?"

"A surprise," replied her mother.

We reached the car, and her mother pulled out a wrapped box. Angie opened it, seeing a special made cake celebrating her return.

"Mother this is great! But didn't you remember that I don't like chocolate?"

"Oh, I'm really sorry about that," replied her mother, "I'm sure we could go get it fixed for you."

Angie had always been worried about her weight. She avoided sweets and other desserts. I had never really understood why. She was short and fairly thin, but her weight was something she had always worried about.

"Hey Angie, I got you something too," I said.

I took a small box out of my pocket, which contained a bracelet. It was made of glass and different jewels. It had been quite pricey for me; I had saved up the money I earned mowing lawns over the summer to pay for it.

"Oh my god Marcus!" she exclaimed. "It's beautiful!"

She leapt into my arms pecking me with kisses. I was glad she liked it. Seeing her happy made me smile.

We got into the car and began the drive back home. Along the way, she talked about her trip. She had visited Paris, Rome, and Barcelona, seeing various attractions, trying different foods and buying plenty of souvenirs. She talked about how gorgeous the views were, and how fresh the scenery and nature felt.

We arrived home, and Angie's parents dropped me off at my house. She kissed me goodnight, as they drove off.

I went upstairs to my room, my father once again passed out on the couch, as my mother called to me.

"How was it, Marcus?"

"It was fun. Seeing her again was great."

"Alright, just don't forget about what you have to do."

"Ok."

Mother was always concerned about my schoolwork. She was supportive of my dream of becoming a lawyer, but she was always adamant on me finishing my work so I could get a scholarship to university. She had felt a heavy burden with our recent struggles, and she hoped that I could bring our family out of it.

I went upstairs to my room, as I felt my phone buzz with a text message.

NYC tmw night? , Angie had sent. We loved to take trips to downtown New York along with other friends. We would drive through the streets, admiring the city views. Ridgefield had some nice scenery, but it was nowhere near the beauty of the city lights at night.

For sure. I replied.

I put my phone away and opened my computer, pulling up my English assignment on Romeo and Juliet. I finished the essay with a smile on my face, absolutely ecstatic that Angie was back.

4

I got to school early, having been lucky with the intersections I was crossing. It normally took 20 minutes to walk there, but when I didn't have to wait to cross, it could take less than 15. I walked into my English class which I had in the morning, where a group of my classmates were already there, planning how they would work on their presentation next week. My group didn't present until next month, so I never really worried about it.

I could distinctly overhear arguing from the group as I sat down and pulled out an Anthony Kiedis autobiography I had been reading.

"No, there's no way you're doing that part Sarah, your analysis was horrible. We can't risk being asked a question about it."

"But Francis, all you do is boss us around. What have you worked on?"

"Excuse me? I'm the reason this project is still afloat. Do you want to do well?"

Working with Francis in any project was like that. As much as I wanted to help Sarah, after four years of school with Francis, everyone knew there was no way around it. He would go to the teacher behind our backs, making complaints, and while never doing the bulk of the work, he would use his speaking skills to give the impression that he had led the team and should deserve credit for the work. Unfortunately, he seemed to always get what he wanted.

The first school bell went, signalling that classes would begin in five minutes. The rest of my classmates funnelled in, along with the English teacher, who also acted as Vice Principal of the school. It was a small town and because of that, teachers often had to double down on roles. He was a knowledgeable yet caring man who was always there to help us.

We discussed our interpretations of the second act of Macbeth, which we had recently read. I had felt that Macbeth killing Duncan and Banquo was something that would come again to bite him. People couldn't do such horrible sins and live unscathed.

Then we moved on to an article we had recently read, on magical realism, something I had looked forward to discussing.

"So," Mr. Thomas said, pacing around the room, "what exactly makes magical realism special?"

Francis' hand shot up immediately, like always.

"It's a complex juxtaposition of the real and the magical, combining the aspects to make a fantastical atmosphere."

"Right, Francis, but what makes it special?"

I thought about it for a second. Could it be the combination of aspects we didn't normally perceive, put into our daily lives?

The class sat silent.

Mr. Thomas began to speak again.

"It's because it captures what we desire, fantastical features that we only wish existed in reality. We dream to have those feelings, to encounter these myths, as we seek the magic that we long for in our lives."

The class remained silent, processing what he had just said.

"And with that thought, have a nice day," Mr. Thomas said, as the bell rang, signifying the end of class.

The rest of the day was bland. My other teachers weren't as pleasant, and the courses I had to take were often boring. Although chemistry and math had their interesting moments, the geography course I was taking was straight out boring.

At the end of the day, feeling sluggish from my courses, I took my time walking home. I didn't share any classes with Angie and she often had clubs after school, so I really only saw her when we met during our free time.

The path home was fairly straight. I walked down the main street of the town for around 20 minutes before turning onto a smaller street that led to my house. The walk along the main street passed most of the town; I went past the main supermarket, the recreational centre, as well as several parks.

Our town was quiet and I saw similar things every time I took the walk. The supermarket would be busy in the afternoon, with the parking lot of the market always being full of cars. The parks were quiet, mostly used by children accompanied by their parents or babysitters, and several seniors who strolled around walking their pets. The teens and younger adults didn't bother with the kids. We didn't care to mess with them like they do in the bigger towns. In such a small town, things mattered. If you did something to hurt someone, word could quickly spread and everyone would look at you differently.

I reached the end of the main street and turned onto a smaller street. This was a primarily residential area. The houses near the main street were larger, some with three garages. There would be people sitting on their porches, smoking, or tending to their plants. They were kind and often greeted me, asking how school was. I would tell them that it was going well.

I eventually reached my house, situated in a more run-down area of the neighbourhood. The outside of my house looked bleak, with withering plants that had become neglected. The pillars on our porch were rotting away, and the paint that covered the area had darkened from a solid white to being stained and worn down from the weather. My mother struggled to deal with these parts of our house. With our father unable to help, my mother had to work countless hours every day and she rarely had time to tend to our house.

I walked past the front door, left unlocked, and noticed that my father wasn't in his usual position passed out on the couch. His routines were largely predictable; he would lie on the couch, passed out drunk, for the majority of the day, only leaving to get something to eat from our fridge, or head to the corner store. It had been two years since he had been fired from his office job due to alcohol abuse. Though it was a struggle keeping him around, he was still our family's only hope of getting out of our situation and my mother couldn't bear letting go of him. We couldn't afford therapy, so all the support we got came from our church group. Though they were very generous and caring, he hadn't made any progress in dealing with the situation, making it more and more tempting for my mother to look for other solutions.

I went upstairs to my bedroom and began to do my homework, working through my geography questions about the divisions in the Middle East and the changing boundaries. Next was my math homework, before I finally did my chemistry work. My English teacher didn't give any work, which made it easier for me to finish everything before my friends would come around to pick me up to go to New York City tonight.

It was 8 pm when I finished my work, meaning I still had an hour before they came. I went downstairs, where my dad was stumbling around the kitchen.

"Sonny, did you see the jam?"

"Yeah, it should be right there on the counter."

I walked over to the counter, only to see the jar, smashed and lying on the floor.

"Hey Dad, look you probably knocked it over. But that was the last jar we had. We'll need to get more."

"I didn't do shit. I've never come close to the jar. Fuck this."

My dad promptly went back to his usual position on the couch, and slumped over on it. Neglecting his mistakes had become natural for father. He didn't worry about the struggles he would put us through, and he would even lash out at us when we did something that bothered him.

I cleaned up the broken glass, toasted myself a bagel, and went back upstairs, waiting for my friends to arrive.

5

Angie pulled into my driveway just as I stepped out of my house. With her were my friends Mark and Sally, another couple, who had only recently gotten together.

I got into the shotgun seat of the car, which they had left open for me. As we drove down the freeway we saw the beautiful city lights that illuminated our foreground. To me, the highlight of our trips down to New York was always the drives. In those moments, I felt like I could never be more in love. I felt youthful and happy and I looked over at Angie, smiling just as hard as I was.

We felt the chilly breeze blowing through our windows as we listened to Blondie, Angie's favourite band, playing from her speaker. The car was pretty old and the radio didn't work but regardless, we could always just play from our downloaded songs.

We drove by Rye Lake and looked at the glimmering lights on the horizon across the lake. It was magnificent and I felt infinite. Angie reached over and gave me a kiss as we sped along the empty road. The drive was over an hour long but it always passed by quickly with Angie at my side.

I remembered the words I had read in *The Perks of Being a Wallflower*, a book I had read in middle school. I truly felt infinite and nothing could ever diminish the love I had for Angie. I felt both powerful yet vulnerable, excited yet calm, but it felt like I had some sort of destiny, like some greater power was acting on me. The stars shone brightly and it was always the moments right before entering the heart of the city when the stars were the brightest.

The sky was pitch dark by the time we pulled into the parking garage on the outskirts of the Bronx that had become our getaway spot. We loved to climb to the roof and lie down, staring at the stars. We would talk about our lives, our futures. The view we had felt motivating; I truly felt that my dreams could be conquered and I longed for the day that I would look back at our midnight drives as the highlight of my high school life.

6

As I dozed off in the darkness lying on the roof of the lot, I suddenly found myself swimming in a large pool, feeling the cold water rush by me. I passed by several people in the other lane as I looked down at what seemed to be an infinite vastness that lay beneath me. I knew that the pool could only be so deep, but to me, it felt like so much more. I felt insignificant, tiny, as I allowed the pulses of the waves to flow past me.

I continued swimming, approaching the wall of the swimming pool. I flipped into my turn, seemingly suddenly remember the swimming skills I had learned in my childhood when I swam competitively. I pushed off the wall, floating silently from the momentum of my push, as I felt like I was sinking further and further into the water.

Suddenly I found myself out of control as the pressure from the water felt stronger and stronger. I could feel myself begin to tremble and tighten up. I kicked, I pulled as hard as I could but I could not resist the force pushing me downwards. I continued sinking, unable to breathe, as I turned around and saw what appeared to be a giant platform closing above me where the surface of the water used to be. The platform continued to shut, until it seemed to cover the entire surface of the pool, except for what seemed to be one golden circle away from where I was but within my reach. I tried to push against the force, trying to resist the unstoppable drag that was bringing me to my demise. I kicked and pulled but I was powerless, my drowning inevitable. I took one last look at the golden circle that represented the path out of the water and into the air where I could take one more breathe. My sight began to dim, the glow from the circle fading as I gave up, letting the chasm of force pull my limp body down. Was the circle really there?

7

I woke up as I felt Angie shaking my body.

"What time is it?" I asked her, seeing that the sky was all black.

"4 o'clock. We should head back now."

We drove down the streets of New York back towards Ridgefield. Suddenly as we were driving along a small street, I heard a loud yell from Angie as our car came to a sudden halt.

In front of us was a homeless man, around 50 in age. He had a large dirty beard, originally grey but tainted black with dust. He asked us for change, with a seeming desperation in his dark, haunting eyes. We tried to ignore him, as he walked around to the driver seat, frantically tapping on the window.

The time we spent waiting for the light to turn green felt like an eternity as we wanted to leave the man as soon as possible. He couldn't have been tapping the window for more than 10 seconds, but with Angie acting indifferent and me looking the other way, it felt as if we were being condemned, trapped, locked into a situation of both guilt and resentment. The light finally turned green, we raced past the man, and we never mentioned him again.

It was 7 in the morning when we got back to Ridgefield.

8

Living in a small town meant that although there weren't the most people around my age, everyone was close to each other. The gatherings were always fun; the best part was the parties that would happen Wednesday nights, where almost the entire school would show up. Wednesdays were always just a tradition; no one knew why but that was just how it was. Where the parties were always varied. This week, it was happening at my friend James/ house. We had been close since we were kids, and with his dad being a pastor, his parents always led events and activities at our church.

The afternoon of the party, Angie came and picked me up as the sun was just beginning to set. She was wearing a short black dress, something that she often wore at social events. I liked it and thought she looked great in it; her parents had gotten it for her birthday several years ago.

We drove and picked up Mark and Sally, who both lived between me and James. The drive was somber; we were all excited for the party, but after so many years of experiencing the same things that happened in Ridgefield, it was hard to feel energetic until we were there.

We pulled up into James' driveway a bit late, as the other cards were already there and the driveway was full. The street was dark, with the streetlight in front of James' house being broken. His house was fairly large but it was in a more isolated part of the town. Somehow in a town that was essentially in the middle of nowhere and so remote that we could only be identified as the small place a few hours away from New York, his house seemed to be able to find a place of darkness even in the vast nothingness.

We walked up the cracked stone steps leading up to his house, finding the door half-open with the blasting music seeping out of it. No one wanted to bother with greeting guests at the door, we all knew each other and it was incredibly tedious. We walked into the house into the pitch black living room, only illuminated by the disco lights coming from the room where the music was coming from. In the darkness I could make out shelves with childhood pictures, as well as various artifacts from the church; there were crosses hung up on the walls and a gallery of paintings of disciples. We went into his living room where people were dancing in the dark room.

"Hey guys!" I heard James call out.

His face was red, as he appeared to already by stumbling around from his drinks. Though the parents generally looked down upon drinking at parties, it was something that always happened; there would always be one kid who was able to sneak out some drinks. Even when caught, the parents often didn't mind. It was ironic, given all how religious James' parents were, but no one bothered to complain, and when we got to church, we all knew to act as if nothing was wrong.

"Why'd you guys show up so late? I didn't know that you could ever last that long in your car."

"Oh, fuck off," said Angie.

We went and grabbed some drinks, and before I knew it, the night became a haze. I vaguely remember a brief moment of bliss, feeling as if I was the champion at something but it was something that only drifted away and left my grip. I knew that I kept drinking as it was something that we always did. Soon, faces became blurs and voices became just a buzzing.

I felt like I was losing something, holding on to the last strings of where I used to be, as the lights flashing illuminated what looked to be the sky but I knew was simply the white-painted ceilings that existed in James' house. I felt spinning, my head dizzy, but I felt free and sick, all at once. What was my purpose? What was I going to do?

I walked around the room seeing other faces, other names, others who had always been doing the same thing as me but always envisioned themselves to end up somewhere entirely different. We were born and bred in such a time and we couldn't' do anything about it; I never asked to be born.

Stumbling around, I suddenly remembered vague moments from my childhood. The pieces felt like they were falling into place, like a jigsaw, but as the pieces fit together, the ones around it would drop off and fly away into this void of nothingness that drew everything in and never spit anything out. I saw two pieces join together, forming an image, only stop, split apart, get recycled, and form some other piece that would form connections, only to fall apart again and rejoin the nothingness that made up the basis of the existence we were stuck in.

I suddenly saw a young child, crying in his room, an image which switched into a teenager, driving with his friends, leading into an old man, walking along a park, seemingly waiting in a state of nothingness, anticipating his own death. Was that me? Did it matter? Who was I?

The questions I asked myself could never be answered. The only thing I knew was that I wouldn't know these answers. Then why did I ask them? I felt trapped again, yet free at once, falling apart yet holding together. But things couldn't possibly get worse, there was no point of worry, and all I could ask for was what was happening now.

It felt like ages until I found myself upon James' couch, feeling nauseous. I looked around me, observing the scene. I wasn't sober but at least I was aware. The room was a mess. There were food wrappers and cups littered everywhere. I noticed a particularly large bundle of taco wrappers; that must've been what caused my sickness. I pulled out my phone to check the time, but it was dead. I had forgotten to charge it before I left and I must have drained the rest of the battery in my stupor.

I felt a sudden rush of diarrhea as I continued to try to swallow the vomit I felt was going to spill out. I stumbled around, looking for a bathroom for what seemed like forever. I was too disillusioned to ask anyone, so I resorted to going around the house, banging on doors, looking for a toilet.

It seemed like the two bathrooms on the main floor were filled. Whether they were actually occupied I didn't know. They may have just been closets or laundry rooms.

I felt a sudden relief when I discovered a door that led to a flight of creaky stairs that led down into the basement into a ghostly large unfinished floor only made of dust and cobwebs. It was pitch black, but I had left the door leading into the stairs open so I could use the glimmers of light to locate a small bathroom that was around a corner from the staircase. I was getting sicker by the moment, so I picked up my pace, looking around frantically.

I walked in, turned the lights on (thank god it had lights) and went to the toilet, feeling a sudden rush of diarrhea pass through me. It felt relieving, even in the dire situation I was in. The basements in Ridgefield were rarely finished, with no one really having the need to put out the funds for the construction. My phone was dead so I had nothing to do as I waited for my stomach to relieve itself. I surveyed the room. It felt largely unused and it was small, mostly empty but with a bible resting on a old and cracked porcelain sink countertop. As I felt what seemed to be the last parts of my diarrhea pass through me, it felt relaxing and I felt normal, like I could think consciously.

As I got up to leave, in a state of joyous bliss of having my previous burden gone, I felt another sudden rush of sickness. My stomach growled, and I couldn't process what had happened when another rush of diarrhea came passing through. Then another. And another. And it kept going on, feeling like the peace I had been gifted with was being torn away.

Seconds felt like hours and minutes felt like days. To kill the time, I had picked up the Bible on the sink countertop, and was skimming its pages. When the diarrhea had finally come to a halt and the mess had already been made, I finally put the bible back down and got up to leave. I turned sideways, looking at the wall.

There was no toilet paper.

9

When I was growing up, my biggest fear had always been people. As a child, I remember playing at a park, only to run away when I saw a single person other than my parents approach the area I was in. My parents were supportive, with my father being employed and caring at the time. They didn't mind that I was scared of other people and just brought me to somewhere else to play. After all, in Ridgefield, there was always private space somewhere.

As the years passed on, things changed. As my father spiraled out of control, so did his temper, and as he yelled at me and belittled me for my fear of strangers, my mother could do nothing but follow along. The first times felt brutal; they forced me to be in areas with lots of other people. I felt threatened and exposed, feeling like I didn't belong. It was truly scarring, being forcibly thrust into what felt like deathly situations, with no possible form of escape and being stuck with an acceptance of my doom.

Things got better though, and as I made more friends, I learned to follow along with the crowd and interact with people. I went from playing alone, to having fun with friends, to going to parties with over 50 people. Though I had learned to interact with others, the scars I felt from my early tribulations remained.

I never thought that those isolating fears would ever return, let alone in an isolated room in the basement of the house of one of my best friends.

10

When I was done it looked like almost a quarter of the Bible was missing. The room was a mess; I didn't rip the sheets into uniform pieces and the crumpled up pages clogged the toilet, leaving my light brown diarrhea floating in the toilet bowl, almost reaching the top of the bowl. Inside I could corn pellets, fixed in a macaroni-like sludge. Other sheets of the Bible were flung around the room, which I had thrown in frustration when I couldn't rip out the pages neatly. There was no garbage bin, so the most I could do was throw the sheets into the bowl and hope that it flushed; it didn't, and I was left with a mess of diarrhea and paper sticking out of the toilet.

I tried to calm down and wash my hands, but I couldn't. I was shaking non-stop out of fear, shame, and worry and I couldn't bring myself to leave the room. Upstairs, the sounds of the music had long stopped and I could hear sounds of cars leaving, signalling that it was time for James to start cleaning up the house.

I tried to calm down and consider my possibilities. Could I run out, make up an excuse for why I hadn't left yet, and never bring up the bathroom, hoping he would never figure out who did it? That was a possibility. But how would I leave? His house only had one entrance, as far as I knew. I would have to wait until his family was asleep.

I settled down, sitting on the bathroom floor. It couldn't have been a minute when I heard footsteps coming downstairs.

The steps got closer, as I felt myself shrivel up and tremble with fear.

Closer.

And closer.

And closer.

"James, is that someone in the bathroom?"

"Not sure Mom, no one except for us typically uses it."

"Go and check."

I knew I was dead as he started knocking on the door.

"Hello?"

"Open up."

"I'm going to open the door if you don't say anything."

I opened my mouth but words couldn't come out.

I braced myself, as the door flung open and the two of them stood at the doorway.

"WHAT THE FUCK! MARCUS! WHAT THE FUCK HAPPENED."

His mother let out a piercing shriek and hysterically broke down into tears.

"WHAT THE FUCK DID YOU DO?" he said, looking at the torn up Bible pages across the room and the mess of paper and diarrhea that filled the toilet bowl.

"I-I- had to"

I hadn't finished my sentence when he swung a fist at my jaw as I fell over onto the sink.

"That was from my grandmother. My grandfather gave it to her before he had gone off to war," his mother said quietly in the midst of her tears.

"Get the fuck out of here," James said, holding his mother in his arms.

"I-I-I'm sorry," I mumbled.

"GET THE FUCK OUT."

I stumbled out of the bathroom, went upstairs, and left the house as quickly as possible. I went out to the driveway, noticing that Angie was already gone.

I had no ride home, my phone was dead, and ridiculing the idea of asking James, I began to walk in the direction of my house.

I was alone.

11

I lay in my bed at night staring at my ceiling. What was going to happen to me? I thought about myself as a kid. Once, I had wet myself at church. Scared of the shame of walking me through the aisle with my pants dripping my wet, my mother covered it up and waited until we were the last ones left so that we could leave in silence.

I tried to reason out what would happen. Sure, James' mother probably had a talk with him and I won't be surprised if he never talks to me again. But I knew James for years; I doubt he would do anything much beyond that punch he gave me.

But what if he did? No. He couldn't.

What if he told everyone else? No, no one would do that. That would just be embarrassing for everyone.

You let a kid wipe his ass with a Bible? You're just as dumb as him. I could already hear Francis' voice mocking James in my head. James couldn't possibly do anything that bad.

I was going to be fine. Everything was going to be alright, I told myself.

12

I had always been a responsible kid and was rarely late for anything. My walks to school were consistent; I knew that if I left home by 8:10, I would get to class on time.

I woke up Thursday morning and went downstairs when I realized that the previous night, I hadn't cleaned my clothes. We couldn't afford to use too much electricity so my mother had decided to pawn off our washing machine. Everything was done by hand now for us and I was responsible for my own clothes. I would always wash my clothes the night before wearing them, so that they were cleanest when I wore them.

On my coach lay the clothes I had worn the previous night; a black sweater with a pair of jeans, stained from the drinks I had the night before.

There was no way I could show up to school in those again. My mother wasn't home as she was working.

"Dad, do you know if I have any spare changes of clothes?"

I didn't hear a reply from anywhere inside the house. I frantically began to look around. My house was always a mess; my parents were both unorganized and with my father being the way he was, you could never know where things ended up. I went back upstairs to my bedroom and into my barren closet, where under the small pile of clothes, I found a white shirt that was somewhat clean. I quickly put it on and spotting a pair of grey sweatpants, I put them on and began to head to school.

By the time I had gotten downstairs, I went right to the door, not looking past a corner when I bumped into my father,

"Why did you yell at me?"

"I'm sorry Dad, I was looking for my clothes and I wanted to see if knew where they were."

"You're seventeen. That's your fucking job."

""I'm sorry Dad, it won't happen again."

He took a step closer to me, with a menacing glance in his eyes. His sweater was long and baggy and it felt like the extra space his loose clothes took up only made him more terrifying. I felt trapped as I slowly inched back as he came closer to me. I never knew if he actually meant what he said. There were times when I would find out he was legitimately angry. There were others when even he couldn't remember what he had said.

"That's all you ever say. You always do the same shit over again. Can't you see that you're a pain in the ass for me? Your mother is an absolute mess now. It's all because of your nagging."

I began to feel myself turn red with anger from his accusations.

"You're just going to stand there with your mouth open like a little bitch? That's all you are. People just shit on you and you just take it like the sissy that you are."

I tried to remain calm and defuse the situation. I couldn't risk getting into another altercation, especially now.

"Dad, I'm just trying to get to school, I'm going to be late."

"Fuck off."

"Dad, could you just –"

He slapped me across the face, as I stumbled over, my backpack weighing me down.

"Oh fuck! Why are you always like this!" I exclaimed, now furious with anger. "You're the piece of shit that's fucked us all up. You just can't admit that it's your lazy ass that's destroyed us."

"What the fuck did you call me? Get over here. I'm going to beat your ass. You pathetic little shit."

He began to stride towards me again, looking more red than I was.

"You ungrateful little bitch," he said as he came closer and closer to me, as I became backed up against a wall.

I braced myself in front of his gleaming eyes with a terror that could only be seen in a loved one who was only a shadow of who they were before. I remembered all the times we had when he had a functional life, and thinking about the moments only made me long for them more. He was a mess, but he was still my father.

He took another swing at me, which I anticipated and ducked under. Seeing my chance, I grabbed my bag and ran out of the door.

"I'll deal with you later," he said to me, as I frantically ran away from the house.

It was 8:30 by the time I left.

13

I walked into my first period English class 10 minutes after class had started, completely sweaty from what felt like a marathon that I had ran to get to school. I quietly sat down, trying not to disrupt the class. I sat down and pulled my chair in, noticing that the chair slid smoother than normal. I looked down, and saw a blank sheet of lined paper under my chair, so I reached down and pulled it out, turning it over to see what was on the other side.

SHIT. HOLE.

I turned around to look around. Edward, who was sitting behind me gave me a dirty glance. I turned over to the left look at Ashley. She gave me a glare, then turned away. All around me people were giving me smirks and stares, like I was some outsider who had walked into the wrong class.

"Marcus are you still there?" Mr. Thomas had noticed that I not writing down notes.

"Yeah, I'm fine," I replied.

Edward suddenly got up and pushed his chair back, making a loud grinding noise.

"Mr. Thomas, I need to change seats," he exclaimed loudly. "It looks like Marcus pissed all over himself too."

The class burst into laughter as I got up to defend myself.

"Edward, what in the world are you –

I hadn't finish my sentence when I was suddenly hit in the face by what felt like a brownie, coming from across the room. I turned red with anger and frustration as the class's laughter continued to roar.

"Marcus, is there an explanation for all this?"

"No sir, everything is fine."

I sat back down and put my head in my arms.

Edward bent over and leaned in to my ear.

"This is just the beginning, shithole," he whispered.

I couldn't control myself as I began to feel tears well up in my eyes and dampen my arms. It was the first time I that had cried in an eternity.

14
What was going to happen to me?

I had no idea how news had spread and how everyone knew about what happened. What did they know? How did they find out? What was going to happen?

I thought back to last night. What could I have done? My phone was dead, no one could've heard my yelling. Maybe I should've ran out before James came downstairs. What then? Maybe he would eventually find out. But why? Why me?

It was a load of bullshit. Why did these things have to happen to me? I did everything right. One bad night and a bunch of dumb crap and I was suddenly the biggest joke in the school. I thought about the brownie that hit me. I didn't even know who threw it. And Edward? I never knew he was that kind of asshole. Fuck these people.

If God is so great then there must be a plan for me. I doubted it but I still believed. There had to be some stupid reason why this was happening to me. But why? I did everything right. Good grades, I helped others and suddenly all this dumb crap was happening to me.

I didn't feel like the same person I had been a week ago. Or even yesterday. Or even right before I went into that bathroom. How come you can do something right all your life and one load of crap comes and everything falls apart? It's like everyone only judges you based on that one thing that they hear about. And no one hears about all the good things people do, only the dumb crap that makes stories and gossip.

I thought about all my dreams and aspirations. I wanted to get out of this town. I wanted to become a lawyer, I was going to help my mother get out of all this too. I would buy her a nicer apartment in the city, or maybe a house down in Florida. She liked the warm weather. Could I still do it? I had to hang on. For her.

15
Class finished and I heard the bell ring.

My head had been in my arms for a good part of an hour, which felt like a decade As I finally lifted my head out of my arms, I looked around hazed, seeing what had gone on during class. The board was blank and most of the other students were already gone, even though the bell had just rang.

I noticed something on the chair on front of me. It was another sheet of paper, taped to the back of the seat in front of me, placed knowing that I was going to see it.

CRYBABY SHITHOLE

I slowly got up, not even reacting to the sheet of paper, almost like I had expected it. I got up to grab my backpack, but upon putting my hand around the handle, I only felt a moist and slimy substance. I looked at my now brown hand. It was chocolate syrup, and it had been dripped all over my backpack. The previously blue bag was now stained brown, and the smell of chocolate reeked from it. As I looked up I caught another set of words written on the side board, which was normally used for showing our homework assignments.

SATANIC PUNK

No one could've written that in the moments between the bell ringing and me lifting my head. That meant that it happened before, that someone had gotten up in the middle of class just to write those things so I would see them. Did Mr. Thomas really not care?

I got up to leave, feeling destroyed and lost within. I walked in the hallway, towards my next period chemistry class. As I walked through the hallway I felt a dead silence. It was like the other students were all turning to look at me.

I downplayed it to myself. There was no way they all knew about what happened. I continued to walk with my head down, ignoring the dirty glares I was getting.

I thought to myself,

Ignore them. This isn't about you. Keep walking.

It was like I had escaped from the prison, like I was free, until I reached the end of the hallway and suddenly felt another brownie stuffed into my face, up close.

The entire hallway burst out laughing.

I looked up to see who had done it.

It was Francis.

Of all people, the kid who seemed to only care about his marks, about doing better than other people. This motherfucker finally decided to get into it.

"Really Francis, you?"

"What the fuck are you gonna do about it, shithole?"

"Don't fucking call me that."

"What are you going to do about it? Shithole."

It felt like a crowd had gathered around us, people stepping to Francis' side.

"Francis, you don't want to–

I felt another brownie hit me in the face. He had pulled it out of a bag.

The entire hall burst out laughing.

I hunched over, looking at the ground. What was I to do? I was red with anger. I tried to compose myself.

I lifted myself back up, seeing that there was no way for me to leave. I knew class was going to start to but it seemed like that didn't matter to anyone here, all they cared about was my mockery.

"Francis, just move out of the way, I just want to get to class."

"Not looking like this. I'm not gonna let you get away from this. Satanic devil-worshipping shithole. You're big daddy can't help you now.

I lost it.

"Oh, fuck you Francis, you pussy ass bitch. All you do is shit on people and you're a piece of crap and you'll rot in hell and –"

"Oh you're calling me the piece of crap?"

The entire hallway burst into laughter and the crowd seemed larger than it was before.

I turned red with embarrassment.

"How would you like some of this?"

He pulled out a bottle of chocolate syrup and dumped it on me.

The crowd lost it, laughing hysterically.

I looked at Francis. His smug grin. The menace in his eyes. He loved every moment of this. He was a coward who rose up whenever it meant putting someone down and boosting his reputation. He wanted to see me embarrassed, ridiculed, and with every laugh, he only felt better about himself.

"What now, shithole?"

I couldn't take it.

I threw him a punch that connected with his jaw. And another.

I lashed out at him in a flurry of punches that felt like an absolute blur. I felt consumed, like I was bottled up, and I was finally letting it go. I didn't stop. I kept swinging, thinking fuck you, fuck you, fuck you, he was up against the wall and his nose had been bloodied but I kept going and going and going and I saw him on the ground in a sprawl. I felt arms on my back and hands around my shoulders, my legs, pulling me back but I couldn't stop. I kept swinging at him, his face, his chest, his torso, consumed by my rage, almost feeling justified in what I was doing. It was worth it, I didn't give a fuck what happened, he was a little bitch, he deserved it, it was right, he was getting what was coming, he should've seen it coming, this was just for him.

His face was a bloody pulp by the time someone tackled me and flung me aside. I lay on my side, in blankness, staring at my bloody hands as I heard the yell of Mr. Thomas running over, having heard the commotion.

I was frozen in shock, as I gave an empty glare at the wall in front of me, indifferent to what felt like a mountain above me, pinning me down.

"What happened here?" exclaimed Mr. Thomas.

Everyone was too shocked to respond.

Francis lay on the ground with a crowd around him, blood leaking onto the floor.

What had I done?

16

I was in Mr. Thomas' vice principal office with my head in my arms, worried about what was to happen next.

Mr. Thomas was pacing around the room in silence, preparing what he was going to say. He had phoned my parents but both were unable to come in.

"Marcus, I know you're a good kid, but –"

"It wasn't my fault! Did you see what they did during class?"

"I know Marcus, " he replied. "But what you did after was unacceptable either."

"What could I have done?"

I was flabbergasted. I really had no choice, and he had just been watching them torment me.

"Well you could've talked to a teacher or –"

"Really?" I exclaimed, beyond angry. "You sat there in your class watching them write shit on the board?"

"Excuse me?"

"Could you really have helped me!"

"Watch yourself."

"You don't give a crap!"

"You weren't even paying attention in my class. How dare you!"

I sulked back as his face turned more red than I had ever seen. He was pacing around almost frantically.

"You're disrespectful and if I had any sympathy for you it's gone now."

I sat back down, not realizing that in my anger, I had stood up to meet him eye to eye.

"We're going to expel you."

"What?" I exclaimed, once again standing up.

"No, you can't do that. What about Edward, what about Francis? They started it."

"I'm sorry, you were the cause and it's now clearly a distraction. It's just as hard for me, trust me."

I found myself full of rage. The school didn't care about the kids who tormented others day in day out, but once a god damn honour roll kid gets shit on and defends himself, he gets expelled.

"No! That's bullshit. I do my damn work every day, I do well on tests, this crackheads just screw around all day and I'm getting expelled? Why not just a suspension. One week."

I tried everything I could. If I was expelled my life was over.

"Listen, Marcus. I know you're a good kid but –"

"If I'm a good kid then let me stay!" I yelled, in utter disbelief of what he was saying.

"I can't. I'm not going to argue this anymore."

"No!" I exclaimed, finding myself bursting into tears. I began to pant and found myself hysterically wandering around the room, like a chicken without a head, almost like I was grabbing something I could hurl. Anything.

"No you can't do this. Please. One chance. This is the first time ever. It won't happ –"

"No," Mr. Thomas said firmly giving me a glare. "I'm sorry. Leave."

I stood in silence trying to process what had happened, looking frightened, into his eyes.

There was no going back. It was over.

I gave him one last glare, one last look, hoping he would sense some pity and go back on his decision.

I picked up my bag and walked out of the school, tears in my eyes.

I continued to hear jeers, even as I was leaving.

Hey look, the shithole's crying now.

Well fuck you too.

17

I began to walk home, still shocked about what had happened. As I walked it seemed like my surroundings felt so much more transcendent before. Like I was in some dreamlike state. I looked at the playgrounds I used to go to back when my family was functional.

Back when I had a family.

As I continued walking it felt like everything was brighter. LIke there was some sort of glow I couldn't escape from. It was almost piercing.

I continued to walk but I began to feel a haze, like a bright light shining in an operating room moments before the anesthesia kicks in. I began to feel dizzy, sick, and I felt like I was toppling over. I continued to stride along but I couldn't. I felt myself topple over in a bright blinding light just as I managed to bring myself to sit down on a curb.

I felt like I was falling.

Falling.

Down.

Down.

down

I fell into a dream. Or was it a daydream? Did it exist?

It was one of my happier times

I was a kid riding in my dad's van, cruising down a highway next to a lake. It was chilly outside and I felt the breeze from the open window flow by. I couldn't have been over 6 years old but I was riding shotgun in the truck, listening to a rock album that my dad had introduced me to. Outside I could see the trees and rocks, giving me a mellow yet nostalgic feeling. It was calm and the highway was empty and it was just us. Just my Dad and I. Us and the world.

We pulled into a beach that was made up of a dock with an office shack. It must've been early autumn, because with the temperature, there wasn't really anyone in the water. There were other kids playing on the beach and adults reading, talking, and preparing food. My dad took me over to the shack, where we rented a small motorboat.

Boating had always been a hobby of my father's. His father before him used to take him out on a canoe he had owned, and as I got older, my father took me on more and more trips. It was a great bonding experience; sometimes we would fish, but other times we would just relax out on the open water.

A motorboat was always a treat. It meant that my father was in a good mood, or it was just a tiring day. The breeze felt while riding the motorboat was relaxing and it was incredible enjoying the serenity of the lake. Being in a motorboat also meant we could go out far, knowing that it would only take minutes to come back. We would go out to distances that felt like miles away from the beach, where the beach was only a golden-brown block and the people were only specks. Like dots on a page..

We were out on the lake when my dad asked me,

"Marcus what do you want to be when you're older."

"A fireman."

"Why do you want to be a fireman?"

"Because I want to save people and help people."

"Being a fireman is hard, you know. It's not a job everyone can do."

"What do I need to do?"

"There's lots of tests you have to do. Body tests and thinking tests. Most people can't be a fireman."

"Do you think I can be a fireman?"

"I'm not too sure if you can. It'll be really hard though. As of now I don't think you can, you're not nearly smart or tough enough."

I thought about it for a second. Why did my dad tell me I couldn't?

"Oh. What can I be then if I can't be a fireman?"

"Why can't you be a fireman?" he asked, confusing me. What did he mean? He had just told me I couldn't be one.

"Because you told me I can't."

"And you're going to give up?" he replied. "Just because I said that you couldn't?"

I looked at him in silence.

"Don't let anyone shut down your dreams, not even me. Come on kid, let's head back to the beach."

We rode back towards the beach, stopping around 15 yards out, where the boat couldn't go any further.

"Hop out kid, I'll go and return the boat."

I jumped into the water. It was shallow enough for me to walk, as I lunged back to the beach. Seeing other kids around, I found an area where no one was and began to build a castle.

I started off with a wall. At the corners I put towers, just small bumps where I told myself I would build more on later. The castles I built were always rectangular, like the ones in the tv shows and books. Often I would build them with my father and at the end of the day, when it was time to go home, he would have to drag me away in tears, not wanting to leave my creation.

I moved into the center of the walls I had built. Just as I began to pill sand into what would be the king's chambers, I felt a block of sand hit me on the back. I turned around to see what it was, as two teenagers ran towards me, throwing sand on my face. I fell down, wincing in pain from the sand entering my eyes. I called out for my dad.

"Dad! Help!"

I heard no response, as I slowly got up, only to see the teenagers kick down my castle.

"Loser!" they yelled, proceeding to kick down my walls, laughing at the destruction they were doing to a young kid's creation.

I felt helpless, as I looked around, seeing other parents and adults watch with indifference, as I started bawling, just as the teenagers began to jog away from what was left of my castle.

Just as they began to get away, I heard a thunderous yell.

"Hey! You! Get back here!"

I saw my dad, almost a hundred yards away, sprinting like a madman.

I ran across the beach faster than I had ever seen, giving chase to the teenagers.

He didn't stop, he kept running, but the teenagers were already too far away.

When he realized his chase was fruitless, he stopped and let out a thunderous yell, as I continued bawling.

"You fuckers! I'll kill you!"

His voice felt like a boom, one that everyone heard and stopped. The beach was dead silent, as everyone who was there turned and looked, at a man, who was doing his best to protect his son. A man who would do anything for the one thing that truly mattered to him. His family.

In the dead silence my dad came over, picked me up, and carried me in his arms as we went back to his van and drove away. His grip gave me a presence that seemed to just ease any pain I felt, I could relax and stop crying, knowing that my father was there.

I didn't know it at the time but it was the first time I had heard my father swear. I never saw his rage as a foreshadowing of what he would eventually become; I only saw him as someone who do anything for those he loved. Someone I could count on to support me.

Someone to support me when no one else would help.

That was what I needed.

Support.

Angie.

I still had Angie.

18

I picked myself up from the sidewalk and began to hurry home, anxious to call Angie. She would be there for me, I thought. She could help me, and things would turn around. All I needed was several witness for the school to realize that punching Francis was a fluke, a once in a lifetime mistake that was never going to happen again.

I went straight to my phone once I got home, dialing in Angie's number, which I felt was right at my fingertips, dialing instantly.

Three rings later, no response.

I put the phone down, realizing that she was likely busy with either work or something from church.

I decided to wait before calling her again.

I sat on my bed and picked up the book I had been reading, when I heard a sudden shout come from the living room, as I heard the front door open and slam shut.

"Marcus?" I heard my mother say.

"Yeah?" I replied, unaware that the school had already told her about what had happened.

She walked into my room, absolutely red with anger, shutting the door behind me and giving me a menacing stare. My mother was rarely ever angry, only when she was exceptionally stressed, but even in this situations, nothing ever came close to the look she was giving me.

"Marcus, what were you thinking?"

"Mom, it was an accident I –"

"I DON'T CARE THAT IT WAS AN ACCIDENT"

"Mom please I can explain"

"Do you know what this means?"

She gave me a solemn glance, almost of pity but in a way that made it seem like she was the one at fault. She burst into tears bending over and as I went over to embrace her, she cast me aside, leaving me feeling horrible, guilty, and full of shame.

"Mom, I'm sorry." I said knowing it was beyond repair and there was nothing I could do.

She looked up at me as if to say something, but decided not to, and quietly walked out of the room. I stood where I was, dumbfounded, stricken with grief, wishing I could somehow reverse all this.

All because of a dumb shit.

19

I had been sitting in my room, staring outside the window for hours until I decided to call Angie again.

Three rings.

And then her voice.

"Angie?"

"Sorry I'm busy right now."

"I really need you right n–"

She hung up and all I heard were beeps.

What had I done?

The possibilities began to spiral in my head. What if Angie left me? She was all I had left.

No, I told myself. We had promised to each other. She just didn't understand what was happening.

I picked up the phone and called her again.

"What do you want, Marcus?"

"I really need to talk to you."

"I told you already, I can't right now."

"Please, Angie," I begged her. "Did you hear about what happened?"

"Yea, I heard."

"Angie, I need you right now."

"What the fuck Marcus. What do you think we are?"

I was shocked. I couldn't believe it. After all that we had done together, this was how she was going to be?

"What?" I replied, dumbfounded.

"Marcus I'm not gonna put up with your shit."

"But Angie! We promised each other. We'd be there. No matter what."

"Yeah, but that was before you decided to be the biggest fuckup in the school. No way I wanna be known as that dumb chick who decided to fuck with the satanic dick at our school. We're done."

"No, Angie," I said, trying to reason with her. "I'll fix it. Don't worry."

"Fix what? You haven't even apologized to me. I'm the one who's been stuck going around fixing things, telling people I had nothing to do with it. You're an embarrassment, and I never knew you."

I thought about everything we had done together. The midnight New York City drives. The calm nights we would spend lying next to each other in the park, feeling like it was us against the world, that nothing else mattered.

And I lost it, realizing that it was something this dumb that would end it.

"Oh, fuck you Angie. I should've known it from the start. You're just an attention-seeking whore. I never should've done any shit for you. Ever."

"Well you're the one who's fucked up now. Go away and don't talk to me again. I still have work to do and a career to follow. You're the eternal fuckup."

With that she hung up.

I wanted to cry but I couldn't bring myself to do it. I didn't even feel empty or saddened, only enraged. As if I had seen this coming.

I should've seen this coming.

20

The playground wasn't always so sparse like it was these days. Back then, the graffiti wasn't there, the cracks in the concrete seemed not to show, the playground had a vibrant gaze to it, a feeling of liveliness.

As a fourteen year old there was nowhere better to play. Long gone were my days of bad social anxiety and it seemed to be a celebration everytime I went to the playground.

It was also where I met Angie.

As a pretty active kid, grounders was always my expertise; something I could always win in, regardless of how I was feeling or the conditions of the day.

The game was simply: the person dubbed "it" would try to tag the others, while only being allowed to open their eyes when on the ground. If they wanted to climb onto anything they'd have to close their eyes.

One day I went to the playground, the summer before the start of high school. August was nearing its end and it had already started to cool down, with leaves blowing in the wind.

I walked to the park in the afternoon around 2:00, the same time that my friends always went on Fridays. A group was already there, waiting for the rest of us.

Once we had all showed up, we began to play. I went to my usual position: the playground was made up of a castle-like structure, with three large tower-like domes, each one larger than the next. The third-highest tower on the side of the playground was always my go-to spot; it was tall enough that no one could catch me with their eyes closed, but it was low enough that I could feel comfortable up there.

I sat there as we played, by-passing three rounds without ever coming close to being caught. Everyone knew that I always went up there but no one bothered to climb it with their eyes closed.

By the time the third round had finished the crowd had gathered to become much bigger. Not only were there almost 30 kids, playing, there were others sitting on the park bench or under trees, watching the rest of us frolicking.

I climbed down from my spot and joined the rest of the group as we decided who was going to be "it" next.

As we we spun a bottle as we stood in a circle, the custom we followed, someone said out of nowhere:

"Marcus, can you climb to the tallest tower?"
I froze for a second. The third tower was easy and i could easily climb it but the tallest one was something that I had never attempted before.

Before I could say anything a chant had begun.

"Do it! Do it! Do it!"

I stood there, red in the face, scared of trying it but feeling as if I would be a letdown if I didn't try it.

"Ok. I'll try," I said, as the group burst into applause.

I walked over to the base of the structure and steadied myself. First there was the regular platform up above, that we would walk upon. That was an easy climb. I jumped up and grabbed the top of the handrail along the edge of the platform, locking my feet on the gap between the handrail and the bottom. With my feet locked in, I heaved myself up, bringing one leg, then another, over the handrail and onto the platform.

Now came the hard part.

On the four corners of the platform were four beams going upwards, around 10 feet up, with a pyramidal roof on the top. That was where I had to go.

I knew that standing on the top of the handrail, I wouldn't be able to reach the top of the roof and propel myself upwards, the way I would climb the lower tower.

I had to climb the beam itself.

I readied myself, took a deep breath, and stood up onto the handrail, the grow of kids clapping and cheering me on.

"Let's go Marcus!" "You can do it!" I heard, along with the occasional "Don't kill yourself!"

Fuck, if I didn't want to kill myself why did I attempt this.

I grabbed onto the beam. Feeling the friction between my hands and the beam, hoping the friction would be enough to keep me on the beam. I propped my legs around the beam, taking a deep exhale.

Here we go.

I inched my hands up slowly, following upwards with my legs. At first it felt fine. It was going to be over soon. I continued to inch myself up until around 8 feet off the ground.

"Marcus I love you!"

I turned and looked, suddenly seeing the crowd of kids, now seemingly far below me. I traced the origin of the voice, looking towards the right side of the crowd.

Standing there was a short girl with blonde hair, wearing a puffy light green jacket. She was pretty, with a charming glow in her eyes and a smile on her face. I didn't particularly know her; I felt like I had seen her around with other girls but she didn't go to my elementary school.

Suddenly I felt like I was trembling, at the sight of the ground below me, and the captivation I felt from seeing the girl. Maybe it was just my hormones, a teenage thirst acting up but I felt tingly, engaged, like I was doing something of god-like significance in front of a girl I thought I had now adored.

I took a deep breath, and while shaking, I inched my way up.

What if I fell down the beam?

No way I could do that, it would make me a disappointment.

Up.

Up.

The roof was almost within my reach now and though my legs were slipping and my hands were sweaty, I knew I was almost there. I continued up and up and up.

The roof was now in my reach and I put my hands over the top, letting out a gasp of relief. I pulled myself over to a roar of applause from the rest of the kids.

I took a deep breath, admiring the view from the top. I had done it, something I never thought was possible. I felt relieved and accomplished, as I began to head down from the tower. I placed my feet on the handrail, stepped onto the platform, and jumped down onto the ground.

I was greeted with cheers and high-fives as I walked towards my friends, feeling like I had broken down some immovable obstacle, something to be revered. Time had passed by quickly, and it was already getting dark, signalling it was time for everyone to go back to their homes.

As the crowd dispersed, I found myself walking home, tired, yet with a sense of accomplishment and proud of myself. As I walked

I heard a call, and the same pretty blonde in the green jacket came running up to me.

"Hey Marcus!" she called, as she ran up to me.

She was even prettier up close, with her glowing brown eyes imprinting a softening glare.

"I haven't really seen you around but I think you're pretty cool," she said to me.

Glad about the compliment but shocked at how blunt she was, I replied solemnly.

"Thanks."

"Where are you going for high school?"

"Harvey Clemson Secondary."

"Oh wow that's cool! I'm going there too!"

I felt glad, almost relieved, knowing that I would at least know this girl for the next few years.

"What's your name, by the way?"

"Angie. Everyone thinks it's short for Angela but it's not, it's just Angie."

"That's a cool name."

"Anyways, I've got to go home now, but I think you're pretty cool doing what you did. Hope to see you at the park again sometime."

And as she said that, she trotted away, leaving me stunned yet also glad. She was so pretty, but I hardly knew her. Still, I felt a tingle, like I was attracted to her already, like she could be that puzzle piece in that teen romance that everyone so drastically seeks.

That was the first time I met Angie.

What if I didn't make it to the top?

Would I have still met her?

Maybe I would've been better off falling off the beam.

I wish I had never met that bitch.

21

I sat in my room, alone. I looked around my room, at the certificates hanging on the wall, the awards I had gotten for character trait recognition, the awards I had gotten for my achievements. My young lawyers' conference plaque. My English award.

Was all this going to just be wasted?

It's like I could do all this, go through all this, do well in everything, and at the end, just get kicked off the giant mountain I was climbing.

But even if I fell, how could I fall all the way down?

I couldn't.

Who cares if I didn't have a high school diploma? I could go get a job now, and who knows, maybe I'll even be ahead. Not that many people went to college anyway.

I would fix this, I could fix this, I told myself.

Oh, how wrong was I.

22

Two rings and I finally heard a voice.

"Hi, this is Principal Louden speaking."

"Hi Mr. Louden, this is Marcus I —"

"No, Marcus, we're not going back on our decision."

He didn't even hear what I wanted to say.

"No, please, just listen –"

"You heard me the first time Marcus. I'm going to hang up."

"This is bullshit! I didn't –"

"Marcus, goodbye. This should be the last –"

"No! Fuck this shit!" I yelled, losing control, frustrated. He wouldn't even hear me out on what I had to say. "Just please let me explain!"

In all honesty, I was shocked he let me finish my sentence.

I wasn't shocked at his response.

"Marcus, do you really think this is excusable? Stop being ridiculous. You just swore at the principal."

"But please, Mr. Louden. It was a one-time thing. Do you see what the other kids do?"

I was almost glad that my swearing had led to the continuation of our conversation. But I was begging now, and I felt the hope slipping away.

"I don't care. But maybe you should've thought things through before you assaulted Francis."

"But he was –"

"I DON'T CARE WHAT HE WAS DOING."

He said this firmly, with authority, almost giving me a shock and a roar that left me stunned in my place.

"THIS IS OVER."

And he hung up.

Great. Now I had burned a fucking bridge with our principal.

23
It was Sunday now.

Which meant church.

And oh my.

I did not want to go.

Let's ask for forgiveness, my mother had said.

Great, like that was going to work.

24
I walked behind my mother, silent along the entire journey.

The church was closer than school so we got there quickly.

Only 10 minutes of unbearable silent agony.

25
We walked into the church, as others had turned around and gasped, almost as if they were waiting for me to come in just so that they could show disgust.

It was like the entire church knew what had happened and turned around.

How the fuck did it spread so quickly?

My mom pulled at my arm, gesturing for me to sit down.

We sat at the back and didn't talk to anyone.

Three gruelling hours of boredom.

It was like the occasional dirty glares were the only things that sparked some life.

It was almost like I liked them.

Stare at me.

Yell at me.

Beat me.

Just fuck me up already.

26

As the pastor had finished his sermon and the songs had all been sung, everyone finished with a prayer.

I don't know why I was expecting to get some sort of blessing. Like the pastor was going to bring me up. Tell everyone to give me a second chance.

But that wasn't how this fucking church was.

We got up to walk out, as the rest of the crowd followed behind, almost like they were storming us, like I was the target of some protest, some rally.

Did everyone legitimately know?
I walked out to the occasional glare, jeer.

I had almost made it to the door when my mother was interrupted by a yell.

"Margaret!"

My mother turned around and so did I.

"Repent, Margaret. You have been cursed but you can break free. Your son may have been lost but you don't have to be. Come back to your true family."

It was the Wellingtons.

The same people who had helped us out when my dad turned into a drunk bastard.

The same people who always asked me how my life was going, keeping an eye on me.

And now they were speaking like I didn't exist, I was some outsider who did nothing but taint the rest of the town. Like I couldn't be fixed.

Someone could fucking down a bottle of gin a day and fuck up an entire family and he'll get helped.

I take a fucking shit on a Bible and now I'm scored.

But what was worse, what she said or what my mother responded?

"Abigail, I will speak to you later."

I don't know why I expected her to defend me, to tell Mrs. Wellington that it was bullshit how they were treating me like crap.

I stormed out alone.

Why the fuck did she bother chasing me?

27
I stormed away, walking along the sidewalk.

I didn't know where I was going but I didn't care.

The playground, the school.

Maybe I would go home and burn some of my dad's alcohol.

"Marcus where are you going!" my mother yelled, as I realized she had followed me out.

I acted like I didn't hear it.

"Marcus, don't you see what you've done. We're an embarrassment."

I kept walking.

"Marcus, you've brought shame."

I turned.

"Is that all you care about? Our reputation? Your only son, who's going to keep this family alive, has been expelled because of bullshit and you just care about your reputation?"

She walked up closer to me as I had stopped moving.

"Can't you help me in some way, do something?"

She came closer to me.

"After all that's happened with dad this is –"

She slapped me.

"Ah fuck! What the fuck was that for!" I yelled, clutching my cheek.

"You can't think everything is about you Marcus! There's no way out of this. You've ruined everything. And did you just swear at me?"

I stood in silence.

"Marcus,"

She stopped, glancing down.

"I don't want to do this, but I really can't support you.

"What?"

"Marcus, we just can't do this anymore."

"No what are you talking about? Let's get a lawyer. We'll get this fixed and it'll be back on track. I'll go back to school, I'll go to college. I don't care how the kids treat me, I'll keep –"

"You know we can't afford a lawyer. Or college."

"Well how's it helping that my old hag is lying on the couch–"

"MARCUS! This isn't about your father. You just blame others for what happens. This is you!"

With saying that she drove a finger at my chest pointing at me.

"You! You brought upon this. This is your fault. And don't you dare bring up your father. He's going to get through this, you won't. You're the embarrassment."

"Mom, can't you just help me with this?"

"No! I'm going to get my life back on track. With you I'll starve to death. It just doesn't make sense. I'll go back to the church, tell them that you've moved on. And they'll help me get back on track. You've hurt us enough, the last you can do is never bother me again."

I was stunned at what she was saying.

"Marcus, if you ever come back to the house again I will call the police."

"Mom, what are you saying?"

"I'm saying that I can't handle you anymore. Get a job and leave."

"But you're my mother!"

"And you were supposed to be my son. But you're not anymore. And I'm not going to babysit you and drag you around anymore."

And she turned around and went back in the direction of the church.

I wanted to yell at her.

I wanted to chase her.

Put her in her place.

Wake her up.

I was her god damn son.

This was her fault, I had simply made a mistake. And now she would be willing to throw everything away. Her fault. Her fault.

I couldn't do anything about her, it was pointless.

How far was this going to spin?

28
She was running away from a group of people, chasing after her. They had sticks and lights as they illuminated the dark alleyway. She screamed for help as she slowed down in her sprint, losing grip from her handbag.

She called his name.

"Joseph! Joseph!"

She kept running, reaching the end of the alleyway and making it onto the street. The group followed closely behind. Though it was a major street, it was late, and in a small borough of the city, there was no one around at 3 am. It was a dark street in perhaps the worst part of town, the part that wasn't safe, where parents would never take their kids.

She reached the end of the street, deciding to turn right, feeling the group behind her come closer.

Suddenly, a black sedan pulled up and the passenger door flung open.

"Get in!"

She got into the car and it quickly sped away, with her closing the door as the car accelerated.

"Margaret, everything's going to be ok," he said, as he held her hand.

She leaned against his shoulder and let out a gasp of relief as they drove to safety.

Perhaps that was what happened.

But I'm not sure. I made that up.

What else do I need to make up to justify why she was still with him?

29
I walked into the supermarket, hearing the bell ding as I opened the door.

It was the largest market in the town but it was by no measure large; there were 6 aisles and I guessed that they probably had around 10 people working there at once.

I was hoping they could add one more.

I walked to the back of the store, having known where the manager's office was. He was inside the small and packed office, sitting at his desk.

I knocked, and he gestured for me to open the door.

"Mr. Klabowski, could I speak to you for a moment?"

"Sure, son."

I didn't know him that well but from what I had heard he was a caring man.

"I was wondering if you had any openings for a job."

He looked to think for a moment.

"How old are you, sonny?"

"17."

"Why aren't you in school, boy?"

I hesitated for a second.

I couldn't lie and tell him I had finished early or something. If he found out I would be even worse off.

"I got expelled. And I need a job."

He almost seemed unbothered, to my surprise.

"What for?"

"I got into a fight."

"Ah, ok. Well you know what they say, eh? Boys will be boys."

I gave out a small chuckle and a smile.

"What's your name, boy?"

"Marcus Smith."

He looked like he froze.

"Ain't you Margaret's boy? Ain't you the one who get ridiculed for doing that –um – what did you do? Was it taking a crap on a bible?"

He gave off a small chuckle, amusing me. Was he not insulted?

"Yes, sir. But it was small and an accident and if you hire me nothing will happen again. I'll work hard and be on time and –"

"Look, sonny. I ain't so much of a Christian myself, but the rest of the town is," he said, interrupting me. "And I can't hire a boy who'll just piss off the townspeople."

I turned red and I felt my heart beat faster than before. I honestly thought our conversation was going in the right direction.

"What if I work in the back? I'll check stock. I'll do anything. I just need a job."

"Look, sonny. Ain't nothing I can do to prevent the word from getting out that you're working in here. I'm sorry, son. Can't hire you."

"Please, sir, you're my only option and I really need this."

"Look, I told you once, maybe come back in a few years and your name'll be all clear. But I can't hire you now, boy. You seem like a good kid but I just can't risk it."

"If I'm a good kid, why won't you hire me?" I noticed that I had raised my voice and he reacted in surprise.

"Look, I won't be arguing this, boy. It's a no."

"Please, please please," I begged, feeling like tears were starting to streak out of my eyes. "I need this too much." I grabbed his hard with my plea. "Please sir, my mother's kicked me out, my school's gotten rid of me, I can't afford college, I need something. I can go live in basements and couches but I need money, sir. Please."

He flung my arm aside.

"I ain't going to listen to your crying. You need to leave now, sonny. I said no and I mean it."

I began to bawl. Wildly.

"No you just don't get it. Mister Klabowski! I have nothing else! I'm going to be homeless, no one's going to take me! Just please!"

"If you don't leave my store now I'm going to call the police."

He slammed the office door shut, leaving me, hysterically in tears. He went to sit back down, and gestured for me to leave, through the window.

I stood there, defeated and dumbstruck, still finding myself in front of the office door mirror.

After several breaths and after wiping my tears, I turned to leave.

Someday I would come back and get back at him. Someday. I'll have a job, I'll have a life, and it'll be him begging to me.

30
I don't know why I went back home.

Or what I was expecting.

Was I expecting my mother to have a change of heart? Welcome me back in? Somehow tell me that perhaps everything had been a dream? Or that my father had risen from his couch and fixed all of this?

I walked up to the door and tried to push it open. It was locked.

I knocked several times, before the door opened, with my mother standing in front of me.

"Leave," she said coldly, her arms folded.

I tried to come up with something, continue the conversation, so that maybe she would change her mind.

"I'm just here to get my stuff."

She silently stepped to the side, allowing me to walk through.

I slowly walked into the house and walked over to the stairs, which were directly in line with the entrance to the house. I stepped up the first few steps before turning to say something to my mother.

I turned back after seeing her directly glaring at me.

I walked into my room, unsure of what to do. It was like I had come back home expecting welcoming arms and a place to stay until I found something to do. Looking at my laptop, my phone, the charger, it was like I was actually here to pick up my stuff, though I had just told her so as a conversation starter.

I sat down on my bed.

Was this is?

Was I actually leaving?

31
We drove along the street that connected most of our town.

"Mom, are we there yet?"

"Almost there Marcus!"

We passed by rows of houses with gorgeous trees hanging over the street, providing a darkening yet also illuminating shade that seemed to shroud the neighbourhood in both mystery and joy. It was soothing, feeling the air wind blow across my face.

"And, we're here!" my mother yelled as we pulled up into my driveway.

I had become so interested in the surrounding trees that I never bothered to look in front oy me.

"C'mon, Marcus, let's get out!" yelled my father.

I sat in silence. I was shocked.

"Mom, I thought the house was going to be bigger!"

Since my parents had said we were moving and talked about the new neighbourhood and the new school I was going to, they had always described it in such a desirable way.

Instead, in front of me, was an old, crumbling shack that lay at the end of the street, outside the beautiful flury of the trees that shrouded the neighbourhood.

"Hey Marcus, I promise it'll be bigger once we go inside."

I liked around me. There was no big garde. I doubted there was a big backyard either. There were no basketball nets around.

"I don't wanna live in this place for old people!"

"C'mon Marcus," my father replied. "Let's go in."

We stepped inside the house, to the creaking of the front door. It looked old. I could see a spiralling staircase right in front of me. To the right led directly into the kitchen, to the left was a lounge room that was as bare as the outside garden.

I stood in front of the stairs utterly disappointed in what I was seeing. I had imagined a mansion, with rooms for me to play, and a beautiful nice garden in the front, with a huge backyard in the back that I could play baseball in.

I walked towards the back and towards the small, worn out white door that led to the backyard. I stepped out. It was small, with patches of grass here and there, all in a haunting yellow colour, bland and depressing.

There was nowhere near enough space for anything; not long enough to simulate the distance from a pitcher's mound to a batter, not wide enough to make a small soccer net.

I walked back into the house, disappointed. I had expected an upgrade from our old house, instead it was a downgrade to a tiny shake in an isolated part of town.

"Marcus, let's check out your room!" my mother told me.

I followed her upstairs. Sure, the backyard and the garden might have been plain but perhaps things would get made up as long as my room was nice.

The upper floor was small, with 3 doors: a washroom, a master room, and an additional bedroom. They led me into my room.

"This is my room?" I asked my parents.

"Yes, son," replied my father.

It was tiny, like it was an extended closet. There was little room for anything beyond the bed against the right side of the wall, and there were inches of room before the leftmost point of the bed and the edge of the desk that was against the left side of the room. Outside the view was bleaker than it seemed from the back door. Beyond the fence bordering the outside of the backyard was just patches of grass in a yellowish hue that signalled boredom and nothing else.

The house was tiny, the garden was bleak, the backyard was unusable, and my room was a disappointment.

Did anyone ever live in this house? Ever?

My parents came back up.

"Marcus, we understand that this might not be what you expected but—"

"This isn't even close!" exclaimed, completely disappointed with what had happened. They never told me we were downsizing, they had only stressed just how amazing our new neighbourhood was going to be.

"Maybe, you'll get used to it eventually," my father replied, "but somethings just take time. Often a drastic change can be a good thing!"

"No, this house won't change!" I exclaimed.

My parents began to back out, and I could feel the guilt they had, seeing how disappointed I was. I didn't understand just how much my parents were suffering because of issues at work, which forced us to downsize; I was just a kid who thought I would be getting a bigger place to play.

"Mom, I don't ever wanna live here! Ever!"

It was like I had always longed for the day when I could leave.

Why did it have to happen like this?

32
I sat on my bed, looking outside the window.

The picture was the same as it was 10 years ago, when I had moved in as a 7 year old.

Yellow grass, a word down wooden fence with a chain-link row behind it, separating the backyard from a vast patch of yellow grace, now littered with cans, bottles, and all sorts of other garbage.

33
I walked downstairs.

The very steps that I had done thousands of times, through joyous times, through worse times. Running downstairs to go play with my friends. Walking down to check on my drunk father. Walking out to go to school the day I got suspended.

The walk never felt longer.

Perhaps it was the bags I had in my hands, with all my belongings I cared about. My laptop, phone, charger, and a bag I had stuffed with clothes. Perhaps it was the creaks from the steps that only seemed to be apparent now.

I turned into the living room, where my parents stood. My father's arms were around my mother, in a gesture of comfort, as I would like to believe. It seemed like this was the only time they had shown any sign of affection, the day they were supposedly going to leave me behind.

It was like I saw a silhouette of them standing there, only a reflection of what they were once like.

But they were real, and soon I would be gone.

"Mom?"

"What are you still doing here Marcus?"

"Can you just think again about -"

"No," my father said firmly, as if he was out of his perpetual drunken stupor.

"Please, I have nowhere to go," I begged. "Every manager knows about what happened, the church won't take me, I'll be alone. My friends won't take me, there's nowhere for me."

My father was now standing in front of my mother, almost like he was shielding her, like I was some big threat. They acted like they didn't hear my pleas, didn't want to acknowledge how helpless I was. Like the child they had raised for years was repulsive, was toxic, was something that my mother couldn't even bear eyes on. He hadn't even been in my life all those years, and now he felt like he was the one who had to protect my mother from me?

As I thought about these ideas I could feel my face redden, unsure if it was anger, or disgust.

"What are you still doing, standing there with your mouth open," he said condescendingly. "Leave. Now. We won't take you anymore."

I looked at him, a vicious glare in his eyes. I tried to meet eyes with my mother behind him, but she turned her head away, not wanting to make contact with me. If only she could see my struggle, if only she could see that I had nothing now and that if they cast me out I would be nothing forever.

"Mom, please?"

"Your mother came to this decision with me. We're not going back."

I just couldn't stand how he acted like he was the head of the family, like he was some sort of chief spokesperson. It was disgusting. I tried to tell myself to calm down, accept that nothing was going to change. But I hated him and I just wanted him to be gone.

"Stop acting like you control everyone," I murmured quietly, wanting to say it louder, but feeling like I was scared, like after all these years, my father was still able to strike a fear into me that stopped me from standing up to him. Though it happened before, he was always just as menacing, just as terrorizing.

"I don't want to have you here anymore. Get out of here. You've ruined our lives."

"Really, dad? Me? You've been drunk for the last -"

"Shut up!"

He yelled loudly, with a fierce thump of his foot accompanying his howl.

Silence.

I froze in shock, as everything went quiet, and I felt as if I could hear the air in the ventilation, the water in our pipes. With the silence was a sense of loneliness I couldn't explain, like I was trapped, yet also free in a realm of nothingness, where I had an unlimited sense of freedom but nothing to do. Like no matter what I did, I would end up in the same place.

When I came to my senses I found myself looking down at my feet, in fear. After all these years, all these thoughts of how pathetic my father was, how I was far greater a man than he would ever be, he still controlled me, he still had power over me.

He had won, and now I was lost.

I grabbed my bags, opened the door, and left.

34
First and third, one out.

I stepped up to the plate, little league bat in hand, as I adjusted my helmet.

With the number 8 and 9 hitters on the team miraculously hitting a singles in a row, I had the chance to tie the game, or even win it with a walk-off hit.

I steadied myself, taking a deep breath, facing the pitcher.

As the rest of my team in the dugout looked on in hope, I braced myself as the first pitch came.

I quickly read it, like I always had. It wasn't too hard at this age, since kids always made distinct movements for certain pitches. Cocking an elbow out before throwing a curveball. Having a more direct overhead delivery for a fastball.

The first pitch came. Outside, ball.

I stepped back, taking another breath. I was the leadoff man, and all I needed was a single to score the runner from first. A single. A light hit beyond the infield but in front of the outfielders. Something I had done countless times before. Something I had even done today, twice.

I tapped my bat on the plate three times, my sign of good luck.

Second pitch. Outside again, ball.

2-0 count now. No way they were going to walk me. This was my chance, like things had fallen in my favour for me to win the game for my team.

The pitcher readied himself, as I did too.

I caught a fastball coming dead center, and I instinctively took a big swing at it.

It chipped off the edge of my bat, going backwards for a foul.

2-1 now. Still a hitter's count.

Another pitch outside, just low. A curveball I didn't bite.

3-1.

The catcher called a timeout, going up to the mound to chat with the pitcher.

This was my chance, my opportunity to win it for the team. I could take as big of a swing as I wanted, being safe regardless.

The catcher made his way back.

The pitcher began his wind up. Knee up, then down. Arm extended back out. His arm came around the top, releasing the ball.

I saw it clearly with my glaringly open eyes. A backwards spin, a fastball coming up in the zone.

I began my swing, taking a huge windup, with a rapid release.

I saw the ball align with my bat, right in front of me. I almost blinked and flinched for a moment, as I felt a thunderous contact.

Time seemed to slow. In my mind, I was already rejoicing, feeling the huge hit. But then I began to see something different. It was sudden. As I felt the contact of the ball, the hardest I had ever hit it, in front of me was a blaze of shrapnel, a splintering of wood.

I watched, dumbfounded, as a splinter of my bat flew leftwards, hitting the ground.

And I watched, as the ball bounced towards the shortstop, who threw it to second base. And then to first.

I was still standing at home plate, as the other team began to jump around, in celebration of the clutch, last-minute defensive heroics against the opposing team's leadoff man. I felt a brush on my shoulder as the catcher ran by me, embracing the pitcher.

The kids who had been on first and third solemnly walked by me, not uttering a word, heads down.

I had costed us the game. My stupid bat had broken. It was my first time ever breaking one. And it turned a surefire game-winning double into an inning-ending double play.

It felt like a whirl, like everything had reversed so quickly. I was so sure that I had made contact and gotten a hit. And now I was the only one left on the field, wallowing in disappointment over the double play that costed my team.

My team had already left by the time I stepped out of the field, as kids were all in their parents' cars, having driven away.

I grabbed my bags, and stepped into my dad's car.

"Dad, I want to die."

Looking back, it's funny how many times I thought I had hit rock bottom, how I felt like I had no one there for me.. Like there was nothing I could ever do.

But now I was walking alone down the street, with my only belongings in my arms, with an uncertain future and unknown plans, lost within a vast world that felt like it had no place to me.

If only this was a dream.

35

Dream.

That was my only hope.

Seek out those fantastical elements that don't exist in reality.

Was this magical realism?

A mystical feeling, a sensation of a cloud surrounding me, covering everything, preventing me from seeing what was really there.

But instead, the fairies were replaced with ghosts around me, pots of gold were replaced with the bag of disheveled, mixed up stuff I had with me.

A darkness, clouding what should have been a normal life, now thrown apart, in the midst of nowhere, surrounded by nothing yet lost within my surroundings.

I had nothing, I was alone, I was lost, but still I had almost this surreal feeling, like I couldn't wrap my head around the reality I was in.

I couldn't accept it. No. This wasn't happening.

But as I looked at the dim streetlights, and the houses around me, it was happening. All before my very eyes.

Why the fuck did I punch that kid. Why the fuck did I even show up to school that day. Why the fuck did I have to use that Bible. I could've just waited. I shouldn't have been gone to that party. I didn't even like those parties all that much.

It was like there was an infinite number of paths I could take, an infinite number of possibilities, and I had stumbled upon the one shitty sequence that led me to this road, completely alone.

Only weeks ago, I was with my girlfriend, I had good grades in school, I had a good relationship with my mother, and I knew I was well on my way to a good college.

Now it was nothing. And I still couldn't believe it.

No, this had to be a dream.

I pinched myself.

Wake up, wake up.

I squeezed harder.

WAKE UP. WAKE UP.

And more, and more and more.

WAKE YOURSELF UP. WAKE YOURSELF UP.

I squeezed with all my might, until I let out a yell, my body instinctively pulling my right arm away from my left, ending the gashing pain.

This was real.

I had nothing.

I was alone.

WINTER

36
I tried to scream but I couldn't.

I don't know what it was in my mouth, a sock, a towel. But it drained my screams, as I gasped for air, knocking out another one of my senses in an already dark room.

I could feel hands going all over me, and bearing the futileness of my shouts, my mind wandered to try to keep track of the hands, counting them as they came on, trying to latch on to any dignity I had remaining.

I tried to let the cool wind of the New York sky, the shimmering reflection of the moonlight on the ocean cleanse my mind, but I couldn't, as the scene s of the horror kept coming back into my mind.

I could feel the hands move slower, get tighter, along with a whispering around me, with several distinct voices without any phrases I could pick out. The muffled sounds of my voice and the almost glistening transversion of the hands across my body must have left a haunting silence, but the exhilaration of the moment, the fear, bombarded in my mind with screams, with voices. I could hear my own shouts inside my head, but to my ears, there was nothing, to anybody that could've possibly saved me, there was nothing.

As I felt my undergarments come down, and a pair of hands move towards my crotch, my screams turned to whimpers, my struggles in escaping turning into the soft pawing of a baby cat, something that could be felt by my attackers but was completely ineffective. And in this homeless shelter, even if I screamed, I doubt anyone would have responded. That was just how it was.

I opened my eyes and glanced around me, the dark and dirty bridge that I walked on, heading in an unknown direction, anywhere away from the shelter.

Forget about it, I told myself. Stop thinking. I knew I would only make it worse, that my mind would be infected, that I would crumble, that I couldn't bear it anymore, but I had this temptation to relive it, to think back to it. Perhaps to envision what I could have possibly done, maybe paint the scene from the perspective of an outsider. But these explanations were fucked up, and that the fact that i kept thinking back to it was fucked up, and what happened was fucked up.

The first finger went into me, almost as a teasing knock, a doorbell rung before a murderer brings out an axe to murder a family. The second was the breaking down of the wall. My whimpering turned into wailing, but to the outside world, it was still silence, a silent prisoner waiting for his execution.

The hands began to move upward, and get firmer, as I felt myself bent over. In this darkness of the room, I could only make out the wood in front of my rubbing on my bent torso, my hands pinned behind my back, with my ragged shirt being the only article still on my body. I felt a hand push my head down, my chin tucking into my neck, with that hand now moving across my face, pushing on it, keeping whatever was in my mouth still. In the deafening screams in my head, I could make out some snickers behind me, as I felt the fingers leave me, and I knew to embrace myself for the worst.

I saw what was coming, but I didn't think it could be worse.

It went in then out, in then out. And the pain of it going through my body was only amplified by the brief pauses between insertions, as I figured my assailants were changing spots, taking their turns. The moments gave a false hope, like perhaps everything was over. And then it would come back, the cycle would stop.

I could feel myself sweating, as I screamed louder and louder, knowing that no one would save me, but still hoping someone would, that someone would eventually come in and end it, some sort of saviour.

It continued, and went on and on, for what felt like several lifetimes to me, with every break feeling like a potential ending, only to find it coming in again and again.

This could be it, I would tell myself. But then no, I would be wrong, I even set numbers, perhaps only 4 more, but as the numbers counted down and my hope went up, it would only shatter again, at the end.

And then it ended, as all the hands and penises left my body, and I could hear the pounding of footsteps as the assailants left the dark room. I was still blind, hunched over some wooden frame with some cloth in my mouth, my pants pulled down.

It took me several moments before noticing that I could spit whatever was in my mouth out, that my hands were freed.

I refused to open my eyes, as I stayed hunched over the frame. I could feel myself weeping.

I opened my eyes again, looking up at the moonlight. I turned around and looked at the dark, grim area of buildings I was coming from. Never again. But was it possible? It felt like it had been happening every moment since, for the last three days, as I felt the memories of the moments rewind in my head, like I was experiencing it again. I tried t o bring in other memories, other moments from my old life, but I couldn't, as everything else was clouded, tainted.

I had only been in the shelter for weeks.

I don't get how the other people stay in there. The ones who spend entire lifetimes in the shelter.

I would never find out who the assailants were. But that wasn't even the worst part.

I had to take a breath every time before even thinking about it.

Angie's parents had been strictly religious, and they never allowed us to do anything together, even after being together for so long.

That made it my first time. In a homeless shelter, with people I'll ever know, forced into me, in an attack that would never leave my mind.

37

Whatever I had previously thought about homelessness was wrong.

Previous thoughts about the homeless in the heart of the city, sitting on street corners, getting enough loose change to survive, that was wrong too.

I had always thought somewhere in my mind that if the worst was to come, I would head to the heart of the city, the busiest places, where the most people would pass by.

Instead, the heart was where the trash was, where the danger was, where all the horrors you hear about the homeless experience actually occur. Like a convoluted mess of the worst that there could be.

Though I only spent part of a week in the downtown areas near Times Square, I saw what I needed to. Muggings, beatinges. It was every man for himself, people attacking others and stealing belongings to survive, all layered over a mess of drug addicts, stoners, alcoholics. A pursue left out would quickly become money for cocaine, an open car would become a shooting range for a gun.

It was a mess, like a terror zone, and those who remained were simply addicted to the horror, using the grind of the struggle to survive to give themself purpose, grant themself a drive to survive.

And the notion we had in our town, the feeling that I had anywhere I went, that no matter what happened, the police could help, and at the least, bring justice, was absolutely diminished. No one cared about what happened. People would get beat, robbed, and as long as we were just seen to be junkies, no one gave a crap. If junkie 1 even killed junkie 2, well to them, it was one less problem to deal with, an issue that cleansed itself.

And now I was nothing but a junkie.

38

I had drifted to the outskirts of the city, still in the New York area but away from the perpetual violence, the terror of the downtown areas.

During the day, the streets were more clear, contrary to what I had believed before. Even the homeless would roam around, leaving their perches on the street corners. But at night, the streets would will, as it became quiet, and people settled down to sleep.

The shelters were all garbage, either being overcrowded, or completely ignored, understaffed, without resources to help anybody.

And outside of them, I was thirsty, hungry, and lost, not knowing what to do. I still held on to some sort of hope though, that this would all end, that I would find my way back. I just had to give it some time, and everyone would forget what happened, and everything would be back on track.

But for now, standing at the outskirts of the city, I knew this was my new home. For now.

39

I first met him on a Saturday afternoon as I was walking along the sidewalks, scavenging for food. He sat in a corner between the wall of an office building, and a staircase that led up to the entrance.

I must have been staring at him, at the sandwich he was eating, because he called out to me first.

"Hey buddy! Want some?"

I stood dumbfounded, having never been offered anything by anyone who was homeless. The man was older than me, but not by much, likely around 30 years old. He wore a toque, had a light brown beard, and a large brown leather jacket that went around a dirty green sweater. He had a pair of baggy sweatpants that were originally grey but had become a more brown colour. With his clothes, he almost looked like the stereotypical homeless man you saw on TV, just 20 years younger than what you'd expect. But from the way he looked, and the way he seemed to handle himself, he already seemed like a veteran, one who had spent many days on the streets.

I shuddered at the possibility that he had came from a situation like mine. A stupid mistake in high school, and now ten years later, he was still here, still going about, never leaving his life as a homeless person. It shocked me, frightened me, and for a moment I began to imagine a bleak future, one that replaced my hope of restoring my life.

I must have been standing still for at least 20 seconds, as he called out to me.

"Are you mute, man? You want some or not?"

He had a friendly chuckle in his voice, but the doubt still lived within me, the terror that anyone could do anything to me. I began to walk away, not wanting to take any risks.

I was trotting away, as I felt a tap on my shoulder, and I turned to see the man standing right next to me.

"C'mon, man, no worries, just a bit of salami."

I wanted to leave, perhaps to shout out, or to run away, but his friendly chuckle, and the fresh smell of the sandwich kept me in. I truly was starving, and after a week of scraps, the smell of the sandwich enticed me. And besides, it was the daytime, and it was only him, so if he never tried to do anything, I could just run.

I went to sit down beside him as he broke off a piece of his sandwich and handed it to me. The bread was hard and somewhat moist, but the salami inside was still cool, and smelled fresh. Starving, I quickly devoured it.

"Man, you must be a rookie," he said, after watching me eat the portion of the sandwich he gave me. "How old are you? 18? 19?"

"17," I replied.

"Man, shouldn't you be in school or some shit. Why are you here?"

I sat still for a second.

"Because I got fucked over. And it really wasn't my fault, the people I knew were really just fuckers who just ruined my life."

"Well, I guess you're here now, so whatever, that's all I gotta hear," he said, before I could move on to my next sentence. "By the way, I'm Chris."

I sighed with relief, not really wanting to ever describe what had brought me onto the streets. And if he had really wanted to know, I probably would've lied, perhaps painting a picture of myself as a badass, being expelled and being screwed over by the principal after defending a friend in public.

"Marcus," I replied.

"But hey man," he said, "spending your days out here can be rough. And judging by the way you ate that sandwich, you seem pretty shitty at it."

He waited for me to digest what he had said. It was true. I struggled to find food, spending hours digging through bins to find anything to eat.

He saw that I was thinking, and continued.

"Hey, if you wanna tag with me, I'm down for it. Two of us can cover twice the ground. Who knows what we'll find."

I thought about it for a second. He seemed friendly and trustworthy, but I knew not to make any light judgements, now knowing that anyone could screw me over in any way.

I knew that I shouldn't follow him, after what had happened. But I really had no option. I was struggling to find food. I was starving all the time, and anyone's guidance could help.

"Yea, sure," I said.

"Welcome to the party, man," he said. "You'll learn all there is to learn about living on the street. Come on, follow me. This is gonna be lesson one. Finding food. Good food, not that rotten crap the rest of these hobos eat."

He got up and trotted away as I stood there, thinking about what had happened.

"C'mon man, what are you waiting for?" he said.

I looked around at the empty and quiet street, and began to follow him. I considered leaving, running away from him, but I knew that to survive, I had to be reasonable. I figured that he didn't seem dangerous, and that if it was just him, I could escape even if he attacked me in some way. And I really needed food to survive.

I felt like I now had a friend, and even though I knew nothing about him, it felt like even this random, unknown man could plug a hole within me. Sure, he was nothing but a junkie, and he was the only person I really knew now, but after even just a week of loneliness, it seemed like a lifetime since I had felt any human connection.

40
"Now people always think that the key is to cover ground, go through as many bins as possible, spending the time in between getting money from the corners. Sure, you might get lucky and find an unfinished sandwich in it's wrap, or perhaps get a generous donation from someone on the street. But you follow that route, and you'll really fuck yourself over after some time."

I looked at him confused, having thought that begging and dumpster diving were the only options to survive.

"The key, kid, is that it isn't the number of bins, it's the quality. You gotta find a stakeout."

"What's that?"

"It's a bin you can count on. Here, I'll show you mine."

He led me along the sidewalk, into an apartment complex. We were now in a cleaner part of the city, with less graffiti lining the walls. Cars filled the streets and the constant buzzing from engines and car horns created a mellow backdrop for the city experience. He walked into an alleyway, and I found myself frozen outside of it, not walking in.

The darkness of the alley plagued me, and brought back vivid memories of the darkness and all that happened to me in it. I could feel the haunting attacks come back to me when I so much as thought about stepping into the darkness. I feared the dark. And the sounds rang in my head, muffled shouts, the grooming of hands over my body, and I stood there frozen, staring at the back of the man as he walked down the alley.

He walked for several metres until he noticed I wasn't behind him, as he turned around.

"Hey, what are you waiting for? Come on!"

I took a deep breath, but I still felt like I couldn't walk through. But I really needed food, and this was likely my only option. I began walking until I caught up to him, and I continued following him.

"Now the thing here, is that there's a really rich family that lives in one of these apartments. Sure they might not be millionaires or anything. But they've got like 6 spoiled kids or something, and they throw away a shit ton of food. Hey if we're lucky, today might have been taco day.

The courtyard led into an open area behind the apartment complex, that featured several dumpsters, with compost, recycling, and garbage bins.

"And the other amazing thing about this dumpster," he continued, "is that the kids often take down their garbage, but they're always scared of touching the garbage. Now typically I would say, fuck them, but given that it means that the food stays clean, I guess it's a blessing for us."

"So you just wait around here to grab food?"

"Yep. But you can't actually be here when they come with the food, or else you might creep them out. But once they drop it off, you can come here around 8:30 every night, and you'll have a nice meal waiting for you. There's sometimes drinks too, ranging from juice to if you're lucky, some whiskey or rum. Sometimes there's even so much food left over that I can't carry it without being robbed. That's what you're here for."

I thought about it. If I could have a steady source of food, that could really ease the worries on my part. I could just wait some time, before going back to Ridgefield to show everyone what I could do. I would just wait my chance, almost like a hibernation, before going back to destroy the lives of those who messed mine up. I grinned at the idea of Francis being homeless, having anything to do that lied beyond his fragile bubble. And Angie? I would go back and embarrass her, the way she did to me. I didn't know what I would do, but I would shame her, get back at her for messing my life up. And then I would get a job, show my dad that I would be more useful than he ever was. I now had a plan, and I knew that after just a bit of time, I would go fuck everyone who fucked me up.

"Hey, so you know how it is now, eh?" Chris asked.

"Yea, I think I've got a sense of it."

"Ok, I've gotta go do something on my own with someone else. Tomorrow's Sunday, so wanna meet me right here, in front of the entrance alleyway, at around 10 am?"

"Yea, sure," I replied, so caught up in the idea that I had a stable source of food that I didn't question his antics.

He left, leaving the same way that I entered, leaving me in the courtyard to wait for the food to be dropped.

And that night did turn out to be taco night, as a boy no older than 15 went to the bin and placed a bag next to it. Part of me wanted to go to the boy, tell him to be careful, tell him that his teachers, his peers would fuck him over. Another part of me wanted to beat him, upon seeing the naive, careless grin on his face, dropping off the leftover food that his parents had spoiled him with. But I didn't, and instead, when he left, I helped myself to several empty hard taco shells, as well as a half-finished bowl of salsa that after a week of sandwich scraps, tasted like an absolute feast.

And then I took the shells I couldn't finish with me, retreated to the alleyway, and gathered up on a dry part of the ground to sleep.

41

I woke up in the changeroom of my school's gym, as I was putting on my clothes to prepare for gym class. I was late for class again, after an altercation with my parents in the morning that made me leave home late.

I could hear the sounds of basketballs bouncing outside, as the class warmed up. The all-too-familiar rings of the rims of the nets, the loud bounces off the ground, I picked up my pace to get out into the gym and join my classmates.

When I had my clothes on, I put my feet into my shoes, and began lacing them up, tying bunny ears like I had always done.

I got up, to walk to the door, prepared to flail the door aside and walk into gym to join the warmups. But when I got there, I couldn't. The door was locked, and though I pulled, it just wouldn't open. I couldn't unlock it, and even putting my foot on the wall next to the door, I couldn't pull it open. I began banging on it, first a calm knock, hoping that someone on the other side would hear my pleas, would come open the door for me. But no one came, no one was coming, and soon my pleas turned into wails, as I was banging on the door, hoping to be let out.

I frantically pounded it, as I cried hysterically, there was nothing, nothing to help. Filled with anger, I stepped back, lowered my shoulder, and charged at the door, hoping to knock it down, but expecting to be held by the hard wall, that didn't budge before.

But it came through, as I felt the door cracking, then breaking apart as I broke through to the other side. But that wasn't the only thing I felt. Suddenly I found myself covered in something, like some sort of sludge that was all over my body. It felt all too familiar, and I couldn't bear looking at myself. But as my head turned to look at my arm, I knew what was coming, but I still couldn't look, the terror still consuming me.

And when I finally turned, I knew what I was going to see, but the brown sludge all over me was still terrifying, still shocking. I looked up and down all over myself, and saw that my whole body had suddenly been covered with diarrhea. The smell made me want to vomit, but I couldn't. I stood frozen, in shock, wondering if it was real or not, but knowing myself that whether it was a dream didn't truly matter.

But after staring down myself, I came to the realization that what I expected to hear never came. With my head pointed down towards my feet, I realized that I didn't hear snickers, laughter. I hoped that it meant nobody cared, that I was having a hallucination and no one else saw what I was seeing. But I also knew that it could be something worse, something worse than utter humiliation in front of my classmates.

I slowly lifted my head, bracing myself for what I was going to see.

And it wasn't laughs, but it wasn't fake either. My classmates were standing in an arch around me, with the teacher firmly in the middle, serving as the keystone. And instead of joyous snickers, there were straight faces, with each and every student staring me down, with haunting, enlarged eyes.

And then they began to march, with the arch closing in on me, each kid coming closer to the other as they cut off the space separating them from me. They walked towards me, all at once, and I could feel shivers in my body, I could feel the fear as they came closer and closer. I couldn't see what they were going to do, but I knew what it was, and I knew it was all too familiar. My worst nightmares, my scarring experiences, all coming together as one in the peaceful sanctity of the school gym.

They began getting closer, and I couldn't look, closing my eyes against the sight, even though I knew it would be worse. The thumping of footsteps, getting louder and louder, the breezes of air going by me, reminding me of the horror that was to come. The fear had drowned out the stench from the diarrhea, but that didn't make it easier, as I felt a hand come across my mouth, sealing me off from air, as I began to breathe frantically from my nose, with my eyes still firmly shut.

I felt hands move across my body, more than I could count, and I couldn't bear connecting the hands to anyone, guessing who was doing what, among my class. I felt hands move across me, tearing my clothes apart, evilly caressing my body, as I was stripped fully naked, hand still over my mouth, eyes still shut. I wanted to cry but my shut eyes wouldn't let me, I wanted to scream, but my mouth couldn't open. My body was oozing sweat, as I felt several hands go down my body, to my hip and to my butt. And as a finger traced down it, in between my cheeks, I felt a whimpering inside of me, a desire to end it all, a reluctance to keep living.

And then the fingers began moving to the side, hands going in opposing directions, as I felt my rectum exposed to the chilling breeze of the gym, which felt colder than ever. And fingers circled around, in a haunting tease, as I braced myself, knowing that I had reached my extent of pain, yet knowing that there was always something that could be worse. That no matter what I had endured, something could be worse, and nothing could save me, that I would be subjected to this torture that would scar me eternally.

Once this nightmare ended, and it had to, I would get revenge on everyone who ever wronged me. Every single one.

42

I woke up in the alley, covered in sweat, to the sounds of a familiar voice.

"Hey yo! It's 12 already!"

I opened my eyes, looked at my arms, to see that I was alive. My back ached from the hard pavement I slept on, and I felt lethargic from my sweat, but as I slowly opened my eyes, I could see Chris, and more importantly, I could see the beaming sun behind him.

"Man, I thought I lost you for a sec. Died in your sleep or whatever."

I took a deep breath, savouring the fact that my limbs were mine, that my head was mine, that I had a voice.

"Well," I slowly said, "phew."

"Hey, you want some blueberries?" he asked, pulling out a small box from a plastic bag in his hand.

I didn't want to ask him where he got them from, with it being the second day I had known him, but I begged to know.

"Where'd you get those blueberries?"

"Oh, man, you won't believe this. I was heading over here, and I just saw a shopping bag outside a grocery store. Sucks it didn't have more, and I feel bad for whoever forgot it there, but I don't mind a nice box of berries."

I didn't question it, I just devoured them, with the refreshing taste of the fruit lighting up my mouth.

As I was eating, Chris sat down next to me, and continued talking.

I noticed something dangling from his pocket. It was a small golden key.

"What's that key?" I asked, pointing at his pocket. I wondered why he ohad one. He was homeless. What did he need a key for?

"Oh, it's just for a mailbox. But yea, it's nothing. So, kiddo. You told me a bit about someone fucking you up. What's the story."

He was so great at changing the subject. The mailbox didn't add up and I wanted to question him, but I didn't. I was also skeptical of him asking about me, and I didn't feel comfortable sharing, so I didn't tell him much.

"Oh, there was just an accident with my parents, and they got pissed at me, and a fight made them kick me out."

Part of me was almost preparing to say more, but I didn't want to, and I figured he would ask, so I tried to prevent it.

"What about you?" I immediately asked, preventing him from asking more about me. What had happened truly frightened me, and in my head, I always had a worry that he somehow knew about everything, making me feel even less inclined to mention the bible, or the breakup, or the rape.

"Was almost hoping you'd ask," he said, as he grinned. "How about I show you? It's Sunday and it doesn't seem like you're up to much. Come on, let's go."

"Where are we going?"

"Just a couple of places that would be cool to see. Come on."

He got up, and as I remained seated, I really questioned what he was doing, why he was doing it. But the boredom within me really ached, and he seeemd friendly enough. And though I didn't want to believe it, I really did long for the company of just having someone.

I got up and followed him, as he led me along the sidewalk, down the road.

43

We had walked for at least twenty minutes before we stopped, as he led me in front of a school, the first one we had seen along our walk. The school appeared old, with basketball hoops missing nets, and the chain fences around the basketball court seeming battered and damaged. The school was fairly small, with it's brown brick foundation giving an old feeling, of the weather that had been endured over a long period of time. In front of the school was a sign that read "Midwood High School," and behind it a sign that had a list of school events, with parent teacher interviews and a pa day listed.

"So why are we here?" It was weird that he had brought me out here, like it was some movie or something.

"Well, you know man. I figured that we weren't too far from here. And really, when you picture a school, you might imagine it all pristine and shit, but man, fuck this place, yo."

"What happened?"

"Well, sit tight kid. Come, let's go this way."

He began to lead me around the school, which was empty on the weekend, as he began to tell me his story. By this point I realized that I truly was interested. I wanted to hear how someone like him, who had such an easy-going and friendly personality had become homeless. Maybe I could find solidarity, perhaps even a partner, as I pictured the idea of the two of us, embarking on a quest together to get back at those who harmed us, like it was some action movie or something.

"Well, it was eleventh grade, and I was a pretty good kid I'd say. Played on the football team as a linebacker with all the jocks, but I also joined the quiz club. My marks were pretty good too. And you know, because of football, I guess I was pretty good looking too."

He had led me towards the school's football field, which we were now heading towards, with the towering yet visibly old field goal posts standing at each end.

"Well anyway, there's also this guy named Mark at the school. Black dude, tall as fuck, pretty big too. Still remember him as if it was yesterday. Pretty cool guy, but he was one of those guys who probably had a massive dick, since the chicks were all over him. And I'm sure he was all over them too. I think he played small forward for the team, but yea whatever."

"Anyways, um, there's this chick named Courtney. Blonde, pretty, she hung around the popular girls, the ones who went to concerts, all that shit. But then I met her once at this volunteer event for our school, I think it was some fundraiser. And we kinda just hit it off from there. She turned out to be pretty smart too, and really into books and shit, so we got pretty close."

We were now inside the fence area, with the basketball court being free to enter. Chris walked at a fairly swift pace, and I never really interrupted him as he was talking.

"So," he said, slowing down his pace. "Anyway Mark was pretty into Courtney too, and he was always around her. But then I really did start to like Courtney. And one thing led to another, and soon, I was meeting her parents, dating her completely. And oh, I didn't say it but I should. She had the nicest ass I had ever seen. Like really. Ten years later, still haven't seen a better once."

I winced at his description, but I kept listening.

"So because of that ass, Mark was pretty into her too. But then word got out that I was dating her, and things weren't too great. And oh, by the way, this all happened in junior year. So turns out Mark was more into her than I had known, and naturally, his basketball friends, and the rest of the jocks all sided with her. Man I should've just given her up yo. But yea. And then later I fucked Courtney since we were still into each other and shit. And then Mark got real pissed. Like he hated my ass, and I could really only avoid him, and our principal was pretty strict and there were cops all over our school because of the fights that would come up. And remember, I was clean at the time."

He paused for a second, and I felt inclined to prompt him to continue, now being genuinely interested in his story. I knew I wanted to guess what happened, but I didn't, I held my mind back, waiting to hear what was next.

"And?" I asked.

"Well so Mark fucking hated me. So he thought it would be funny if he got some weed and planted it in my bag. And I know he fucking did it, I didn't touch that crap. And then someone snitched me out, and one day, there's a bag check, and I get busted for the weed that wasn't even mine. And worst part was that I tried to get Courtney to back me up, but she wouldn't and she didn't really want to get into any of the shit, since she thought it would hurt her uni chances or something."

"And so my parents wouldn't take any of that shit, especially with the suspension I got, so they signed me up for some drug prevention shit. And huge mistake yo. So I went in there clean, being framed, but then things just went to shit. The counsellor kept judging me, and he was just an asshole, saying that I was a waste, and it really just pissed me off. So I hated him, and one day, I yelled at him. And then my parents found out, and shit just really got worse."

"And then the funniest shit, is that you know how I went in clean? Well so one of the guys at the centre is this dealer. And then he hooks me up with some coke. And really, I was stupid, but I figured some wouldn't hurt. I was in rehab already, and I just really needed something to take my mind off my parents and the punishment and shit."

"So it was drugs?" I asked.

"Yea. But wait let me finish."

Part of me felt relieved that he didn't have a similar journey to me. But part of me also felt angry. This guy shouldn't have done drugs, and he brought it on myself. He wasn't like me, in the way that I had hoped. He wasn't. He didn't just get fucked over, he played a part in it. I didn't.

"So yea, I get addicted. And it's just real painful you know. I ended up going back to school, but by then I was already a fucking crackhead. And the second punishment is always worse. And soon the third, and I was expelled and shit. That coke shit really consumed me for years, you know. Years. I would find some way to get some money, taking some short job, and soon that money would all be gone. Took me fucking years. And I still feel cravings now, man.

"What does it feel like?" I asked, really wanting to know.

"Man, it's just bad. Trust me. But yeah I got through it, but now I've just lost so much man. But you know, I try to stay positive and shit. Things are just great, eh?"

I now felt sympathetic to him, feeling almost proud that he had gone through such a battle. Here I was with a man who really had a struggle, really had some issue. Perhaps he was more like me than I had thought before. Perhaps we could help each other, even though he was older.

"But yea, man," he said. "Some bad shit."

I felt sympathetic to him, and now I was sure he could be my friend. Though it was surprising that I had met someone like this after only a week or so being on the streets, I felt glad, I felt reassured that I would get through it, make my way back to Ridgefield, and show everyone what I was made of.

44

After leaving the school, we went back to the stakeout, where we were able to pick up some leftover pasta that the family had eaten for lunch. The walk back felt shorter, as I was thinking about what to say. I wanted to ask him about how a cocaine dealer had been in the drug help center, or perhaps what happened to Courtney and Mark later, but I didn't bother. Nor did i bother asking why he had been on the streets for so long, why he hadn't worked his way back, now that he was clean. Why he still roamed the streets, picking up food from a dumpster, even though he was more than smart and capable enough of making his way back, having gone through the struggle that he did. It puzzled me as to why he was still on the streets, talking to someone like me, as he seemed fully recovered, and prepared to take on the next stage in his life. But I didn't want to ask, it felt too personal, so I let it go, letting myself just stay with this man, whose story didn't seem to fully add up, but seemed to have the skills and personality to really help me get to where I wanted to be.

It was the late afternoon by the time we had gotten back to the alley. Listening to Chris's story had made me lose track of time, as we walked around his high school. The sun had reached its apex and was now venturing downwards, with the days becoming shorter and shorter as winter began to near.

We went back to the dumpster, where we found that there wasn't any food left in a box. But in the dumpster there were several sandwich scraps, and leftover salads from other families, which became our afternoon snack. We didn't talk much on the way back, so we ate in silence, sitting in the alleyway, as I stared at the wall across from me.

Finally, Chris spoke.

"Hey man, I know we just went out for a walk. But there's some place that you gotta check out. We should honestly go tonight."

"What is it?"

"Sorry to do this to you man, but Imma just say that's it's a surprise. But no worries, I'm sure it won't let you down."

Though I felt slightly exhausted, I didn't mind going to do something. My days had become boring, and any excitement would really help me, I felt. I just needed something to let the days pass, something that could eat up my time before I was ready to go back to Ridgefield.

"Where is it?"

"Well the part that sucks is that it's kinda far. So we should really get going soon. About a 45 minute walk?"

"Well, um. Yea let's go."

So we got up, walked out of the alleyway, and began once again walking down the road, this time in the opposite direction of the one we had gone in to reach the school.

45

As the skies got darker, the streets began to crowd out more, even on a Sunday night. Traffic was always there, but at night, it was far more apparent, either because there were simply more cars, or because the headlights of the cars radiated more, against the backdrop of the cloudy night sky.

Suddenly, at this time, walking with someone else, it began to feel like there was an element of the streets that I had never seen before. A feeling of radiance, a feeling of life. A certain freedom, that couldn't be found anywhere else. The strict routines that governed a working life, even the lifelong habits that dictated retirement. But here, in the open. Everything was all access, everything was anyone's game. Sure, it brought some pains and struggles, but it also brought freedom and life, something that if appreciated, was incredibly worthwhile.

We spent the walk there talking softly, about nothing too personal. Sports teams, hobbies, all those things. We were walking in a completely dark, older, run-down neighbourhood by the time he stopped me.

"Hey, we're right here."

I stopped and looked around at the emptiness. On one side of the road was an open park. Not one that was vast and beautiful, one that was old and grim, yet still extended far beyond, almost reaching the horizon, where several apartments were perched. And on the other side, a series of seemingly abandoned housing structures. They were attached townhouses, old and discarded, with wooden boards that covered the doors. The townhouses were narrow, but tall, many up to 3 stories high, with few windows.

"Where are we?" I asked.

"Here, follow me," he said.

He led me up to one of the boards that covered a door of a blue wooden townhouse. He put his hand around the edge, and pulled, revealing a hinge behind the far left side of the board. The board served as a door, and upon being opened, I saw a small room, with a big, fat, bald bouncer sitting in a chair, in front of a staircase that led upstairs.

Chris turned to me. "You ever fucked a hooker before?"

I quietly shook my head, still in awe at what I was seeing, hidden inside an abandoned townhouse.

Chris walked up to the man, reached into his own pocket, and placed something in the hand of the man, which the man had stuck out.

"Friend's first time," Chris said, as the bouncer gave a nod.

The bouncer got up from his chair, and dragged it to the right side of the room, away from the staircase he had been in front of. As he did, a girl began to descend the staircase, slowly coming down from an upper floor.

She had blonde hair that was dyed with black streaks, giving a dirty yet captivating impression. She wore a dark mascara and eyeliner that brought intensity to her glare, that was further highlighted by her light pink lipstick. She wore a green and red flannel shirt, tied in front of her torso, revealing her navel region, as well as a white bra underneath her shirt. Below she had black leather pants, that led into black boots with gold rings on the sides. She was tall, which was only augmented by the long heels of her black boots, which gave her a feeling of youth, as she strided down the stairs and towards us. She couldn't have been older than 25, which was odd, considering where she was, but I figured that given how I was, I wasn't really in the position to judge.

"Oh, you can't have her man," Chris said. "She only does girls."

The girl gave Chris a dirty stare, before replying.

"You're the reason why," she said.

And she walked by Chris, me, and out the door.

She had walked out the door, before I dared to ask anything.

"Is she lesbian?" I asked.

"Nah, she's bi. Apparently she's actually more straight though, just doesn't like to fuck guys in her, um. Profession. Do you believe she's only 19?" he asked, rhetorically.

I looked back at the wooden board that served as the door, before turning my head around again to look at the flight of stairs that led up.

"You want some or not," the bouncer asked, after Chris and I had stood there for a couple seconds.

"Yea, show us up," Chris said, as the bouncer began to lead us up the stairs.

That girl was pretty, I thought to myself. But I realized that since leaving school and seeing Angie for the last time, it had been a while since i had seen a girl around my age, and perhaps I was just seeing things I wasn't. I knew better than to get infatuated with a girl who worked as a hooker, especially considering how anything with her, or anyone in general at this point could really bring me down more.

The truth is that I wasn't even all that interested in a hooker, but as Chris wanted to, I followed him, with me thinking of it as an act of thanks after all he had shown me and taught me. I never had sex with Angie, and she had been my only girlfriend, but figuring that it would likely be long before I could be in a true relationship again, i didn't mind having sex with a hooker.

We had reached the second floor, when the bouncer gestured for me to go into a room.

"There's a girl for you," the bouncer said, before continuing to lead Chris up another flight of stairs.

"What about you," I said to Chris.

"Oh, I've got mine up there," he replied, before turning his head, and continuing upwards.

I opened the door and walked in, seeing a red-headed woman, around 30 years old, waiting for me, all dressed in black lace. She sat on an old and small bed that was up against the wall in a tiny room, which had likely previously been a small bedroom. She also wore dark eyeliner and mascara, but with her age and facial structure, she was nowhere near as pretty as the girl I had seen before.

I closed the door behind me, as she began to walk towards me, silently, staring me in the eyes.

It was something in that stare that scared me off, as she had knelt down to the floor, and was beginning to caress her hands around my waist, about to pull my pants down.
"Sorry, I can't do this," I said to her, looking at her face, which was now right under me.

"What's wrong?" she asked.

"Sorry, um. I just can't."

Perhaps I had gotten nervous, perhaps I had some moral lapse. But I just couldn't do it.

Dixun Cui

"Is it something with me? I could find another girl for you."

"No, it isn't, I just really can't, I'm sorry."

My face had turned red, and after finding myself staring at the ground, I turned around, opened the door, and left the room, flustered with embarrassment.

I went to the staircase and began walking down, talking to myself, wondering what had happened. I really just didn't feel comfortable, I really wanted to leave. I felt disgusted, like I wanted to puke, but also guilty, that I had felt fine before but had a sudden change of heart. I just couldn't bring myself to have sex with a hooker. Maybe it was the rape in the homeless shelter, maybe it was something with Angie. But I felt nauseous, and as I stumbled down the stairs to the ground floor, where the chair still sat next to the stairs in the absence of the bouncer, I lumbered over to the wooden board that served as the door, and opened it to step outside, desperately craving a breath of fresh air.

When I had gotten outside, I saw the blonde girl, sitting on the curb. She had turned around to look at me, having heard the sound of the board opening and closing. In one hand was a package of cookies and in another, a cookie that she had just taken a bite of.

"What's wrong with you?" she asked. "Did you really come that fast?"

She had a seriousness in her voice, a strictness, that froze me where I was, standing on the steps that led to the townhouse.

"No, I just couldn't. Um, I'm not sure what it is. I just…"

"Yea, I know. Happens all the time. Kid goes in there, wants to be all badass, two seconds later, he's out.

"No, I wasn't trying to…"

"Yea sure, whatever. What are you doing standing there? Come take a seat."

I went over and sat next to her on the curb.

"You want a biscuit?" she asked.

I shook my head. Before turning my head away from her, looking straight across at the park across the road. I was scared to look at her, for she truly was beautiful especially from where I was, right next to her. She had pretty green eyes, that showed a flash of innocence, veiled behind the hardships of living as a hooker at such a young age.

"So," she said. "Why Chris?"

"What do you mean?" I replied.

"Why are you with Chris?"

"Oh, well. I haven't been on the streets that long, but I ran into him and he showed me how to get food and get around and stuff. Pretty cool guy."

She gave a sarcastic chuckle.

"What?" I asked.

"Forget it. Doesn't really matter."

"So what happened to you?"

"What the fuck are you asking. Really? You're the one judging. You have to pay for your fucking sex.."

"I didn't want to, Chris made me," I interjected, unhappy with what she had said.

"Well sure, whatever. But don't judge me. I'm not here asking you what you've done in your life. So why do you care."

She said that with a disgusted smirk on her face, like she had been taken aback by what I had asked. Like I had asked something forbidden, something that shouldn't have ever been mentioned.

"Sorry about that," I replied.

"Yea, whatever."

She took another bite out of her cookie, while looking straight across the road, at the park.

I was hoping she would say something to continue the conversation, but she didn't.

It seemed like she didn't really mind what anyone did at all. If I spoke, she would too. But if I didn't, she would just eat her cookies, minding her business. If she had something to say, she would say it. If not, she wouldn't.

"By the way, my name is Marcus," I said.

"Ok cool. Hey Marcus."

I was surprised she didn't introduce herself.

"What's your name?" I asked.

"Diane," she replied.

I nodded my head when she replied.

"That's a cool name," I replied, my face turning red with awkwardness. I wanted comment something, but didn't know what. I probably would've been better off saying nothing at all.

"Well. I guess you can thank my parents. If you ever find them. But good luck. I haven't had any."

"Oh, I'm sorry for what happened."

She chuckled.

"No, please don't say that," she said, grinning, with a light laugh. "Doesn't really help. And honestly, I'm kinda glad how it turned out."

"Why?"

"Well I get to do what I want. Spend my money on whatever. People always have those ideas of having some job or family or something. But then they end up depressed and divorced. Depressed and divorced. The only two Ds you'll ever need. I get to do what I want, fend for myself, and I'm fine right now. My parents definitely didn't want that. And people say, yea sure, you're a hooker. Well, first of all, I don't fuck guys. Since they're cunts and they really just don't care about anyone. And honestly, what makes being a hooker any worse than anything else. I show up to work, get paid, and get home with money."

"Hey, not all guys are…"

"Nah everyone is. Me, you, Chris, Mr. Bouncer Bob, everyone. cunts. People she just go about their jobs, not giving a crap about others. But whatever, we're forced into it. Might as well take it."

As she reached into her package for another cookie, I felt footsteps come behind us, along with a familiar voice.

"So, I see you guys are hitting it off, eh?" Chris asked.

"Fuck off," Diane said. "I was just telling him about how you were a cunt."

"That's not nice for a girl to say," Chris replied, jokingly.

"Well fuck you," Diane said.

Chris chuckled, as Diane wrapped up her package of cookies.

"Anyway," Diane said. "Time for me to go."

And with that, she left, and I watched, as her trailing blonde hair hovered behind her, as she walked down the road, opposite from the direction we came.

"She sure is a special one," Chris said, after she had left.

Yea she is, I thought to myself. Real special. And as her blonde hair faded into the night, I couldn't help but think about what she had said and how she had acted. She felt like an asshole. But I also sensed a free spirit, an outcast who really didn't care what others thought. She was working in such a shunned job, but she didn't seem to mind. Maybe if she could be okay with this, I could find a way too.

"Well," Chris said. "You know the way back, right? I'll come see you tomorrow night or something."

"Ok."

46

When Chris didn't come for two days, I didn't worry. Maybe he got caught up in something, had some issue. But two more days, and I began to feel both worried and suspicious. Perhaps something happened for him. Or maybe he was living some double life. I had no idea, but I just couldn't take waiting for him anymore. The dumpster stakeout had been consistent with food, but I was craving something else, maybe some fresh snack that Chris would bring, or maybe just some social interaction. The neighbourhood around the dumpster alley was quiet, and being alone and dressed in dirty clothes, there wasn't really anyone to talk to.

I reached into my pockets and felt the change I had collected over the past weeks. I had never been too active in begging, especially after discovering the stakeout, but feeling the variety of different coins and 1 dollar bills in my pocket, I figured that I had enough to get something for myself.

I walked down the road, looking for the first market there was. I realized that since meeting Chris, it was the first time that I really was walking alone to go somewhere. His companionship, though at times awkward and mysterious, had been nice, but getting the chance to just walk around myself on a weekday afternoon was nice too. There was an occasional car or cab that passed by, but overall, it wasn't too loud.

It was several blocks before I ran into a market, located at the corner of an intersection. It had a green sign with white letters that simply read "general market." It was fairly large, extending down the perpendicular road against the one I was walking on. In it, I could see bright lights and several people, browsing around.

I walked in, as I heard a bell that rang every time the door was opened. At first I didn't notice it, but after several steps into the store, I realized that everyone's eyes were on me. I looked down at myself, seeing the dirt that covered my pants, my sweater. Perhaps it was the fact that I was so young, or maybe it was just because it was so rare to see someone homeless in a store. But everyone, including the cashiers at the registers next to the door had their eyes on me. No one said anything, but for once, I realized just how much of an outsider I was. I had never really been in a public setting in the past few weeks and it really was a shock to me, how far I had fallen.

And after their initial shock, no one dared speak to me, giving me glares in silence. The silence was deafening, and no one would reach out, not one.

Except for her. As I ventured into the back of the market, browsing the packaged snacks, I heard a familiar voice come from behind me.

"Not used to it, huh?" the voice said, in a surprisingly easy-going tone. "Guess it's your first time getting looked down upon by everyone."

I turned around to see Diane, dressed in a light jacket and sweatpants. In her hands was a shopping cart, filled with several snacks. Her blonde hair flowed across her neck, in front of her shoulders, and without her mascara and eyeliner, her face had a pretty glow to it, like some sort of hidden innocence that was behind her.

"What are you doing here?" I asked, surprised at seeing her.

"Just getting some stuff."

Her voice was a lot calmer than it was the last time we had met. She didn't feel uptight and rude. But she still had this feeling of independence, like whatever she said was definite and you couldn't change her mind.

"Do you come here often?" I replied.

"Yea, sure. This place has the most stuff in one place, so yea I guess so."

"Yea, I just wanted to come by and get something. Chris didn't show up, so I wanted something beyond the normal stuff from my dumpster."

She nodded, in a way that showed that she understood what I was saying.

"So what are you getting?" I asked, trying to continue the conversation.

"Some fruit, some drinks, and a bunch of crackers."

She gestured over to the shelf that was behind us.

"Those biscuits are great. I get them all the time. Just a buck. Really worth it."

I looked at the biscuits on the shelf. They came in a blue package, each package being fairly long, reaching perhaps 1 foot each. They were a plain flavour, but they looked fairly cheap and worth it, so I took a package off the shelf.

"Thanks," I said. "These look like they've got great value."

"No worries," she said, as she began to walk down the aisle, towards the side of the market.

"Are you, um. Working tonight?" I asked, not wanting the conversation to end in silence, with her walking away.

"Working as in fucking? Yea. Not sure why you care though."

"No, sorry, that's not what I meant. What I meant is.."

"Yea, whatever, I don't care. Anyways, I'm done here. Bye Marcus."

And with that she walked back towards the front of the store, towards the cashiers.

"Bye Diane," I called out.

I was angry with myself. I just shouldn't have asked her, and I wished she knew that I just wanted to continue the conversation, and not knowing much about her, it was the only thing I could think of to ask. I was just curious as to what she was doing, and I should've thought more before I spoke. I really hoped that she didn't care, or worry. But I was glad that she remembered my name, glad that she knew who I was.

And she felt different. Perhaps she had been putting up a cold personality as a guise last time. I hoped she was.

She looked even prettier under the lights of the market. I knew that seeing her was never going to amount to anything, and I didn't want to go seek her out or anything, but I knew deep down that I wanted to run into her again, like I did, I wanted to see her. I felt like a child with his first crush.

I reached into my pocket, took out my money, and counted it. I had $11.73. And with roughly 10 dollars in excess after subtracting the cost of the biscuits, I bought myself several soft drinks and a boxed salad, before paying a cashier that never said anything to me except my total price, and I walked out of the store.

47

It was Saturday evening when Chris finally showed up, this time with a bag of bananas and a box of croissants.

I was angry, annoyed, and I tried to ignore him and not to talk to him.

He came over in the afternoon, as I was sitting in the alley, just letting time go by.

"Hey Marcus," he said.

I tried to stay silent.

"Marcus, I'm sorry man, but just talk to me, ok?"

"Really, Chris? Fuck you man. What the fuck is even up with you. I honestly just can't fucking trust you anymore."

I thought about just leaving him, finding a stakeout and getting by myself, not having to give him any thought anymore.

"Hey, I'll explain, just let me, don't worry about it."

"Well you better fucking explain," I said.

"Yea, I will, don't worry."

"Now," I said, with a fierce tone to my voice. I was fed up with him, fed up with his disappearances and reappearances, without any explanation between them.

"Woah, man. It's just that…"

"Now," i repeated myself."

Chris's face had turned red, and now his voice had a softness, a weakness to it that was hidden before. Part of me felt bad, but I was also pissed, and I felt like I had gotten to the breaking point.

"Fine, Marcus," he said softly. "I've been lying the whole time."

I wasn't even surprised, so I didn't say anything, letting him continue.

"That stuff I said about being over coke? Being done from it?"

"Yea," I replied.

"Well, I'm not. And, um. I'm still working on it. I got to rehab still, every weekday. But it isn't just that. Back when I was an addict, I did some things. And now I need to settle them, repay them, and …"

"What things," I said, interrupting him.

"It's just things that …"

"Tell me," I said boldly.

"I robbed some stores, and I just need to repay them some way. So I just help out with work, stuff like that."

I suddenly began to feel sad, and disappointed that I had gotten angry at him.

"I'm sorry for getting mad. I understand," I said, feeling ashamed. He was simply making up for his past actions.

"No worries. If you don't mind, I'm just gonna go take a piss," he said, as he walked back out of the alleyway.

I looked down at my hands, disappointed at what I had said, and the tone of my voice. Part of me wondered what Diane would've thought. *You fucking psycho*, I envisioned her saying. I thought about it. Chris was just a guy who had gotten into some bad shit. And he was truly trying his best to make up for it. He had done some bad things, but now he was making up for it by working in a store.

Making up for it by working in a store.

Part of that didn't add up.

I thought about it more. Why on earth would a store owner get a coke addict to help in a store, after robbing it?

And if he claimed everything happened in high school, and his addictions happened then, was he really trying to sober up, after something like 10 years of addiction? And I never sensed any coke, nor did he ever feel high.

His story didn't add up.

He was a liar.

Fuck.

48

He came back around the corner that led into the alleyway.

"So, Marcus, any plans tonight. Wanna go get some more, if you know what I mean."

"No, I'm fine."

I wasn't going to ask any more from him, anything. But I knew I had to leave, I had to distance myself from him.

"Ok, I guess we can just chill here," he said. "I think I'm gonna sleep here too, if that's alright with you."

"Yea, that's fine," I replied. He could stay here for the night, but early in the morning, or late at night, I would wait. Yeah, that was it. I could wait for the night to come, I would wait for him to sleep, and I would leave, I would perhaps go somewhere near the abandoned townhouses, somewhere close to Diane. Perhaps she could help me. Even if she couldn't I'd still have someone with me.

"Is anything wrong? I'm sorry about lying. But I just really hope you can forgive me," CHris said, noticing my cold expression.

I tried to fake a smile. Tried to prevent him from suspecting anything.

"Yea, it's fine. Everything's fine." I said, trying to force a grin.

"Well, ok."

He seemed to have a haunted expression on his face. He looked ghastly, partly from fear, partly from disappointment. But I really didn't mind. One more night and I would be gone, one more night and I wouldn't have to deal with him, I wouldn't have the lingering fear of being with a perpetual liar. I wouldn't have to question his motives, his actions. Just one more night.

And so we sat in awkward silence, eating the bananas and croissants, waiting in the alleyway for the night to come.

49

I lay on my back, staring at the dark night sky, waiting for the right moment. I knew that to be safe, I had to wait until Chris was in deep sleep. And once he slept, I would just leave, head down the road, and never see him again.

Sure, I should've left several days ago, when he wasn't here, so he would have to show up, expecting me but seeing nothing. But this was good enough. He would wake up to see no one there. Perhaps he would come looking for me, to no avail. I would be long gone.

I thought about what had happened to me in the past weeks. Just three weeks ago, I was bound on my way to college. I would have a career. All the things that could have prevented this. If I didn't go to that party. If I didn't eat and drink as much. If I had just waited in the washroom for the party to end, so I could call out to James. But it was fine. I would go back and ruin their lives. Just some more time, perhaps a few months. They would be past it. I would go back, revive my career, become the lawyer I had dreamed of becoming. And perhaps later, I would have the freedom to embarrass them. James, Francis. Maybe even Mr. Thomas. Everything would fit into place.

50

I don't know how long it had been, but I found myself beginning to fall asleep. But I couldn't. Just a bit more. Just a bit more.

I thought about all the mistakes I had made before. Perhaps I just shouldn't have started anything with Angie in the first place, if I knew what it would turn out to be like. Maybe I never should've chosen the courses I did, so I wouldn't have classes with Francis, and I wouldn't have Mr. Thomas as my teacher.

So many possibilities, yet that one option led to where I was. But soon, everything would go back, I would get a fresh start, and this time. I knew how to make it.

Just a little bit more.

51

I was just going to count down from 100, and I would leave. Quickly, silently, I would slowly walk down the alleyway, and out. I lay down against a wall, and turning my head, I could see Chris further in front of me, lying down, closer to the exit. I had to go by him. Would I run or would I slowly walk?

80 more seconds.

Perhaps it would be best to walk slowly. Walk slowly, and if he noticed anything, I would sprint away. Or maybe I would keep walking slowly, and with the silence, he would never truly be awakened, and even if he was, he would just think it was a gust of wind.

60 seconds.

Just one more minute. Crew it, why not do it now? But no, I told myself I would wait. Besides, it doesn't really make a difference.

50 seconds

It was almost here. Just calm down, nothing's going to go wrong.

40 seconds

39…

38…

Deep breath.

37….

Suddenly I heard a rustling. And before I could lift my head, raise my body to look over, I felt a hand on my mouth, and I saw Chris's eyes, looking at me, right in front of my face.

No, no, no. This couldn't happen. Not now.

I tried to break free, but I felt another strong hand on my body. Pinning be down, just half a minute away from my mistake. I should've acted earlier, I should've gone.

"Still awake, huh?" he whispered.
He opened his hand, giving me enough room around my mouth to speak, but still preventing me from getting up, trying to do anything.

"Who the fuck are you," I whispered back.

"Hey, I won't do anything to you, I just need one thing. Please. I've been dying for it forever."

I remained silent, thinking about what I was going to do. As much as I didn't want this right now, I figured that I could still escape, still get out of it.

"Marcus, have you ever just felt. Impulsed by someone. Like someone your with."

I remained silent.

"Marcus, I just need one favour. One favour and that's it, we can go back to normal, you can forget about this night."

The darkness was haunting, but I didn't feel scared. Somehow, I felt stronger, more willing to do anything it took to protect myself.

"Marcus," he said, as he began to move his body up towards me. With his right hand against my neck, preventing me from moving, he brought his left hand down, and began to pull down his pants.

"Marcus, just blow me. Please."

I don't know whether it was because I was so deep in thought about my escape, or whether I was somehow expecting it, but I somehow didn't feel shocked about his demand. He always had some part of him that was questionable, something that didn't add up, even beyond his lies.

He glared at me, expecting an answer.

"Fuck you," I whispered, as in a burst, I sprung my arms up, pushing his right arm aside. The force sent him over to my left, onto the ground. I pushed back on the ground behind me, leveraging my body over my feet and legs to get up and run away. Halfway through my leap, I felt his arms around me, as he swung me around him, onto the ground.

I quickly turned my head towards him, placing my eyes on his face, as I lifted my back up, and threw a punch at his face. It connected, as he stumbled over, with a groan. I shuffled backwards, knowing that running forward would be futile, and I would only get stopped by him. I figured that I would just need to defend myself one more time. Just one knockout blow to him, and he would be stunned enough for me to run away. And in this dark night sky, he would have no way of catching me.

He lunged towards me, with anger in his face.

"Fuck you," he said, coming towards me.

He came at me and swung his arm, as I stepped back and avoid it. I gave him a shove as he stumbled backwards, but he regained his footing, standing up tall again. We looked at each other for a few seconds, eyeing each other down in the darkness of the moonlight. Suddenly, he began to charge at me, and without enough time to react, I felt him tackle my torso, as I flew backwards. Hitting my head on the hard paved ground.

He was now above me, as he raised his fists and began launching a flurry of punches to my face, that I tried to dodge and block to no avail. I groaned, as I felt each fist, and I could hear his heavy breathing, as he continued to swing his hands.

"You didn't need this!" he exclaimed, as he continued to hit me, with my hands now covering my face.

He slowed down to a stop, as he continued to hover over me.

"I helped you. And that was all I needed. I hope you fucking die."

And with that, I felt his breathing leave, as he got up. I continued to lie on my back, on the ground. It was like our scuffle had been such a fury that I didn't feel anything during it. The back of my head still hurt, and my face felt bruised, and my hands felt numb, as I continued to lie there, frozen on my back.

I breathed heavily, as I felt my senses come back to me, as I felt my mind bend back into form.

My mind was so focused on what had just happened that I didn't bother to think about who Chris really was, or what he aimed to do.

When it felt like my head and my back finally came back to me, I rolled over, before crawling towards the front of the alleyway, where a bag with my stuff had been. All I wanted was a drink now, to calm myself down. But when I got there, the bag was almost empty. Chris had taken everything when he left.

But not everything. He had left the package of biscuits.

I took them out of the bag, and held them in my hand, looking at them. They didn't have a brand, simply reading "BISCUITS," in a white font over a blue package.

I put the vertical package between my legs, as I opened the package from the top. The biscuits were brown, and though some had gotten crushed, the rest were still in shape. I put a piece in my mouth. It has a simple, yet good taste. There was a hint of gingerbread, as well as one of vanilla. I could see why Diane liked them.

And so I sat there, in the alleyway, alone, knowing that I would never see Chris again. Sure, I had gotten rid of him, but it had never really occurred to me before that in losing him, I lost one of the two people I knew.

And eating those biscuits, I couldn't stop thinking of Diane, wondering where she was, what she was doing. I sat there, thinking, until I felt a cold speck on my neck.

Reacting to it, I looked up at the dark night sky.

The snow had begun to fall.

51

Winter was something I had never considered before. The cold air and snowflakes were something I never considered, with the prospect of being on the street being enough for my mind to think about already.

In New York, it gradually got worse. And with the cold already being harsh enough in Ridgefield in the past years, I couldn't imagine how it would be on the streets of New York.

I had to quickly find a new stakeout, and ideally one that had somewhere I could live.

And not wanting to venture far from the only person I knew, I began to walk in the direction of the townhouses, looking for somewhere to stay.

Although the precipitation had stopped, the roads were now covered with a thin layer of snow that by the morning, had turned into slush on the intersections. The wetness of the roads really gave the city a different feeling. It felt more constricted, with a lack of openness that had been present before. It was scary in a different way. Though before, the barren emptiness of the city made me feel lost and alone, the wetness caused a dreary effect, one where I wasn't necessarily alone, but I was still uncomfortable, restricted by my surroundings.

And though walking on the street before was hauntingly silent, walking now was far louder. Honks from cars were far more present, with the slushy conditions causing more traffic trouble. This felt more like the picture of New York that I used to think of before. A mess, with people struggling to find their place among it all. A random mix of different elements, creating a feeling of both liveness but also emptiness, in a haze of unknown discovery and a perpetual search for purpose.
And I was lost in the middle, without a home, with the cold of winter approaching.

52
I had been walking for at least 15 minutes until I caught sight of something familiar that could maybe be an option for me. The alleyways I had passed by all didn't have enough shelter to get away from the cold. There was no way I was ever going back to a

homeless shelter, figuring that the shelters would probably be even worse in the winter, as more people packed in.

But as I saw the familiar green sign of the market I had gone too, I realized that perhaps I had an option. The market would always have expired food, and I figured that maybe, in the back of the market, I could find somewhere to curl up to sleep at night. It wouldn't be perfect, especially the smell, but this put me in a place that was busy enough that it wasn't dangerous, was likely warm enough, and though not a primary concern, put me closer to Diane.

The market was at the bottom of an apartment building, one that went at least 10 stories up. The apartments were brownish red on the outside, laced with black fire escape staircases that ran outside the side of the building. I walked to the end of the road that had led me from the old alleyway, and turned right on the perpendicular road, going across the face of the store, looking for some sort of alley that led to the back fo the store. I figured that even though the market was located under an apartment building, and it was connected to the neighbouring buildings, there had to be some way to get to the back of the store. There must have been an alternative exist, perhaps one where the garbage would be taken out. After walking across the face of the store, I went past one entrance for the apartments above, before seeing an alleyway between the apartment building and the next one that was down the road. I walked down the alleyway, and was delighted when it led to an open square that was directly behind the market.

The square was decently large, perhaps the size of a tennis court. Upon passing through the alley, to the left, where the back of the store was, there were three or four steps that led to a green metal door. That was the only thing on the back wall of the store, the rest being the brown brick that characterized the market. To the right, on the far side of the exit of the store, were several large garbage dumpsters and a large recycling dumpster. And staggered across to me, a bit to the right, was another alleyway. It was closer to the dumpsters, and presumably, it led to the road on the opposite side of the market. With its positioning, I could only see the entrance to the alleyway, being unable to look across to the street from one alleyway to another.

In the middle of the square was a sewer, and several flat pieces of cardboard, likely originating from boxes, spread out around. The rest of the ground was dark pavement, with several small craters resembling small potholes.

And though it was still the afternoon, I felt relieved, having found somewhere decent for me to stay, likely with a good food source. Exhausted from all the walking, I crouched down, against the wall surrounding the square. And tilting my head back against the wall, and feeling the cold and rough texture of the brick wall, I slowly began to fall asleep.

53

Ridgefield was a small town, so when we could, our family would always try to escape somewhere. Some sort of wilderness adventure, to see the world beyond our limits.

When my parents told me that we were taking a trip to go camping, I was excited at the prospect of living in a tent, in the open wilderness. In grade 5, we had learned about what camping was, and upon seeing pictures of a tent in school, I knew it was something that I wanted to do.

The drive up north was somber and peaceful, yet also interesting. Though our town was fairly mellow, there was was a strong of an exposure to nature as there was when we went up North. My father had been an avid camper when he was young, and though those days were behind him, he still loved nature, and loved taking our family up north.

When we got there, we pulled up to our campsite and began to set up our tent. I wasn't old enough to really help, even though I wanted to. But once my mom and dad had the tent set up, we could go explore, whether that meant swimming in a lake, or perhaps finding a park to go to.

But nothing would ever be as good as the marshmallows around the campfire. Sitting with my family around the open flame, I loved the flickering with the ashes, the dancing of the blaze.

And in those moments, looking into the fire, it was like everything could be forgotten. All the pain, all the anguish, could just float into the flame. To be consumed, and released, as an invisible smoke, set to rejoin the great atmosphere of the world. To be consumed, burned, and then reborn, in a new state, in peace and harmony with the heavens around. Everything was only temporary, all darkness would pass, and in the end, no matter what, everything would return to nature.

We finished up our marshmallows and afterwards, we cleaned up and it was time to sleep. Bunched together in sleeping bags inside the tent, it was warm and comfortable, lying under the darkness of the northern night sky. But as we were settled in, I realized that I wouldn't be able to sleep. I had to poo, and while getting up to go, I told my parents.

After a long day, they were both extremely tired, with my dad almost fast asleep. In a haze, my mother told me to take the flashlight and go, as she closed her eyes again, with her head on her pillow.

I took the flashlight, unzipped the opening of the tent, and began to walk in the direction of the washroom. I remembered where it was from when we had gone to brush our teeth. Our campsite was in a lower area of the park, so stepping out of the tent, I knew that I had to walk up a hill. I followed the hill up, leading me to an intersection. I knew that I had to turn left, so I followed the path.

Though it was dark, the flashlight was bright enough to lead me. I wasn't too scared, but part of me knew that I should take the trip as fast as I could. I followed the winding path, intertwined with other paths, until I reached another hill. At the top of that hill was the washroom. I rushed up the hill, quickly entering one of the opened stalls, placing the flashlight on the ground, still turned on. The washroom smelled bad, but there were enough lights that I could see.

After I was done, I quickly washed my hands, grabbed the flashlight, and left. I scurried down the hill, and began walking back in the direction I had come from. Suddenly, I came to a stop upon reaching the bottom of the hill.

117

There were two paths. And on the way to the washroom, I had been on such a hurry that I didn't pay attention to where I was coming from.

I tried to think about it, picturing what I had seen as I was coming to the hill. I stood from the entrance of both paths, looking at the washroom. But they looked too similar, and the paths were too close to each other.

I began to panic. What if I never got back? What if I got lost forever? I couldn't just stand there. I took the left path, and began walking down, trying to get back to our campsite. I looked around me, trying to remember what it was like coming. Did the path look this way. Were the trees like this. I couldn't remember. I kept walking. No, I should run, I began to jog, looking around me. Some signs would reassure me, remind me of something that looked somewhat familiars. Other trees and sections in the paths just felt wrong. No, it wasn't here. I turned around, thinking about whether or not I should go back.

I was in full panic now. Now I was on a path that I wasn't sure about, lost in the darkness. I couldn't figure out which way to go. I was lost. I should've just stayed at the washroom. But that wouldn't have helped. I was lost. I was going to get kidnapped. No, no, no. I kept walking down the path. Maybe it was right.

With my heart beating, I looked on my horizon for a hill I could go down, one that could lead me to the campsite. I knew there had to be a hill. I kept walking, at a fast pace. I could feel my eyes start to well up, in fear. I was lost, I was going to be lost forever. I would never be able to get home. This stupid park. There should have been signs. But now I was going to die here, I was never going to see my mom or dad again.

I kept walking, looking for a hill, but it never came. I didn't know whether I simply hadn't walked far enough, or if I was on the wrong path. Hill, please, please. I kept walking at a fast pace, and it had already felt like forever. But still no hill. I realized I had taken the wrong path. Now I was doomed. I began to scurry back, now almost running at a full sprint. The darkness was absolutely frightening. I just wanted to wake up. It felt like a nightmare. But I couldn't. I was lost and I had to get out. But I never would, I was stuck here, forever and forever. I had to get out.

I had been running full speed, until I ran into another intersection. There was no hill ahead of me, no washroom in sight. Here I was, lost again. Another intersection, after having gone down the wrong one. This couldn't be, this couldn't be. It couldn't be like this. Luck couldn't possibly be this bad. This couldn't be.

But it was. It was, I was lost for good. I could feel tears coming down my cheeks now, in fright of never being able to return. Soon I was bawling, afraid, crouched down on the side of the path, near the intersection.

I cried and cried. I was never going to make it back. I was lost forever. I was just going to be stuck here. I cried, thinking about how this would all end here. The park had no signs, and going out alone, this was going to be my doom. If only I had paid attention to where I had come from. If only the park had some sort of directory. All these little things, and if one of them had gone my way, I wouldn't be stuck here.

And I kept crying, my hands now fully wet from my tears, as I felt them drizzle down my cheeks, down my neck. I sniffed to keep my snot in, as I bawled, whimpering for my parents to somehow come find me. I was going to have to spend the night out here all alone now, and who knew if I would ever reunite with them. I sat down on the ground, continuing to cry.

The tears came in bursts. Bawling until I physically couldn't anymore, before waiting a period and starting to cry again. I couldn't bear it, being alone. The darkness was tormenting me, ripping me apart, as I continuously shuddered with fear. I was going to be left out here all alone forever and ever.

It felt like it had been ages until the tears finally stopped for good. And now I sat in silence. And it felt just as haunting before. Sitting there, eyes still wet, just waiting. Not knowing what for. Perhaps I was waiting to somehow doze off and fall asleep, to escape from this horror. Waiting for someone to come to me, anyone. Waiting for any help that could possibly come.

And it felt like I waited even longer in silence than I did with tears. With nothing to do, the time seemed to pass even slower, and I could even feel like perhaps I would eventually just wait it out, just wait for the sun to come up so I could eventually find my way back. I could somehow get out of this dark shadow I was now entrenched in.

I had almost come to peace with the darkness and silence when I heard the wailing of sirens, accompanied by a voice on a loudspeaker. I could hear someone calling my name as a truck drove by me, as I got up and began to yell hysterically, getting them to notice me.

With its flashing blue and red lights and loud siren, I could hear the commotion as the lights turned on in the tents around the intersection I was on, as people were woken up by the commotion. The truck had stopped, turned sideways, as I saw my parents jump down from the back, coming forward to embrace me.

Their eyes were filled with tears, as my father picked me up in his arms, holding me close, making me know that I was safe. He carried me back to the truck and slowly and quietly, we drove back to the campsite, as I stayed in his arms in the back of the truck the entire way.

If only my parents could somehow save me now. If anyone could pick me up and hold me, telling me that everything was going to be okay. But those days were gone. A figment of the past that would never come back. Forever.

54

I woke up to a tap on my shoulder, as I was slumped up against the wall.

I opened my eyes to see a man, around 20 years old, standing in front of me, wearing a uniform from the store. He had short brown hair, a thin, long face, and bushy eyebrows.

"Sorry, man. Can't loiter here. Lots of people do it, but you can't. It's fine if you come by to grab food, but if you loiter again, we'll have to report you."

I was still in a haze, so I quickly nodded several times, as he walked back to the door.

At that moment, I realized what he had just said. After the searching, after Chris, after the shelter, I couldn't just let anything get away now. I ran up to the worker before he walked in.

"Hey, is there any way I could stay here? I just need something temporarily. Soon I'll be gone."

He turned and looked at me, as if he was thinking about something.

"Actually," he said, as I felt myself get more hopeful yet nervous. "Come inside for a bit."

He opened the door and let me in, as I saw the back of the store. There was a small room with several steel shelves with boxes. In the front of the room was another door, the only other exit of the room.

"So I tried this with someone older, but it didn't work," he said to me. "And to be honest, for me, it doesn't really matter if I keep trying."

I stared at him blankly, confused about what he was saying.

"So I work the last shift here four days of the week. We shut down at 12 am. Now on those four days, I can let you come into here and sleep inside as long as you leave before we open at 8. But in exchange I need something in return."

It sounded like a perfect chance for me.

"What is it?" I asked.

"So, um. I've kinda got a career on the side. Selling some stuff. I'm just gonna need you to transfer some things for me."

"Transfer as in carry?"

"Yea, it's something small. See the thing is, I get nowhere near enough money for college. So I sell weed on the side. But it's hard for me to reach my dealer. I need you to bring money to him, and bring weed back to me."

I thought about it for a moment. Part of me was disgusted that I was even considering the idea. Weeks ago, I would have spat in his face and walked away. But I realized that if rape wouldn't be punished in the homeless world, transporting some drugs wouldn't either. And I needed the shelter, especially in this cold. It was four days a week, but that would always be better than nothing.

"How would it work?" I asked.

"So I work Monday, Wednesday, Friday, and Saturday nights. So what could happen, is that on those days, I'll leave some money in a plastic bag and I'll put it somewhere we decide on. I'll do that when I start my shift in the afternoon. You take that money, and some time at night, you go to my contact. Swap the money for the weed. Then when you come at night, you show me that. And then I let you in. No weed, no room for you. And if you ever think about stealing my money, I'll kill you."

It sounded like a good plan. It felt dangerous, but I figured that I really had no other choice. This wouldn't ever end up on any record of me. And it was just weed and the offence wouldn't be too great anyway. I just needed protection from any harm from other homeless people. I had always thought that citizens were my enemy, but after the shelter and after Chris, I knew to think otherwise.

"I'll do it," I said.

He did a fist pump and smiled.

"Well today's Monday, so come here tonight at 12. I'll let you in and explain what to do. See you then."

And with that, he went back into the store.

I felt hopeful. It was risky, but I figured that in exchange for a warm shelter, this was definitely worth it. And I could just do this for the winter, and when the spring came and the ice thawed, I could go back to Ridgefield to show all of them that I could make it, that I was better than them, and that they couldn't ruin my life.

55

The sun set around 6 in the winter, so by 12 am, I was almost used to the dark. As I ventured into the back of the market, there was a thin layer of snow on the ground, on that clearly showed footsteps from where people had been.

As I went in to the square, I saw him standing outside the door, waiting for me.

"Hey, what's your name, by the way?" he said.

"Marcus," I replied.

"I'm Jack," he said.

He led me over across the square to the back right corner that was furthest away from the door of the store.

He crouched down near the corner and pointed to the sprout of a rain gutter. It was a rectangular metal opening that led down from a pipe that was connected to the edge of the roof of the apartment right above. The opening was moderately sized, probably small enough that a baseball would fit snugly. It was also hidden from sight, as the grey-white sprout blended in with the grey wall behind it.

"In the afternoon at 7, when I start my shift, I'm going to stuff a plastic bag in here. It'll just be a shopping bag. It'll be sealed, so just rip it open. In that I'll put an orange envelope. In it will be $600. You take that money and you take it to my supplier. Then you come here at 12 am and I'll be waiting for you. You give me the weed in whatever package he gives it to you in and I'll let you in. But don't ever touch the weed or try to steal my money or else I'll kill you."

I nodded.

"Also, another thing. There's an alarm that's on from when I lock the back door until the morning. That means that you can't leave the room at the back. I'll put a bucket in there for you in case you gotta piss or shit. But what'll happen is that once the first guy in the morning comes at 8, he'll disable the alarm from the front. You'll probably hear a sound or something. Once you know he's inside, you can leave from the back. No one will know you were there. Does that make sense?"

He looked at me with a glare of seriousness that pierced the dark night sky. When we had last met, he seemed laid back, but this time, I could sense that what he was describing was really important to him.

"Where do I take the money?"

He took a deep breath before looking at me.

"I have this supplier, his name is Kevin. He's around a 20 minute down the street that runs horizontally from the market. He has this office up in this townhouse there. You just find the black townhouse, say you have something for Kevin. Go up to his office, tell him that you're running for Jack. He also runs and owns a hooker place right next door. So don't you dare fuck up and use my money on those hookers."

I took a deep breath, digesting what he had just said. I was now going to work with the man who ran Diane's place. Part of me wasn't even surprised that he was a drug supplier. But I wasn't sure if I should have been glad that I would be able to see Diane or if I should have been haunted by the prospect of seeing her again. I knew she wouldn't care about what I did. And I wanted to see her again, talk to her, as she was one of the few people I really knew.

I must have been standing still, thinking for a while, as Jack spoke again.

"What, is the hooker part fucking with you?"

"Nah, it's fine," I said.

"Ok then. We'll start tomorrow. Here, I'll let you in," he said, leading me to the backdoor.

He opened it and I stepped inside. The room was dark, though with the light from the moon and the lights outside, I could make out the empty steel shelves that lined the sides of the room. I reached down and felt the ground. It was a hard tile, but it was warm. And so was the room. And I figured that the warmth was all I needed right now.

"Make yourself comfortable," he said, as he closed the door and left the store.

I lay down on the ground in the complete darkness, thinking to myself. But there was only one thought capable of making its way into my mind. Diane.

56

I woke up to the opening of lights in the room I was sleeping in. Lying down on my back, I could see the fluorescent light tubes directly above me. I shook myself to my sense and sat up, staring at the door in front of me that led into the store. I could hear sounds from beyond the door, meaning that someone had entered and opened the store in the morning. Looking up at the lights, I was relieved they had turned on. Jack must not have known, but the automatic turning on of the lights in the morning would definitely wake me up in the morning, so I wouldn't have to worry about being caught.

I opened the back door, and like Jack had said, there was no alarm. The back square was empty, except for the thin layer of snow that seemed to perpetually cover the ground.

I let out a yawn, feeling relieved that I had somewhere to stay to endure the cold nights, at least on half of the days. But to keep this, I had to figure out what I was going to do with the job. I had to make sure it ran smoothly, so I could keep it up.

I figured that I was going to spend the day collecting food and just travelling around, before going to the townhouses at night to scout them out. I wanted to know which townhouse to go to beforehand. I had to be careful, and I had to be ready.

I walked in the direction of the townhouses, stopping at dumpsters along the way. In one, I was able to find a box of expired croissants that didn't smell the best, but were still clearly edible. In another, I found a half-finished cola drink and a full and new plastic water bottle, which must have been thrown out accidentally.

Satisfied with what I had, I settled for a nap on the street, before venturing to the townhouses.

57

I woke up in the late afternoon, feeling far more energized than I had been before. Looking around me, I remembered that I was around halfway there, between the market and the townhouses. In total, it was roughly a 20 minute walk, so I knew that I was close by.

It wasn't snowing, and the light snow that had fallen the previous night was now melted away and gone.

The buildings that led me in the direction of the townhouses seemed to get progressively older and worn-down. The landscape went from ten-story apartment buildings to low-rise, three-story buildings that spanned several blocks. Fire escapes sprawled across the buildings, adding complexion to the uniform nature of the brown brick buildings. The buildings were interspersed with convenience stores, a car repair garage, and several small and dirty take out restaurants, before the gradient of buildings led into the townhouses. The initial ones, close to the restaurants, were normal. There were old sedans parked in the driveways, and occasionally, a woman sitting out on the small porch. But getting closer to the makeshift brothel, the townhouses were largely abandoned, waiting to be torn down, but never actually being demolished. Perhaps it was because these buildings were so insignificant that destroying them wasn't worth it. Or maybe it was that some things forgotten by society were just meaningless. Like people didn't even know these townhouses were here, as no one dared venture into this part of the city. Maybe this was what happened to humans too. Left behind. There was no point of even getting rid of us. That was how worthless we were.

The thing that signalled the makeshift brothel and apparently, the drug supply office was actually on the other side of the street.

Across from the gradient of apartment buildings and townhouses was a series of small and old houses that began to parallel the side I was walking on once the apartment buildings shifted from ten stories to three. And those houses extended, getting older and more worn out, until reaching a point of abandonment that mirrored the opposing townhouses. But several of the houses had chain-link fences around them, with signs signalling planned demolitions. But the worn down houses soon stopped, as they transitioned into a park.

I would follow the park for about 2 minutes, before seeing a large fountain, made of the stone. It was no longer functioning now, but the sheer size of it allowed it to still served as a useful landmark. It sat around 50 meters away from the sidewalk, near the edge of the vast, dirty park. The base of the fountain started wide and round, before becoming thinner, until it reached the bottom of a bowl-shaped structure. The bowl was large, and was where the water would have stayed. Protruding out of the middle of the bowl was a straight tube, with several petal-like structures that sprouted out of the sides of the top of the tube. The water would have come out of the tube, dripping down the curved petals and into the bowl.

I tried to imagine the fountain, as it functioned. A constant stream of water, bringing life to a lively park situated in a fresh neighbourhood. But now, it was just a large stone that lay across from the blue townhouse with a boarded up door that secretly led to a brothel. And just like Jack said, two townhouses over, there was a black townhouse, similar in appearance to the blue one, that housed an office and in it, drugs.

The townhouses were quiet. There were no women on the street smoking, nor any men or women venturing inside the brothel, looking for sex.

With time on my hands, I decided to cross the street and explore the park.

First, I walked up to the fountain, looking to inspect it from a closer range. I noticed that up on the bowl of the fountain, there were carved humps, forming a uniform pattern that extended around the bowl. The fountain truly was big. The rim of the bowl reached my shoulders and with my arm extended as far as I could reach above my head, I couldn't come close to reaching the top of the sprout.

Moving away from the fountain, I walked forward, away from the sidewalk, onto a paved walking path that ran horizontally, parallel to the road. I followed it horizontally, walking for a short time before the path curved left, away from the road and away from the townhouses.

In front of me, there was an old metal playground that the path would eventually lead to. As I walked closer to it, I began to notice more features, as the playground revealed itself to be even older than the ones we had in Ridgefield. The swings were on a rusty metal frame, that appeared to have been red in the past but was now just grey and brown, the colours of rusted iron. To the right was a tall metal slide. The slide was rectangular in shape, featuring seemingly uncomfortable vertical segments along the edges of the slide designed to prevent kids from falling up. The slide was fairly tall, perhaps reaching just over 2 meters in height.

As I got closer to the playground, I began to notice the ground it was situated on. The slide and the swing set both sat on in a wooden frame, that formed a rectangular one-inch high boundary around the park. Inside the boundary, and under the slide and the swing set was now just wood. I figured that it had once been filled with sand, but was now empty, completely gone. Maybe it had blown away, or maybe someone had stolen it for some mysterious purpose. BUt now the parts of the park sat on a plain wooden base, marking a forgotten area that likely hadn't been used by kids for years.

I climbed the ladder behind the slide, reaching the top. From there, I could see across the entire park. It was vast, and it extended far across the townhouses. It was mostly plain, with paved walking paths and patches of grass here or there, all long and yellow, having not been cared for.

Deep in the upper far right corner, as I looked at the apartments on the horizon across from the townhouses, I could faintly see a structure that seemed to resemble something different from what I had seen already.

Though the sky was beginning to darken slightly, I figured that I had enough time to go and see what it was. I began to walk in the direction of what I had seen.

I walked across the patchy grass area for a while, scaling across the vast, plain, open park. I wondered why the park was still here, why the land wasn't used for something else.

Eventually, after around 10 minutes of continuous walking across the seemingly endless park, I was close enough to realize that far in front of me, there was a paved pathway that led to a stone, arched bridge. I couldn't see any water under it, so I figured that it had dried. But perhaps what was more surprising was the dispersed streetlights around it. There had been none on the other side of the park, where the townhouses were. But beyond the bridge, as I looked to the parallel road that sat across from where I had come from, I could make out newer apartments. The streetlights weren't on yet, but in the distance, I could see lit up signs on buildings and stores.

And to the right of me, I could see trees. They weren't dense or crowded, but they were there.

I walked up to the bridge. It was made of cobblestone, forming an arc over a now-dry riverbed. Looking forward, I still couldn't clearly make out the sidewalk that connected the other road to the park, meaning that the bridge was situated fairly deep into the park. However, it still sat significantly closer to the opposite side of the park, far away from the townhouses.

The riverbed was now more of a slight crater. It led into the grass on either side of the bridge. I wondered if there had ever been water in the first place, realizing that there was no possible source. The bridge was there for decoration, to provide something for people to walk on for enjoyment.

I looked at the dispersed trees that lay around this area of the park. Though I barely noticed it at first, it was clear that the park wasn't what I thought it would be. Instead of being a continuous, barren land, it was almost like a divider between a more lively, almost important part of the city and the forgotten areas across from it. Near the townhouses, there was a broken fountain, an abandoned playground, and patches of yellow grass. Yet here, there was a decorative bridge, concrete walkways that led from the edge of the park, and many trees that populated the area. It reminded me of the nicer areas of the parks in Ridgefield, that I would go biking in when I was a child.

As I lifted my head up from the bridge that I had been inspecting, I noticed something new. A bright veil of lights emerged across from me, as I noticed that the streetlights had turned on. I had been so caught up in the new and prettier nature of the park that I didn't realize the dimming of the sky, that seemed to happen so quickly in the winter. The tall streetlights that sat around the park let out a soothing glow that illuminated the walkways. There weren't too many of them, but they were tall and black, reaching modest heights. I wondered if the lights were visible from the other end of the park. If the people on the other side could make out the lights in the horizon, dreaming of a day when they could live on the other side of the park.

The park was like a sea that divided two different worlds. Connected, yet separated in every way, with no contact between them.

Turning around and trying to look back at the townhouses, I couldn't make them out int he dark, even with the light behind me. Instead, I only saw what I thought was the only thing that was here. A long, barren field of grass. But where I was standing, it was like something you saw in a movie. A beautiful area, that definitely featured people walking by, enjoying themselves. But people from either side never crossed into the other world. Perhaps they both tried to pretend that the other world didn't exist.

Which world did I belong in? A month ago, the answer would have been clear. But even now, I wanted to believe I was part of this one. The side of the park with lights, with the bridge, with the trees. But I knew I wasn't anymore.

I was a world away from my old life.

58
The sky was dark by now, so I figured I could make the walk back to the townhouses. It was like I had almost forgotten my purpose

of being here after being so caught up in the amazement of seeing the other side of the park. It was something I never could have imagined. I wondered if the people from the townhouses knew. If they knew that right across the old park, there was life, there was hope.

Or maybe they tried to pretend it didn't exist.

I began to walk back to the townhouses. Thinking about it, I didn't realize just how vast the park was before. It took several minutes of continuous walking until I could clearly make out the dim glow that came from the townhouses. Turning around to look backwards, the glow of the streetlights was still far more apparent, more powerful.

But walking back through the field, the light from the streetlights slowly became less apparent, as I reached the deserted playground, and the streetlights became light specks in the background, something that I wouldn't have bothered to care about if I hadn't ventured over to see where they came from.

I reached the fountain, and from there, in the darkness, I could make out several people standing around the townhouses. There were people sitting along the curb, and on the sidewalk leading to the townhouses, I could see a man walking towards the house, opening the wooden board, and entering the brothel.

And as I got closer, I could make out the sounds of the townhouses, In particular, there was a single source of sound that seemed to paralyze the rest.

Out in front of the stairs that led up to the wooden board of the blue townhouse, I could see two people. I was now standing on the sidewalk across the road from the townhouses, watching the people seem to argue.

Looking closely, I realized that I was watching Diane and another larger man. In fact it wasn't really an argument. He was yelling at her, but she stood up straight against him, seeming to ignore what he was saying. I wanted it not to be her, but seeing her long blonde hair, I knew it couldn't be anyone else.

"That's not what you're supposed to do!" he yelled at her.

"Do you realize what the fuck this means, you bitch! You can't keep fucking this up like this!" he continued to yell.

She remained silent, looking at him.

"You're just a fucking whore," he said, with a quieter yet still serious tone. I was now standing at the edge of the sidewalk, watching him yell at her. I wondered if Diane knew if I was there, if she knew I was seeing what was happening to her.

"Fucking bitch," he said. He seemed to calm down, until suddenly, I saw him raise his arm up, with his hand extended. He swung his arm across her face, as her head flew over to the right, and she stumbled for a few steps.

I wanted to scream, I wanted to run over and do something, but I knew I couldn't.

"If it wasn't for your tits and ass, you'd be fucking dead," he said, as he walked up the steps opened the board, and walked inside the blue townhouse.

I quickly ran across the road, going up to Diane, stunned at what had just happened. I wondered if this was a one-time event, in fear that this was something regular, something that repeated.

"Diane, what happened?" I asked her.

She turned to look at me, having recognized my voice.

"Marcus, what are you doing here," she said softly, behind her outstretched hand that clutched her face.

"I came by to check something out. Why did he do that to you?" I asked.

"Oh, you saw that," she said. "It's nothing. Here, I'm gonna go."

She began to walk forwards, away from the townhouse, as I put my hand on her shoulder, holding her back as I walked up next to her.

"Diane, tell me. This shouldn't happen," I said, trying to help. I didn't know her well, but now, I guess she was still one of the few people I did know.

Her hand was still held up to her face, as she held her left cheek, where she had been hit.

"It really isn't your business," she said, trying to walk away.

"No, Diane, tell me."

"It's something small," she replied. "I was supposed to fuck this girl, but she fingered my fucking ass when I didn't want her too. So I slapped that bitch. And then he got all pissed."

"Does he do that often?" I asked.

"Just don't worry about it Marcus," she said. We had been walking the whole time, and now, we were almost a block away from the brothel. She had turned her face to be away from what I could see, trying to prevent me from seeing the sore part of her face.

"But Diane.."

"This is my life, Marcus," she said boldly and loudly, interrupting me. "Sometimes you just gotta do what you need to. And stop worrying about things. Shit like that happens. Besides, why are you here anyway?"

I paused for a moment. Part of me wanted to abandon everything, abandon the weed carrying. But I had to do it, and there was no sense in lying to her.

"I found a deal with someone. I'm shipping weed and money in exchange for somewhere to stay."

She just nodded.

"Is there something wrong?" I asked.

"No. If you're looking for Kevin, well guess who you just saw."

I didn't want it to be true. I didn't want to work with him, I didn't want to do anything for him, after seeing who he was.

"But no, Marcus, just go ahead with it. He's a cunt but you gotta find a way to live."

"But I don't want to be with people like him. People like him shouldn't be able to do anything. They should be put in jail."

"Yea, that's wishful thinking. But this is just how shit works, Marcus. Thanks for worrying about me. But people like him fuck others over and nothing happens. It's pointless to try to do anything. You just need to deal with him. Just forget about others and do what you need to do. Now go, Marcus, do whatever you came here to do. Maybe I'll see you tomorrow or something."

And with that, she walked down the road, away. I was shocked at how calm she was, how she could go through that, yet be more unaffected than I was. Like she didn't care that she had just been slapped across the face by a man who used her sex to earn money. I wondered how she managed to carry on that way. Just living like this, getting thrashed, but continuing on.

And who knew what kind of shit she had gone through. No one ever would. She would all just hide it, never letting anyone see.

I wanted to tell her that this wasn't how it was. I wanted to tell her that her life could be better. That she could be treated better. But I knew I couldn't because I didn't know if it was true.

I turned around and walked back towards the black townhouse, as I stopped before it, looking at it.

Perhaps what it was what i had just seen, but something about the townhouse made it feel haunting. I didn't want to ever go in, I didn't want to ever be around here. I didn't want to ever see Kevin. I wanted to destroy him if I could.

But this was my life now, and this was the demonic reality that I had to now face.

58

Seeing the news channel station in the coffee shop hit 7 pm, I walked directly to the square behind the market.

Going to the sprout of the rain gutter, I reached my hand inside, and as expected, I found a plastic shopping bag that had come from the market. I took the bag, ripped it open, finding the brown envelope Jack had mentioned. I opened it, seeing several one hundred dollar bills inside. Relieved that what Jack had told me was true, I rolled up the envelope and stuffed it into my pocket as I walked out of the square, on to the road.

I realized that by 7 pm in the winter, the sky was almost pitch black already. Diane was likely already in the brothel by now, and who knew what else was happening in those townhouses. But I had a simple job to do, one that i hoped would lead me quickly in and out of the black townhouse. And finishing the exchange, I would get a warm place to sleep at night, something that I desperately needed.

I began to walk down the road that led me to the townhouses. After the 20 minute walk, I found myself walking towards the townhouses. Once again, with the sky dark, it was already busy, with people hanging around the areas. There were people smoking on the curb, and others just leaning against the outside walls of the townhouses.

The area outside was somber and quiet. Prostitutes sat smoking in silence on the curb, as if they were waiting for something to happen. Maybe a customer to come, maybe something else. They didn't talk between them, but they sat close right next to each other. I wondered how Diane would have fit in. Would she smoke with the rest of them? Or would she be on the side, eating her biscuits.

I walked up to the black townhouse. There was another bouncer standing beside the door who called out to me upon seeing me walk to the door.

"What are you here for?" he asked.

I was nervous, but I tried to just follow the plan I had, the instructions Jack gave me.

"I have something for Kevin," I replied.

The bouncer walked towards me as I shuddered, preparing to run away if he attacked me.
"Just need to check you," he said.

He felt the sides of my body and my pockets. He also went around my arms and my ankles, before standing back.

I wondered what other people had done to make these checks necessary.

"All clean," he said, as he opened the wooden board, once again serving as a door, that was behind us.

The townhouse was identical to the one that contained the brothel. The stairs were to the left, and the bouncer directed me up.

"Go to the top floor. Knock on the door before entering."

And with that, he stepped back outside.

I proceeded up the stairs, which followed a similar structure to the other house. They were light brown wooden steps, with dust that was collected on the sides. The middle of each step was clear from dust, from people walking. The house was dimly light, with several incandescent bulbs on the ceilings of each floor.

The second floor of the three-story townhouse was empty and silent. The stairs led into the middle of the floor, just like the other townhouses. Around was a ring with many doors, each leading to bedrooms. But these weren't used to house prostitutes like the other building. The stairs that led to the floor were right next to the base of the steps that led to the third floor. That was the floor Chris had gone to before, alone. I stepped up the stairs.

The top floor was much smaller. The stairs led to a small area that only had one door, which appeared to have previously led to a master bedroom in the old design of the townhouse. Back when it was used as a home. I walked up to the white door, and knocked.

"Come in," I heard the familiar voice say, the same voice that was yelling at Diane the other night.

His voice was raspy but also very low and powerful. Someone who I didn't want to mess with.

I walked in, expecting to see an absolute mess, with drugs on the floor and perhaps other guards standing around. Instead, there was only one man sitting at a desk on the right side of the room.

The room was empty with the exception of the wooden desk at the right, and several cardboard boxes at the back of the windowless room. The only light source of the room was a lamp on the far upper left corner of the desk, farthest away from the door.

On the desk was several papers, as well as a cup at the top right corner, holding several pens. Kevin sat on a black fold out chair, right in front of the desk.

Everything about the room felt more like an office of a company than the room of a brothel owner and drug trafficker. Kevin wore a polo shirt and a pair of black glasses. He was white, around 40 in age, with a medium build. He wasn't particularly muscular, but he wasn't too fat either. His hair was gelled so it was swept towards the middle. Everything about him screamed office worker to me, or even manager. He didn't appear to have the personality that I saw when he was yelling at Diane. I was expecting a rough man, perhaps sitting in the corner of a messy room. But this office was clean and organized, and nothing like I would have expected.

He only looked up to me after I stepped into the room.

"What can I do for you?" he asked.

He asked calmly, smoothly.

"I'm delivering money for Jack."

"So he got a runner," he said. He looked like he was thinking. "Will I expect to see you every time?"

"Yes," I replied.

"Ok. So what happens is you give me the money. I count it. Then you leave the townhouse, head around the side of it. You open the fence gate. THere'll be some guys there who'll give the product to you."

"Ok," I said, taking out the envelope from under my sweater. I handed it to him.

He sat back in his chair, opened the envelope, and counted the money inside.

"You're all good," he said. "And tell Jack that I'm expecting him to come see me."

"Ok," I said.

"What's your name?" he asked.

"Marcus."

"Marcus what?"

"Smith," I replied. "Marcus Smith."

"Ok, Mr. Smith. Head around to the back."

I turned around, walked out the room, and closed the door behind me. I was relieved, having expected someone far more terrifying. But Kevin was still intimidating, even with his calm demeanour. I feared he would lash out, given what I had seen last time. Perhaps that was what made people fear and respect him.

I walked all the way downstairs, leaving the townhouse. The bouncer stood where he was before, giving me a look as I walked to the right side of the townhouse. There was a small gap between the two townhouses, and between the gap, a wooden fence. It had a door with a metal design on the front, one that looked like an interlocked web in the shape of a spiral.

I walked to the fence door, pushing it open. I walked into the backyard of the townhouse. It was small, just like the size of the backyard of our family's old house. Encompassed by a wooden fence on all four sides in a rectangular shape, there wasn't anyone there. Only the patchy grass.

Suddenly, at the back fence, a man climbed over. He jumped over the fence, his arms perched on the top of it, swinging his body over. I could make out a blonde bear under a beanie. He was wearing a dirty grey hoodie and loose jeans. He ran up to me, a bag in his hand.

Without saying a word, he handed it to me. I took the bag, and he instantly turned around, ran back to the fence, and climbed over. I didn't say a word, surprised at what happened.

This was probably how they ran things. They handled the money and drugs separately. I took a look inside the bag as I walked back towards the gate and out onto street. In the bag were three socks. Filled with weed, presumably. I opened the gate by the handle on it. I pulled it open, walking towards the sidewalk. Once again, I stuffed the bag under my sweater, concealing it and protecting it.

I was relieved with the exchange. I had feared that it would be terrifying, that perhaps I might be attacked. I was worried that Kevin would assault me, like he hit Diane. But he didn't. And this felt like something I could do for the near future. Just come here for an exchange, so I could have a warm place to sleep.

Just as I was walking away, I heard a familiar voice.

"Marcus!" I heard a voice call out.

I turned around to look, and I saw Diane jogging up to me.

"What are you doing?" I asked.

"Got bored I guess. Don't have much to do tonight. I'm just gonna head home now."

"Isn't it a bit too early?" I asked. I figured that it was only around 9 now, at the latest.

"Whatever, I'm tired," she replied.

We walked down the street. The night was surprisingly quiet. It was probably because it was a Tuesday.

"Kevin was, um." I thought about how to phrase myself. "Quiet today."

"Yea, that's how he is," she said. "Calm, but then he flips out sometimes. But he manages this shit like a businessman."

"Why does he do that? He had a desk and everything his his room."

"He's careful," she said. "He's a cunt, but there's a reason he hasn't been shut down yet. But then he flips out just enough that people won't fuck with him."

That made sense to me. He did seem clever. But he was also intimidating enough that I didn't dare do anything to him.

"And he never touches the drugs," I said, realizing his plan.

"Yea. So he never really gets turned in for shit. But watch out for him. He's done some bad stuff that he's gotten out of. But no one cares. He'll just keep going on."

"What do you mean?" I asked.

"Well I've been in this for a couple years. He had a partner before. One day he disappeared. Dude's name was Brad. He wasn't as vicious as Kevin. But Kevin was definitely a part of it."

"Oh," I replied. Part of me wanted to live in the ignorance of believing Kevin was someone good who could help me. But I knew he wasn't.

As we kept walking, we passed a man walking by, who let out a big puff of his cigarette, in front of us so we could smell the smoke.

"Ugh," Diane let out. "Fucking caner."

"What?" I asked, surprised at Diane's reaction.

"The smoke," she said.

"You don't smoke?" I asked.

"No," she said, with a disgusted look on her face. "Do you?"

"Nah," I replied.

"Phew. I would've looked at you differently."

"All the other hookers do," I said. "It's typically the first thing I see when I come by."

"Yea. I really don't get it. Why they do that."

I was pleasantly surprised at Diane's reaction. I feared that she was just like one of the hookers I had seen before. But somehow, this gave me faith that she was different. That she was something more.

"It's disgusting," she continued. "Cigarettes, alcohol, drugs. People do it to make themselves feel like they belong. To make themselves feel like they fit in. Just doing dumb shit, poisoning themselves. They indulge in these things because they're insecure fucks who can't handle the world. They do dumb shit, feel like they belong with the others, and make themselves feel better about themselves."

"Oh, wow."

"What, you didn't expect that?" she said, with a chuckle. "Well, surprise."

She used her hands and gestured at me with a smile as she finished her sentence, the same gesture one would use when trying to scare a kid. She was smiling and seemed happy. Part of me was amazed by her but another part admired her. That she could stand so strongly on these things, around such different people.

"Marcus, what do you think is the biggest problem in the world?" she asked.

I thought about it for a second.

"Maybe unforgiveness? Or maybe people don't think about things from other perspectives. Consider how something happened. From someone else's view."

"Ok," she said, as if she was expecting me to follow up.

"What about you?" I asked.

"People don't act like themselves. They try to be someone else. Try and show themselves in a way that they aren't. If everyone didn't care about what others thought, the whole world would be a lot better."

I nodded my head.

"Like just imagine. If politicians did what they actually believed, instead of just going into the system and becoming a system fuck. Or artists, if they didn't just become sellouts. Everything would be so much better."

She looked at me, gauging my reaction. I thought about it. I guess it did make sense. I thought about the people in my life. My mother, who cared so much about reputation. Francis, who just wanted himself to be seen as more than he was.

"But yea," she continued. "By the way, any music you like?" she asked.

"I like folk stuff. Some soft rock. Fleetwood Mac, Carpenters, Neil Young. You?"

"That's pretty cool," she replied. "I was scared you'd be one of those mainstream kids. Pop and stuff. Anyway, I'm into a whole lot. Psychedelic, glam rock. I have a cassette player that still works with some tapes. You can try it someday."

"Oh, wow, that's cool," I replied.

She had an easygoing attitude that greatly contrasted how she was when I first met her when i was Chris. Perhaps that was just a defense mechanism, what she did towards strangers.

"Well, we're almost at my stop," she said.

We had been walking for at least 10 minutes now, and I knew that we were around halfway there to the market. And it made sense that she lived on the other side of the market, considering where she worked.

"Where do you live?" I asked, curious as to what she could afford, and how she lived her daily life.

"I share an apartment with a few girls. I hate them. They get drunk all the time. Two of them work at a strip club, the other is a bartender. But it's cheap, and I can get by."

"Hey," she continued. "I can show you where it is."

We turned left on the street in front of us, as she led me down the parallel street. The block was made up of the low apartment buildings, the ones with three floors, and a sprawl of fire exit staircases. She led me to the door of one of the buildings.

"I live in the third floor of this one. Honestly, feel free to come by. The girls probably won't want you in there because it's pretty cramped. But over there, on the right, there's a fire escape staircase."

She pointed over to the right side of the building. There was a ladder that came from a fire escape platform at the base of the second floor. It hung around 2 meters off the ground, meaning that I had to jump up to reach it.

"The escape platform is right outside my window. So yeah you can come by whenever I want. Chances are that I'm in there."

"Ok sure" I replied.

"Well, good night then," she said to me, giving a small wave.

"Goodnight Diane."

She turned around and walked to the apartment door, walking inside.

And even as she entered the building and shut the door behind her, it was like the moonlight still reflected off her blonde hair that glistened in the dark. Part of me wanted her to be so much more. She could be perhaps a doctor, a teacher, maybe even an engineer. She was smart enough, insightful enough.

But this was who she was.

And maybe that was what made her so beautiful.

59
Stability was something that I didn't think I would have, not in this world. But somehow, it felt present to me.

A week of a routine. Going to the townhouses, exchanging for the weed, bringing it back to Jack so I could be let into the store. And I would leave the store in the morning as the lights turned on, before going around the dumpsters in the area, looking for food, keeping my extras in a bag I always kept with me.

And the sleep was warm, inside the store. Sure, it was dark, and sure, pissing or shitting was uncomfortable, but it was possible.

But the only harsh part was the other days. When it wasn't a Monday, Wednesday, Friday or Saturday night. And I would curl up behind a dumpster, anywhere where I could get a sliver of heat. I could count as many sheep as I wanted to, I could close my eyes as long as I could, but not even the light from the stars could help me fall asleep in the wake of the blistering cold. I would lie awake for hours, shivering. It snowed every few days, but there wasn't even a storm yet, and I knew I would never be able to handle one.

The winter was only getting worse. I needed somewhere to stay, perhaps in exchange for some other job. I had to turn to my only source for something to do, some help. I didn't want to go to Kevin, but I knew that I had no choice.

60

The Wednesday the week after my first weed run, I told myself that I was going to go tell Kevin that I needed help. The routine I followed had become normal; every time I went to the black townhouse, I would knock on his door, enter, and give him the money. He would count it and would send me out back, where I picked up the weed in a brown paper bag. The only difference was the man who jumped over the fence to get the weed for me. Sometimes, it was a young white man with a blonde beard. Sometimes it was a black man.

When I picked up the money from the rain gutter behind the market, I once again stuffed the envelope under my sweater. The previously brown and green sweater now had smudges of black all over it. It was snowing today, and every bit of frost that I felt on the back of my neck reminded me more that I needed somewhere to stay on the other days.

Eventually, trudging through the slush on the sidewalks, I reached the black townhouse with the familiar line of prostitutes sitting on the curb. Uniform, like last time. But part of me couldn't tell them apart. I tried to recall if they were the same ones I had seen before. But I honestly couldn't.

The bouncer let me into the black townhouse, and I made my way up to Kevin's office.

"Come in," he said again, after I knocked.

I walked up to him and handed him the money as usual.

My mind began to race. The settling of my heart rate after the first visit was all gone now, as I thought about how I would ask him for help. Maybe I would ask him in a way that made it sound like I was doing a favour. No. He would see right through that. He sifted through the bills, as part of me hoped it would go on forever. Just keep counting it, count it forever so I never need to ask. Maybe I just wouldn't ask. I could just not ask, walk away after, make this a normal day and maybe I could ask Friday. But no, I had to do it now, I came here to do it, I had to ask. He was now reorganizing the bills, walking over to put them on the far side of the desk. I was just going to bring it up casually, like I had planned. Just do it. Do it. You need to.

"Ok, head around the back," he said to me.

I froze for a second, in fear.

"U-um…," I stuttered nervously. "C-could"

"Is something wrong?" he asked calmly, a piercing glare in his eyes.

"I need somewhere to sleep on some nights. Is there anything I could do for you in exchange?"

I looked at me, thinking.

"Hmm," he murmured, as he walked towards the back of the room. I stayed at the doorway, as he put his right arm on the back wall, his head bent down, looking at the ground. He turned around again, looking directly at me.

He turned around again and went to one of the cardboard boxes at the back of the room. He opened it, took something out of it, and walked back towards me.

"Here," he said, dangling a key in front of me. "When it isn't Monday, Wednesday, Friday, or Saturday, you can use this. Only on those days. You hear me."

"Yea," I replied.

"There's a room available a few townhouses down. Beige townhouse with a boarded up false door. You go to the top floor. The key unlocks the bedroom."

"Ok," I said, waiting to hear what I had to do in return.

"Now go around the back to pick up the product," he said.

I was surprised that he didn't tell me to do anything.

"Is there anything I need to do for you?" I asked.

"I'll keep you posted," he replied. "But only those days. And no one else in the room."

With the key in my hand, I quickly stuffed it into my pocket, before heading downstairs and retrieving the weed from the backyard.

I knew better than to go check out the townhouse today, after what he told me about only going on the days when I wasn't delivering for Jack. But walking back to the market, I could only feel relief. I didn't bother to question anything, I didn't want to worry about anything. I just wanted to live in this mirage of stability. Because this was the closest thing to home I could have in over a month.

61
Part of me honestly looked forward to Thursday night. Sure, staying at the townhouse near that area on a day when I wasn't delivering for Jack wasn't ideal, but compared to the prospect of sleeping on the streets, it was like a sanctuary.

I followed the regular path I took until I got there. When I saw the park across the street in the distance that signalled the start of the townhouses, I began to look for a beige townhouse.

Three buildings in and it was there. Similar in structure to the other ones. The entrance featured a concrete walkway leading up to two steps. Above the steps was a wooden board, just like the other townhouses that used a wooden board to make the house seem abandoned. I looked at it, from the outside. My new home. At least for half the week.

The door was positioned right at the middle of the house. Above it, there was a window on the left wide on the second floor. On the third floor, there was a smaller window on the far right. At the very top of the townhouse, there was a black triangular roof, peaking right at the middle.

I walked up to the board, opening it and stepping in. Once again, the house followed a similar format to the other ones. A staircase on the left, with the rest of the first floor being on the right. I immediately went to the staircase and began walking up. It was a wooden staircase with smooth rails on each side. It went up straight for half of it, made a full 180 degree turn, then led to the second floor. The house was dimly lit, making me wonder if someone was living in it now, or if the lights were perpetually on. On the ceilings there were individual small incandescent bulbs, accompanied by a faint buzzing. Like the other houses, the first staircase led to a ring-like second floor, with the next staircase adjacent to the end of the previous one. I walked up the second flight of stairs, leading to the third floor. Once again, the staircase went straight for half the way, before making a complete turn. The last floor had a sliver of ground, with the wooden rail on the edge of the floor only around a metre from the two adjacent doors. The door on the right was significantly smaller and it didn't have a keyhole. I figured that it was meant to be a closet, or small storage room.

I reached into my pocket and took out the key. I stuck it into the keyhole of the door and turned.

The bedroom was similar in size to Kevin's office. It was slightly smaller than the bedroom of my family's home, but it was more than I could ask for. The walls were painted brown, but the paint was old and unmaintained. In the middle of the ceiling, like the rest of the house, there was a small incandescent bulb that was bright enough that I could see where things were. To the right of the room, where Kevin's desk was, there was a direct entry into a bathroom. And in the back of the room, at the back-left corner, there was a small bed. It lay just to the left of the small square window I had seen from outside. The bed was low off the ground, and probably just long enough for my body. But it was still a bed. With a pillow and a blanket.

In the washroom, there was a toilet that was functional and could flush. Though the shower was old, mouldy, and didn't work, the sink still did. The washroom had white tiles that didn't match the brown walls of the room. The tiles seemed older though, giving the impression that the room was redone but the washroom was ignored. But still, it was a washroom.

I walked over to the window. From here, I could see the street from outside and the park. Some noise seeped through, but it wasn't much. There was no curtain for the window, but I really didn't care. The light that could come in wasn't too much of a hindrance, and compared to where I had gotten used to sleeping, this was an absolute blessing.

I lay my bag down beside the right side of the length of the bed. The left side leaned on the wall, with the back of the bed also snugly fitting into the wall. I walked over to the door, closed it, and flicked the small light switch that was immediately next to the door. I went and sat on the bed. The room wasn't fully dark, with some light from the window coming in, but I felt at ease, and I felt peaceful. I reached at my waist and slowly pulled my sweater off, above my head. It was the first time I had done that in weeks. Though the smell was pungent, I felt relieved. I then took my boots off, feeling a cold tingle as the sweat in my socks that had collected for weeks finally made contact with the outside air. I turned onto the bed, pulling the thin blanket over myself, as I rested my head on the pillow.

I was asleep in an instant.

62

Something felt oddly uncomfortable about my life now. The stability now was uncanny, almost unsettling. It shouldn't have happened to me. But maybe some good things do happen every once in a while.

But two weeks in, part of me just didn't feel right. Kevin hadn't given me a job yet. I was just living in his townhouse half the week, without giving anything back to him.

Even though the nights I stayed at the townhouse meant nights I could hang around and talk to Diane, part of me still wanted to do something for Kevin. Perhaps I was scared of him. I probably was.

63

Though sleeping in the back of the store was nowhere near as comfortable as the bedroom in the townhouse, every time I took the journey from the market to the townhouses, seeing the conditions of the street reminded me to be grateful towards what I had. I had began to take the money down later; though Jack always planted it around 7 pm, I figured that 7 was the ideal time to scavenge for dinner remains. I would keep the money under my sweater, delivering it around 10 to 11, so that I could head back to the market and see Jack without waiting too long with the weed in my hands.

It was Monday again and after picking up the money from the rain gutter, I ventured down to the black townhouse.

Kevin was once again in his usual position, sitting in front of the desk. But before I left his office to go pick up the weed, he called me back.

"Marcus, come in for a second."

I turned back to face him and stepped into his office.

"Close the door," he said.

My heart began to pound, fearing that maybe now he would do something to me. Instead, he only spoke.

"Marcus, I've been seeing how you're doing recently and it's been good. You've followed my instructions."

I nodded.

"I was worried you'd be a junkie. I don't work with junkies."

I nodded again. I was standing just inches away from the door, looking at him, as he stayed put on his black fold out chair.

"Starting now, you might see a note under your pillow. If you see one, you follow what it says on there. I think I can trust you now. If you want to stay in that townhouse, you better follow the note."

"Ok," I said quietly.

"Ok, that's it," he said, as he turned back to face the papers on his desk. "You can go now."

I turned around and walked back outside. Part of me felt relieved. I knew that now, more than ever, my life was still uncertain, especially working for Kevin. But the part of me that worried that everything was a trick seemed to be settled. I knew better than to take anything for free, but now that Kevin was going to give me work, that worry seemed to disappear. It felt like I had been hired for job, even though I had been living in the townhouse for weeks now.

After picking up the weed, I decided to head back to the market. Maybe I would have a talk with Jack. Typically, I would just hand him the bag and he would let me in. At most, we would say "see you," or something like that. Perhaps I would chat with him this time.

I walked until the part of the street that the townhouses turned into small apartments. I looked at the buildings around me, on either side of the street. Somehow, I didn't feel so foreign anymore. It was like this area of the city, this area of the world was now my home. This was where I worked, this was where I lived. Though I would've been frightened by the prospect of these conditions before, somehow this feeling of familiarity was invigorating.

Looking over at the apartments down the left side of the street I had reached, I realized I was looking at Diane's building. And my eyes were fixated on the fire escape ladder that would lead right outside her window.

I had talked with Diane a few times each week, either as we were walking back, or when she was sitting outside the blue townhouse waiting. Sometimes the conversations would even be long, spanning tens of minutes as we chatted about our lives, about the people around us. It was like we were our own bubble. Though we were different in many ways, we both felt like outsiders, and that really brought us together. But I had never actually gone to visit her at night like she offered. I had thought about it, but I always stopped at the last moment, scared that I would do something wrong.

Maybe today could be the day.

I walked over to her building, stopping in front of the black steel ladder that hung off the ground, to the right of the door.

The ladder was vertical for several meters, before reaching a platform next to a window from the second floor. The platform ran across the building, starting from the right side and reaching the left. From the left side, there was a flight of metal stairs that led to a small platform next to a window on the third floor. Diane's window.

I leaped up and grabbed the first metal bar of the ladder. My arms felt weak from a lack of exercise, but I had enough strength that I could pull myself up, grabbing the second bar. Then the third. By the fourth row, my arms were exhausted, but I was high enough that I could place my feet on the first row of the ladder. From there, the climb was easy, and I soon reached the platform on the second floor. From there, I slowly walked over to the other side, as the platform felt unstable and I worried that it was too old.

I climbed up the stairs that led to Diane's window. Each step was tall in height, but the step itself was small. I held on to the thin rail on the side as I reached to the top of the platform.

The platform was small, but large enough that perhaps three or four people could stand on it at once. There was a rail that was waist-high that ran around it, to protect against a fall.

Her window had a beige curtain, but behind it, I could see that the light was on in her room. I knocked on the window several times and quickly, I saw Diane pull the curtain aside.

She was wearing a white sweater over a pair of jeans. Her makeup was off, and I realized it was the first time I had seen her without her dark mascara or her red blush. Somehow, I found her even prettier. The lack of makeup brought out an almost innocent side to her, one that greatly contrasted the experiences she'd been through. She looked far more gentle, far more sweet.

She pulled open the window from her side.

"Marcus!" she called. "Shit, man, for a moment I was worried I'd see a thief or something. Here, the other girls are back there so they'll hear if you come in. But one sec, I'll come out with you."

I moved over, giving her room in front of the window. She climbed out and sat down, her knees bent over the edge of the platform with her feet hanging below it. From there, the guard rail didn't do much. If you slipped forwards, you could easily fall to the ground below.

"What, are you scared?" she asked, seeing me stand there.

"No, it's just-"

"Just sit down. You'll get used to it."

I squatted down until my hands were on the platform, until I slipped my legs over the edge, joining her. The thighs and calves tingled, as I felt the free air below my unsupported feet.

I took a deep breath.

She looked over at me and smiled.

"You know, during the summer, I used to sometimes just lie out here and look at the stars."

"Yea, I used to do that too," I said. I thought about the times I had driven downtown with Angie. The times we had slept on some parking lot roof, staring at the night sky as we fell asleep. These were the same stars I was looking at now.

"It reminds me how alone we are," she continued. "All these stars that look so close, yet are really so distant, so far away."

"So, what's going on with you?" she asked.

"You know how I told you about the townhouse? Well Kevin said he's finally gonna start giving me jobs."

"Oh, ok," she said. "Just be careful. Remember that he's a cunt."

"Yea, I will," I said, as I chuckled.

The stars were bright today. Night as bright as what I had seen before, but they were visible, in small specks across the sky. The moon was present too. Not a full moon, but not a crescent either. Halfway between, on the right side of us.

"You know, I didn't think I would get here," I said. "But somehow, it doesn't feel so bad."

"Oh there is plenty of bad," she said. "You need to kind of just avoid it."

"I always figured that I would be a lawyer or something. That I could have my own practice, and perhaps even leave behind a legacy or something. For my kids if I had them."

"Is that what you really care about?" she asked, softly.

"What do you mean?"

"Legacy."

"Yea, I think so," I said. "At least before. Why? What do you think?"

"I feel like we're too concerned with what we leave later that we forget what we do now. We want to live thinking we have some purpose, but we really don't matter in the grand scale. At most, in a year, your close friends will get used to life without you. In five years, no one will even mention you. When you die, you die. People try to find meaning, with religion and stuff, but guess what, even the pope just gets buried and that's it."

"That sounds cryptic," I said.

"You don't have to think about it that way," she continued. "I actually see it as uplifting. You can think of it it as, oh, I'm going to die and people will forget me. But you can also think of it as, oh,

I'm going to die, so I might as well just find my own happiness or something."

She looked at me, as if she wanted to see what I was thinking.

"Yea, I never really thought about it that way," I replied.

"It's like, I can live thinking that, oh I'm a hooker and I'm shit and society doesn't have a place for people like me. Or I can just take it as it is, and just live my life, free from anything. And yea, it's simple, but whatever. All sorts of people get all rich and successful but never get the freedom that I have and I love."

She felt so much softer now, as we sat at night, alone. Her harsh demeanour wasn't there anymore. And in her now, I could see a girl who had really been through a lot. Someone who was far stronger than anyone could have imagined.

"How are you able to still work with Kevin and guys like that? After what they do to you?"

"Well, I need to. But I get paid a pretty good amount."

"Do you resent him? Like think of any way to get back at him?"

"I really don't see the point in holding a grudge. Holding a grudge is like stabbing yourself in the back. You just hurt yourself and they don't feel anything. Like using yourself as a voodoo doll. I prefer to just let it go. Because shit happens, and assholes are out there. You just forget about them."

"I don't see how you manage to do that. Like, even now, over a month later, I still hate people from before. I still think about how I want to get back at them."

"Well, I guess that's just how you are and how I am. I think I just stopped caring."

I nodded. I wanted to change the conversation to something lighter, something less serious.

"Well, I forgot to tell you before. Those biscuits were amazing."

"Yes!" she exclaimed, smiling. "I told you they were great, right? Plus they're cheap as hell. Wait, I even have some, I'll go grab them."

She quickly turned around, pulled open the window that she didn't fully close, and went into the room.

I felt so comfortable being with her. The initial fear I had of coming, the fear of sitting up with my legs loose, were completely gone. In fact, not once did I even think about the fact that I was sitting so high. I completely forgot about it. She was all I had my mind on, all I was thinking about.

I heard the window behind me slide open again, as Diane climbed out. In her left hand was a package of the 1 dollar biscuits. But cradled in her right arm was a brown box that I made out to be a cassette player.

"I figured I would bring this too," she said, as she was climbing out.

"Why the cassette?" I asked. "A small MP3 probably doesn't cost much more."

"Well with an MP3, sure I can have the files of the songs. But I like having the tapes. There's just something special about them to me."

She sat down, leaving the cassette player on a shelf next to the window inside the room. She pulled over the earphones that were connected to the cassette, and gave me the left earphone.

"Have you heard of the Smiths?" she asked.

"No," I replied.

"Here, take a listen."

She began to play a song from the cassette player. The song began instantly with a combination of drums and a synthesizer-like note played twice. It had an atmospheric feel, a full sound, one that grabbed all your attention.

A few drum beats later, a distinctive low voice began to sing.

"You like it?" she asked.

"It sounds fresh," I replied. "It has a nice atmosphere to it."

"Yea," she replied. We must have been speaking loudly, as I could still hear her voice, even with a playing earphone in my ear on the side close to her.

The lyrics of the song had a longing to them. A desire for freedom, a desire for life. A desire for love. I could see why Diane liked it. It captured that feeling of escape, that dream of just running away, leaving it all, in the hopes of being alive, the hopes of finding joy.

"Isn't the chorus a bit over dramatic," I said, listening to the lyrics.

"Yea, I guess so," she said. "But I think it also gives some hope, gives a feeling that some things are infinite. Like yeah, we're all going to die, but when you feel alive, that worry really goes away. Like it's fine that we're all gonna die, as long as you experience life along the way."

I nodded, taking in what she had said. That was perhaps the most positive thing she had said yet.

"Well, anyway," she said. "I think you get the point."

She pulled the earphone out of her ear and I gave her the other one. She tossed the earphones behind the cassette player and closed the window behind us.

"The song's called There is a Light that Never Goes Out, by the way. Long name, I know."

I nodded again as I sat back, lifting my head up and taking a deep breathe. The air up here felt nicer, cooler, and crisper. There was no pollution from cigarette smoke, or the smell of sewage on the streets.

"Want some?" she asked, as she opened the package of biscuits.

I reached over and took one.

"It's really nice out here," I said, staring at the horizon.

Directly across from us, the apartment building mirrored Diane's, with fire escapes sprawled over the gloomy light brown exterior. But beyond us, in the horizon, we could see beaming lights, coming from the more downtown area. I thought about the late night drives I had drives with Angie. Back then, everything felt connected. I felt like I was part of the world. Like the tall office buildings that surrounded the city could be a part of my future. I could be there one day.

But now, I felt distant, I felt alone. Like the bright lights in the city night were part of another world. But somehow, that made me value my own world more. In this isolated state, I felt even more connected to those around me. And that meant Diane.

"Yea," she replied.

She took a pause before she continued.

"You know, Marcus. Thanks. Just thanks for coming, thanks for being there. It's just that even though I feel fine with myself and everything, it really helps being with you, it really helps having you here with me.

"Yea, I feel the same," I replied. "I guess it's just hard being alone with a bunch of creeps and weird people."

"Yeah," she said, chuckling.

I felt her scoot closer to me, feeling her long blonde hair brush up against my shoulder.

"How long have you been here?" I asked.

"Since I was 16. So 3 years."

"Wow," I said quietly.

"But honestly, I don't mind it," she said softly.

I turned to look at her, only to see her looking back at me.

She began to bend towards me as I mirrored her. I reached my left hand over to her waist, and I felt her hands wrap around my neck.

Our lips made contact, then separated slightly, still holding each other tight, as my right hand was now on the other side of her waist. We kissed again, this time just a smaller peck.

And after that, we sat in silence.

It was the most beautiful silence I had ever heard.

64

We sat quietly for several moments, looking at the horizon.

"Thanks," she said softly.

We were still right next to each other, sitting on the balcony of her fire escape.

"So, what next?" I asked quietly.

"I guess just live in the now."

The now was all I needed.

"Well, it's getting kinda late now."

"Yea," I quickly replied, realizing that I had to get to the market by 12.

"Thanks again," she said, as we both stood up. "By the way, take these. I have plenty."

She handed me the package, which I took.

I turned to walk back down the stairs of the fire escape, as I turned to look at her again, hearing the opening of her window.

"Bye, Marcus," she said.

"Bye Diane."

I walked down the stairs, climbed down the ladder and began walking back towards the market.

As I left, I had my eyes fixed on her building, fixed on her window.

Perhaps I was stunned, in shock, surprised. But she had this naivety to her, a shyness. As if this was her first love. She moved slowly and softly, like she wasn't sure how to act, or she wasn't confident in her beauty. It brought a feeling of innocence, tenderness, that I had never seen before.

Just months ago, I was in a seemingly stable relationship, with a girl from my school who my parents liked.

Now, I was lost in the streets, and in love with a hooker who might honestly spend the rest of her life the way things are now.

But somehow, this felt so much more real.

65
Just like Kevin had said, I found a note under my pillow.

"Back of black townhouse. Thursday, 11 pm."

It was around 8 pm and I had just returned from my scavenging trip. I had planned to get some extra rest in the townhouse tonight, as it was still much more comfortable than the market.

But I knew this was coming, and I had to follow through.

66
I reached the back of the townhouse exactly at 11. Though my bedroom had no clock, one of the prostitutes or bouncers that hung around always had a watch on them.

In the backyard, I saw the young black man, the one who had been there before, delivering the weed. He had a cardboard box in his arms. It was moderately sized; big enough that you couldn't hold it with one hand, but small enough that you could carry it by wrapping your arm around it.

I walked up to him. He had a deep and raspy voice.

"Take this, and deliver it to the Persian restaurant a few blocks down. Turn right on the street in front of us, until you get to the second intersection. From there, turn right, and walk until you see the restaurant with the bright orange sign. Walk in there, ask for the manager. He'll take you to the back. Don't screw up."

He handed me the box.

"You get it?" he asked.

"Yea, I think so. Turn right, second intersection. Another right, and I'm looking for the bright orange sign."

"Yea, you can't miss it."

"Oh, and at the end," he added. "Kevin wants to see you right after you're done."

He quickly said that and turned around, jogging back to the fence in the backyard. I wondered what was over the fence. Maybe someday I would find out.

The box felt moderately light. It was completed taped shut along the openings by packaging tape. I tried giving it a light shake, but I could feel minimal movement. I wondered what was inside the box. Money? Drugs? I wondered why the Persian restaurant was involved.

Holding the box, I walked back towards the gate of the backyard, out onto the street.

I realized that every time I passed by now, I instinctively tried to look across the park. I tried to look at the lights, tried to visualize life on the other side. Somehow, I felt closer and closer. I knew that I was being dragged into the dark more and more, but the stability that I now had made me feel better, more secure.

I took a right turn down the street, following the townhouses down. I didn't see Diane anywhere outside, so she was likely either inside the blue townhouse or in her apartment. I knew that I wanted to see her, tell her that I was going for my first job with Kevin. Maybe she even knew something about the Persian restaurant I was going to.

Part of me felt like I should be disgusted by the notion of her being in that townhouse. The idea of her, working as a lesbian hooker, and having sex with other girls should've plagued me. But somehow, I didn't feel anything. Maybe it was because it was her free spirit that drew me in. Or maybe I just felt like there was nothing either of us could do about it, and I had to accept those things and just appreciate that I had her in the middle of all this madness.

Hopefully she was doing fine and hopefully I could see her later.

I walked down the street, away from the black townhouse. This was really the first time I was going in this direction. I knew that from the other side, the street slowly descended from high apartment buildings, to low buildings, to abandoned townhouses. But I wondered how things were on the other side. Did it go back up? Or did the area of old property just extend?

I thought about the bright buildings and the streetlights on the other side of the massive park. Where did those meet the road we were on? Surely there had to be some perpendicular street connecting the two worlds. I guess I was about to find out.

The stream of townhouses continued, even as the groups of prostitutes sitting on the curb disappeared. They still followed a similar colour scheme, with constantly changing colours between the townhouses that had varying distances between them. But the boards on these houses looked more real, looked more certain. Like the houses were actually abandoned. Though this meant that less shady business happened in these houses, the lack of life made them feel more ghastly, more frightening.

The cigarette butts that lit up the previous area were nowhere to be found. The street was almost entirely dark. Far away in the distance there were lights, but that was about it.

I walked for a while, in the darkness, until I reached the second intersection. Somehow, I wasn't even scared. Maybe I was used to it now. After spending so much time in the darkness, things seem to become more visible.

I looked down the street. Down in the back, I could see low-rise apartment buildings. But behind those, far in the distance, I could see more lights, coming from both streetlights and signs. Though the first block of the street didn't have streetlights, I could see them in the back, further down the road.

The area was still extremely run down, even after I reached the signs following minutes of walking. The stores were below low apartments, and garbage filled the sidewalks. A small of trash constantly reeked from the buildings.

There was a diverse group of stores, though they followed a similar format. They all featured a sign that was lit up, and if the sign was english, the name of the store was spelled out in blocky letters. There were convenience stores, Chinese, Middle Eastern, and Korean restaurants, as well as bike stores and electronics stores.

There were some people walking down the street, most of them walking around to turn into one of the stores or restaurants. There were some homeless people too, sitting on the sidewalk, or just walking around, going through garbage bins. Whenever I walked by anyone, I held the box more tightly in my arms, as I figured that there was a good chance that the box contained something valuable.

After some walking, I saw the bright orange sign on the left side of the street. It was an orange sign with black characters in a language I couldn't read. The front of the restaurant was glass, with signs on the glass showing promotions.

The road was fairly clear of cars, with a taxi or sedan passing by sporadically. I ran across the street, to get to the side with the restaurant.

Up on the glass of the restaurant, I could see pictures of menu items. The pictures were oblurry, and they depicted plates with meats, vegetables, and rice.

I pulled open the door.

On the right side of the entire was a countertop. Behind it were the chefs. On the left side, against the wall, there were several tables with chairs, that continued to the back of the store.

The countertop ended halfway through the store, and the back half of the entire place was for seating. In the back, I could see a few people sitting and eating. Perhaps 3 or 4 tables with 2 people at each one.

I heard the cashier call out to me.

"What you want sir?" he said in a heavy accent. He was of a medium height with a thin build. He had light brown skin and a moustache that ran across, above his upper lip. He wore a white apron over a grey shirt, and on his head he wore a small paper chef hat. To the left of him, behind the counter, an older, fatter man was at a grill, and an older woman was next to him, talking to him in a language I couldn't understand.

"Can I speak to the manager?" I asked.

He motioned his hand for me to go to the back of the store.

"Grey door," he said.

I walked to the back of the store. There was a small hallway that led to the male and female washrooms as well as the storage area for the food. On the far right side of the restaurant, there was a grey door that said "employees only." I knocked, before hearing the cashier call out.

"Just walk in," he said.

I pushed the door open, seeing a desk with a man sitting behind it. He had a white computer in front of him, to the right. Across the desk, there were stacks of paper, and there were several cups with stationery in them.

He lifted his head up from the computer and looked at me.

The man was old in age. He had light brown skin, and his hair was grey, combed backwards, revealing a large balding area in the middle of his head. He was fat, with several chins. He wore an old and dirty white polo that looked stretched after years of use.

"Is this from the don?" he asked me. He didn't have much of an accent, surprising me.

I figured that Kevin was somehow the don.

"Yea," I replied.

"Ok, give it."

I put the box on the desk. From inside one of the cups, he took out an extendable knife. He cut the tape across the top of the box, opening it.

Inside were countless hardcover books, with blue covers. They were packed to the brim, and along the width and length of the box, the books just fit in. The hardcovers looked heavy though, and the box had been fairly light. That didn't make sense. Maybe there was something under the top surface of books.

He quickly counted the books across the top surface. Then, he began to take books out, until he could see the depth of the box. He counted how many books there were stacked on top of each other in each column.

I wondered what the books were.

Finally, he took a single book, placed it on top of the other books in the box, and opened it.

The books weren't books at all. Once the cover was turned, the books revealed themselves to be boxes. Wooden blocks that were hollowed out, and simply covered by the hardcover of the book. The sides of the books were rock hard, and the boxed area inside the book was completely caved in.

And in the open area of the box in the book, there were two rows of bills. Stacked side by side, filling the box.

They were all 50 dollar bills. The books were used to transport cash.

The man slowly took the money out of the book, counting the number of bills there were.

When he finally finished, he neatly put the money back into the book, and put the book back into the box.

He lifted the box up. I worried he would give it back to me. Perhaps something was wrong and there wasn't enough money.

Instead, I was relieved when he picked up the entire box, and placed it behind him, against the wall behind the desk.

He turned to me.

"Tell Kevin I will return the books next week."

I nodded.

"You can go," he told me.

I turned around and opened the door. It felt nice not having to hold a box.

I walked outside of the store, back onto the street. I turned right, and began to walk back.

He had called Kevin Don. He must be some powerful leader. Who knew what Kevin really did, behind that office desk of his. Behind those glasses, I wondered what he really saw.

I wcndered what that money was for. Drugs? Hookers? Who knew. And I didn't dare try to find out. I didn't want to work with Kevin. I didn't want to do anything with him. But I had no option. This was my life, and this was my source of stability.

I reached the road I had come from, and I ran across the road again to get to the other side.

Down the road, I only saw darkness. An entire valley. Only from here could I truly see just how dark this area was. Standing at the intersection on the side of the road I was travelling down, I could only faintly see the buildings, the townhouses.

I walked down through the darkness, heading in the direction of the townhouses.

For minutes, there was silence and darkness. All I could hear was my own footsteps. But eventually, I began to hear whispering, and I began to see lights.

I was almost glad that these brothels and drug trafficking locations existed. Somehow, these operations gave something to these run down areas. Run down areas that would never be fixed, because even if they were, no one would want to live here. Beside Kevin. Beside Diane. Beside me.

Soon, I saw the cigarette butts get closer and closer as I began to hear light chatter. The townhouses became more familiar, as I re-entered the zone I had come from before when delivering the box.

Remembering the instructions I had received, I went to the black townhouse and entered. By now, the bouncer was familiar with me, so I didn't have to tell him what I was doing. He would just let me by.

I walked up the flights of staircases until I reached Kevin's office, and I knocked and entered.

"Did you get it done?" he asked.

"Yea. The man said that he would return the books next week."

Kevin nodded.

"Mr. Smith, good job," Kevin said. "You did well. You didn't get sidetracked."

"Yes," I replied, not knowing what to say.

"Come in and take a seat," he said.

I closed the door behind me, and Kevin stood up. He reached behind his desk on the far side from the door and took out another black fold-out chair, placing it in front of me.

I took a seat.

"Marcus, I worried you'd be a druggie. I don't work with druggies. They can't get shit done."

I nodded.

"What type of future do you want?" he asked.

I didn't know how to answer.

"Um," I murmured. "I'm not sure."

"What do you want Marcus? Money? Power? There's all sorts of things you can chase. What do you want to chase?"

I thought about it for a second. I worried that telling him that I wanted to go back to Ridgefield and living a normal life would cause him to abandon me, or do something even worse.

"To help others maybe?" I said, uncertain of what he wanted to hear.

"Let me give you some advice," Kevin said. "In the end, it's always every man for himself. Do what you need to do to put yourself in the best position. It helps to be kind every once in a while, but when push comes to shove, you gotta be there for yourself. And only yourself."

He took a breath out and stood up, turning away from me, pacing around the room.

"I believe that you'll be free again Sunday. On Sunday, you're going to have a more complicated job. But you're a smart kid so I think you can get it done. You come here and go to the backyard at around 11 pm. There, you'll join up with some guys. One of our dealers has turned into a crackhead. I need you, along with the other guys, to go and get all our shit back from him. Because no one steals. You hear that?"

He sounded more angry, using a voice more similar to what I heard the first night that I saw him, when he was yelling at Diane.

"Ok. I expect you to be here then."

He waved for me to leave, as I turned around and went back out through the door.

I thought about the advice he gave me, and it didn't surprise me that it was coming from him. I wondered what he had done to get what he had now. All the crimes he had committed. Who knew how far he went.

I felt scared of him. Who knew what was going to happen on this job. Fuck. I wanted to leave this now. But just a bit more. I could just hang in a bit more. Maybe once the winter passed, I would find my way back. Perhaps I would.

I walked outside, went down the steps in front of the townhouse, and stepped on to the sidewalk. I heard my name get called right when my feet hit the concrete.

"Marcus!" Diane called out.

The rest of the street was silent, so her voice stood out, like a bright glow in a dark room.

"Hey Diane," I replied.

She walked up and hugged me.

"How was it?" she asked.

I had to take a moment to realize what she was referring to.

"It was ok," I replied. Perhaps I was thinking more about what was going to happen Sunday, because the job I had just gone on went surprisingly well.

"How'd you know I was here?" I asked, as I was fairly surprised to hear her voice. It was already really late, probably past 12, and I thought that by now, Diane was probably in her apartment already.

"I asked around. One of the other girls said that you asked her what the time was before. So I figured that you probably went on your job, and you were waiting for the right time to go start it. So I just hung around. I figured you'd be back. I must have missed you when you went into the townhouse. Here, I brought some biscuits."

She handed me a biscuit from the package she was holding.

"Are you tired?" she asked. "I was bored so I wanted to take a walk through the park."

"Yea, sure," I replied. I was slightly exhausted, but I didn't mind spending time with Diane.

"Have you been to the other side?" I asked.

"Yea," she replied. "I like the light there. I swear no one goes there though."

"Yea, I was surprised to see the other side," I said. "It makes me anxious. Everything's so much more normal on that side, I guess I wish I was there."

"Ah, there you go again Marcus with your career-mindedness," she said with a chuckle.

I chuckled too, as we walked across the street and into the park.

"Has the park always been like this?" I asked.

"Yea, for the time that I've been here."

Her voice seemed to get softer and softer the more time I spent with her. It was like I could now see the inside of her, the part that was still sweet and caring, even though it was hidden behind a hardened shell.

She was beautiful, and she only seemed to get prettier and prettier. With her, somehow it felt like I could get through this all. Like Kevin wouldn't even be that bad. I could have any bad day, and as long as she came to see me afterwards, it wouldn't be so bad after all.

"Diane, why do you like me?" I asked. I wondered why she even bothered with me.

"Well, you're true to yourself. Like aside from you not being a cunt, you don't act in ways to seem like you're more than you are. Like you're someone else. When I'm with you, I'm with you. Not some mirage of you."

I nodded.

"Thanks, Diane," I said, with a smile.

She smiled back.

"Yea, you really help me out too. Like you're just so real, and you're so strong. And I'm really missing that and somehow with you, I feel ok."

She chuckled.

"So what's happening next? With like Kevin and everything."

"I've got another one Sunday. He told me it was something to do with some dealer doing drugs or something. Kevin said he would send me with a few others to go take stuff back or something. Not too sure what we're doing though."

"Just be careful, Marcus."

"Yea, I will."

"I just don't want to lose you after I've only had you for so little."

"I'll be fine. I won't be doing it alone."

She nodded, though I could still sense the worry. But somehow, that made me feel stronger, braver. It had been forever since I had someone care, and just the fact that she did made me less scared.

By now we were around halfway into the park, past the abandoned playground.

"There's a bridge down there that's really pretty," I said.

"Yea. I walk across it often. The backdrop of lights behind it really just brightens it up. Makes me feel alive. Hey, let's head there now."

She picked up her walking pace and I followed, as we ventured towards the bridge.

Soon, we could see it in the background, and moments later, we were standing right in front of it. The area surrounding the stone bridge had a thin layer of snow covering it, and on the sides of the small bridge as well as the bottom surface of it, the snow remain untouched and uniform. The bridge couldn't have be more than 20 meters in length, but it still seemed so grand, positioned in the middle of nothingness.

It looked even prettier this time, as the lights in the back felt brighter in the backdrop of the darker sky. She walked up to the apex of the bridge and I followed.

"Sometimes I like to just stand here and think," she said. "I guess I like coming out here, away from where I spend all my time. It's so noisy near the townhouses and in my apartment. But here, it feels so much better."

She reached over, grabbed my shoulders, and kissed me.

"I didn't think I could find someone like you. Especially here. But I'm just so lucky."

"Don't say that," she softly said, before kissing me again.

Perhaps I would get through this. Maybe I could get her something better too. Sure she may have felt free in this environment, but hopefully someday I could spoil her. Make sure she would never have to go through crap again.

We stood there in silence for a few moments, until Diane finally spoke.

"Wanna go back now?" she said.

'Yea," I replied.

We began to walk back towards the townhouses.

"You know, I saw the weirdest shit today," she said.

"What was it?" I asked.

"Some Jehovah's witness people were outside the market when I was getting biscuits. They tried to give me a flyer. Like really, me?"

I chuckled.

"Yea, I'm sure they would love to have you," I replied jokingly. "You'd fit right in."

"I wonder what those people do. Like it just feels weird that people pay for religion and stuff. Like how pastors are pastors full time. By the way, are you religious?"

"I guess so. My town was really religious so we went to church and stuff. But I guess I'm more agnostic."

"Ah, I see," she replied. "It's just always felt weird to me. Like maybe religion is innate or something. To me it makes no sense. It feels like something people made since they couldn't handle death."

"Yea, I think that believing that there's an afterlife makes it easier. Makes you less anxious."

"Yea, I guess it would. Sometimes I wish I could. But I feel like just accepting that our lives our meaningless actually lets us do stuff we love," she said.

"Yea, that makes sense," I said. I had never really thought about it that way. In fact, I never really thought about death nearly as much as she probably did. I wondered whether she was scared, or if it was just something that intrigued her.

"I've never really thought that much about death," I said.

"Well, I think it's just such a common thing that's so puzzling. Like we all die but no one knows what really happens. And maybe no one will ever know," she replied.

I nodded to her, taking in what she had said. Perhaps it was true. That you might as well just accept death so you could do what you wanted to. Fearing it would only hold you back.

I never thought that someone like her could be so insightful. Like all the previous thoughts I had about people were vanished. Here I was, with someone who I would've looked down upon before, mesmerized by how smart and thoughtful she was.

I looked at her and her blonde hair. By now, my eyes had adapted to the dark and I could see her, as well as everything around me much more clearly. It must have been nearly 1 or 2 by now. I never really noticed how fast time passed by with Diane.

Soon, the abandoned playground came into view and I could see the townhouses in the distance.

"Anyways, wanna come back here at 1 or 2 on Sunday after you're done? It's just really nice being here."

"Yea, sure," I replied. "Wanna just meet at the bridge?" I asked.

"Sure," she said.

We had reached the sidewalk now. We crossed the now empty street, walking towards the beige townhouse I slept in.

"Well, see you Sunday, then," she said.

I walked into the townhouse and went into my room.

I lay on my bed, thinking about Diane.

Diane never would've gotten into what happened to me. Maybe I did think too much. She would've just ignored everyone, even after the diarrhea happened.

If I had been more like her, it wouldn't have happened.

Somehow, I felt excited. I don't know what it was for. But I just was.

It was so great to have her.

68

Initially, I thought I wouldn't be scared, but as Sunday came closer, I realized I was terrified. I wanted to think of every excuse possible for me not to go. I could say I had a stomach ache. Say I was sick. But it wouldn't work with Kevin. In fact, he probably had eyes on me. He knew how I was doing.

I had to do it though. If I didn't, I would lose everything. I would probably lose Diane. Who knew what Kevin would do to me? I had to do it, I had to go.

I spent all of Sunday lying around, waiting for time to pass by. I tried to bring myself to do something. Maybe go and explore the park more. Maybe explore the city in the other direction from the market, away from the side that lead to the townhouses. But I couldn't. Part of me hoped the moment would just come and I could get it over with, but I knew that it wouldn't work that way. I had to just wait for it to come.

I hung around the market area, picking up food, until I could feel the sky completely darken. But it was winter, and that happened early. I had to wait some more time until it was 11. A lot more time.

Time seemed to tick slower and slower. Everything I was scared of in the past, it all looked so easy relative to this. My life had never really been on the line before, but maybe it was this time. Maybe this time would be the last, when everything would finally fall apart and I would wind up dead like I should have the moment I punched Francis, the moment this entire journey began

The wait was torturous. I wondered what I would do in one of those situations where I was trapped for ages. Like if I was trapped inside a cave with ample food, and I had to stay in there for weeks. I used to wonder about that as a kid. But now, it felt like it was no longer just a childish hypothetical, as I waited for the time to come.

69

It was eleven o'clock as I walked through the gates of the black townhouse.

I walked to the back, and like Kevin promised, there were four men. They were all older than me. One of them was black, two were white, and one was hispanic. They were dressed in similar outfits, with the hispanic and one of the white guys wearing hoodies inside vest jackets. The other two wore sweaters like mine.

I hadn't seen the men before. They weren't the ones who delivered the drugs, and they weren't the bouncers either. They looked to be 20-30 years old. The hispanic was of a a large build and a moderate height; perhaps roughly 6 feet and maybe 200 pounds. The others, though were slim. The white man in the vest jacket sported a dirty brown beard, and upon closer inspection, several tattoos on his face.

The black man came up to greet me.

"My name's Ty," he said. "I'll be leading this. You know what we're doing, right?"

"Kevin told me we were taking drugs back from someone. A dealer that started using them."

"Yea," he said. He had a low voice that was intimidating. He was around the same height as the hispanic but was lean.

"Everything's in the truck," he continued. "Come on, let's go."

He walked past me and towards the gate as the other three men followed. They stayed silent, but their facial expressions were tense, fierce. Like they were focused on what was happening.

We walked out through the gate and we turned left, walking down the sidewalk. I wondered where this truck was. Where were we going? I feared for the worst. What if this was some abduction. Some execution. I thought about running away but I didn't. I couldn't lose Diane now, I couldn't lose what I had. I followed behind them tightly, as the prostitutes and clients standing on the sidewalk moved to the side and made way for us.

We walked past the row of townhouses that I was familiar with. The blue brothel, the beige one that I still lived in, alone. It had never really occurred to me until now, when I was truly frightened, just how long I had been living here. It must have been almost a month, and this was only my second job.

We eventually reached the intersection, where we turned left, down a street I had never gone on before. We were still in the area with townhouses, so as we turned, we saw more of them. On the driveway of the third townhouse, I could see a black pickup truck. Perhaps that was the one.

The townhouses in this area were more or less the same. There was more space between and as a result, the driveways were bigger. But still, there were no garages and still, they were seemingly abandoned, as the back pickup truck was the only vehicle on the street.

It looked fairly new, as the black metal exterior shone in the moonlight. We walked up to the truck. The black man took the driver's seat and the white man in the sweater went shotgun. That left me, the white man in the vest, and the big hispanic to sit in the back.

The back of the pickup truck wasn't empty. As we got closer, I began to notice several long objects inside. Upon getting closer, I saw that they were weapons. Not guns or knives, but instead, all sorts of blunt tools. There were two or three baseball clubs as well as several long golf clubs. I froze and gulped, not realizing that I was standing right beside the truck, blocking the passenger door.

"Won't you move?" the hispanic said.

I quickly stepped to the side as he opened the door. He gestured for me to go in, as I was the smallest and only I fit on the middle seat. The white man had gotten in from the other side, and as the hispanic got in, I found myself squeezed in the middle, with my shoulders pushed forward.

I wanted to ask what the equipment in the back was, but I knew what it was for.

Ty started the car and backed out of the driveway. He turned right, driving away from the direction we had come from.

The drive was silent. I didn't dare speak, but I wondered what the others were thinking. The hispanic and the white man switched between looking out the window and staring out in front, through the windshield. I wanted to know if they had done this before. What their lives were like. But I knew that I'd never find out. I wondered if they were scared, anxious, or nervous. Or maybe they were so cold-blooded that they didn't feel anything anymore.

We exited the run-down neighbourhood area, entering a more populated, city-like area of the town. We passed through the lights, blazing by, as there was no traffic and we were all alone in our drive. We drove into an area that more less sparse. This area had a more suburban feel, even though it was still part of the city. In the back, I could see towering highways built above the ground, on bridges that went over roads.

We reached the edge of a residential area. The road we were on led to a tunnel that was under a highway. We were several blocks away from it when Ty began to drive more slowly. He eventually saw a street roughly one block from the tunnel, and he pulled into the street and stopped.

The area around us was surrounded by white wooden houses. It was an open area of the city, next to a major highway. We parked at the entrance of a residential area. The houses were old but the area was decently maintained. There were streetlights every two or three houses, and there wasn't as much garbage lying around. Some of the lights of the houses were on as well.

Ty got out of the car. The drive couldn't have been more than 10 minutes, but with my nervousness, it felt like an eternity.

We all stepped out of the car, as the hispanic went to the back to take the equipment. I tossed a baseball bat to the white man who was riding shotgun. He gave a golf club to the other white man. Ty went and grabbed the other baseball bat. He tossed me a golf club.

I looked at it. It was a long driver, with a big club. It was lightweight but long, around the length of my leg. I hoped I wouldn't have to use it.

Ty motioned for us to gather around the side of the truck.

"The guys are hanging under the bridge. There's some light in there from the streetlights on either side so they'll probably see us. The tunnel's not long though, so we won't really be able to get to the other side to surround them without them noticing. So guys, the plan is going to be to hide our clubs at first and walk in quickly. Once they spot us, we go right after them."

He took a pause.

"There are sidewalks on both sides of the road in the tunnel. We'll all head down the left. I'll go first. You guys follow me, We'll walk until they spot us. Hopefully they'll be high so they won't sense anything. Our goal is to get all their money and get all their drugs, no matter what cost. They die, they die."

The other guys nodded while I trembled. But I tried to show a strong resolve, so they wouldn't single me out. He sounded cold and fearless. I hoped he was scared too. I worried that he wasn't.

"Ok, here we go."

Ty walked down the street and turned back onto the road that lead into the tunnel. We were around one block away from its mouth. In front of us was an intersection, and after crossing the road, there was only grass on either side of the road before the tunnel began.

Ty stuffed his bat into the back of his vest, sticking it into his pants. He crossed the road as we followed, having concealed our weapons too.

The tunnel wasn't too long, perhaps spanning just the width of the highway it was under. It was four lanes wide.

Ty walked down the left side of the tunnel as we followed. Soon, I could see several figures on the right side of the tunnel, across from us. They were standing up against the wall, smoking. I could see their lit cigarettes. I hoped they were high. I hoped we could just walk over, take what we need to, and not have to use our weapons.

We kept on walking, until the figures got closer and closer. They still didn't notice us yet.

Eventually, we were right across from us. Ty raised his hand, signalling for us to stop.

"Pull them out," he whispered.

We all pulled our sticks out from our back.

Suddenly, I heard a yell, as we had been spotted.

"They're here!" a voice yelled, across from us.

Ty began to walk across the tunnel as we followed him.

As we reached the middle of the road. I could see the other figures clearly. There were four or five of them, three of them standing and two sitting. All of them were white and wore old clothes and rags. They seemed nonchalant, even though one of them had yelled upon seeing us. We stood face to face against them, as Ty began to speak.

"You know what we want," he said. "Give us the money and the drugs, and no one will get hurt. Kevin will pardon you, and everything will continue as normal."

"Kevin doesn't pardon shit," one of the standing men said, as he made a hissing noise and spit on the ground, right in front of Ty.

We all stood in silence for a moment, before Ty let out a yell, raised his bat and charged at the man. Suddenly the entire tunnel became an absolute commotion. Ty swung his bat and hit the man who was standing across the face, before another man tackled Ty, as Ty let out a yell. The other white men and the hispanic ran at the opposers, swinging at them, with some punches connecting. I stood in the back, confused and scared, as I watched the men fight. Ty was now punching the man who had tackled him, who was sprawled across the ground. The hispanic held a man against the back wall, and he was swinging his bat, hitting him in the stomach as the man yelled. In the middle, right in front of me, the white man in the sweater was now on the ground. Two men were kicking him, before one of them turned and tackled the hispanic, who had also fallen

"Do something!" I heard Ty yell, as he looked at me as he was punching the man across the face I panicked but I figured I had to do something. I ran up and tried to swing my club at the man who was kicking the white man in the sweater. He grabbed my club and pulled hard, taking it directly out of my sweaty palms. He stepped forwards and punched me in the face, as I stumbled back. He took another step forward and punched me in the face again, this time with his left hand. I stumbled back and fell on the ground, breaking the fall with my hands. I braced myself for another hit, before I saw an arm wrap around the waist of my assaillant and throw him aside. Ty jumped towards the man who was now stumbling to the side, and threw him down to the floor.

I stayed on my back, observing the action. On the right side near the back, the hispanic was engaged in a fight with a man, as I saw the man who the hispanic had been hitting sitting down with his back against the wall, seemingly unconscious.

In the middle, the white man in the rolled around before getting up to face someone across from him. To the far left, Ty was pounding the man who had hit me, and in the back left corner, the white man in the vest was wrestling someone on the round.

Out in front of me, I saw the man who was slumped stand up, seemingly in a haze. He stumbled over to the back, against the wall, where I could see a cardboard box on the ground. He stuck his arm into the box and pulled something out. From there, he stumbled over to the back side of the hispanic man, who was now on the ground, punching someone.

He swung his arm back and I saw the glistening tip. I screamed to warn the hispanic man.

"Knife!"

He stabbed the blade into the left side of the Hispanic man as he let out a yell. The white man in the vest sprinted over as he tackled the man with the knife, before punching him several times and standing up.

"Fuck we gotta go!" he yelled, as he went over to the hispanic man, took his arm, and began to race out of the tunnel, with no one in pursuit.

"Let's go!" I heard Ty yell, as he ran over to the white man in the sweater and made an attempt to pull him up, before realizing he was unconscious. He began to sprint out of the tunnel. Realizing I was still lying down, observing what was happening. I quickly got up and began to sprint out, following Ty. Soon, we caught up to the hispanic and the other white man, who were slowly trotting out.

"Fuck!" Ty yelled, as he ran over to the hispanic's other side. I caught up to them, and I looked at the wound on the side. There wasn't too much blood, but the hispanic was visibly in pain.

"Marcus grab him!" Ty yelled, as he sprinted forward, running to go and grab the car. I went to the left side of the hispanic, where Ty had been, and together with the other white man, we helped him walk as we went in the direction of the truck. His heavy arm was over my shoulder, and I felt his entire weight across my shoulders as we stumbled forward. Soon, the truck came roaring around, and Ty pulled up right next to us, yelling for us to get in. There wasn't anyone chasing us from behind, but now, it was a race against time to keep the hispanic man alive.

I pulled open the side door on the left side of the truck as the white man helped the hispanic get in. The white man ran around the back of the truck to get into the passenger seat. I got in the truck after the hispanic and closed the door, as Ty began driving.

"Fuck!" he yelled as he drove away. "Fuck! We lost Malcolm!"

"Fuck!" the white man repeated. "Marcus why didn't you fucking do anything during all of that!"

I froze for a second. I realized it was the first time I had heard him talk.

"I'm putting all of this on you. I'm telling Kevin this was you. You pussy."

"Now's not the time!" Ty yelled. "Where the fuck is the closest hospital!"

"City centre! But how the fuck are we going to do anything? He has no fucking ID!"

"Just go as a John Doe!" Ty yelled. "How are you holding up?" he asked loudly.

The hispanic groaned.

"Keep plugging the wound, Marcus!'

My hand had been on his side, pushing against the wound. His jacket soaked up most of the blood but my hand still felt slightly wet. I was terrified, horrified. But somehow, I felt glad to be alive, as I tried to keep the man beside me alive. Such a stupid mission for drugs and somehow we could lose one and another could be fatally hurt. This was a bullshit profession. I had to leave. There was no other way. This was bullshit.

"We're almost there!" Ty yelled, as we sped through the residential area. In the distance, through the windshield, I could see the hospital. It was tall, and the blue "H" sign radiated through the sky.

We quickly pulled into the area that led to the emergency wing.

"Josh, take him in," Ty said.

The white man pulled open the right side passenger door, as the hispanic man scooted over and stepped out. They slowly and painfully stumbled inside, through the automatic sliding doors. "Fuck," Ty muttered again. We sat in painful silence, waiting for Josh to return. I felt like starting some conversation, perhaps asking Ty what we would do. But the words froze right before they left my mouth, and we sat there waiting. I hoped I could go back and see Diane like we had promised. I hoped.

This had to be it for me. I couldn't take it anymore. Delivering packages and even transporting drugs was fine, but this violence was just unbearable. This time, it was Malcolm and the hispanic. It could easily be me next time. And all of it was to get some drugs and money back for a fucker who does the dirtiest shit but gets away with it. This was the last time I was going to do anything.

"Fuck, what are they doing," Ty muttered. "Fuck we're fucking dead." I looked out the window towards the left side. Outside of the drop-off arch of the hospital, there was a parking lot that extended from the main lot. Around it were many trees that looked thin and pale, looking meagre against the grand hospital.

"Finally," I heard Ty say, as he sighed. I saw Josh coming back from the doors. He opened the passenger door and got in.

"How'd it go," Ty asked.

"I put him in as a John Doe. They brought him into surgery. Should be all good."

Ty sighed again. "Ok, let's go."

He drove back slowly, as if he was savouring the slow drive he could take. He rolled down the windows as we drove, passing back through the city area. The drive took longer, as the hospital was a detour from our route. But eventually, we got back, and Ty parked where the truck had been parked before.

"Ok, let's go. Kevin won't want to hear about this."

Ty led us down the path, and towards the black townhouse. This was it for me. I was going to go tell Diane that. I would come up with some sort of plan to secure myself, and hopefully her as well. Maybe some other stakeout. I had to find a way.

Ty led us to the black townhouse. The bouncer stopped us and patted us all down. He told us we were clear, and we went into the house and up the stairs. This walk felt worse than all the other ones I had taken, even the first one. Even though I was with the other two, I worried that Kevin would snap. He would take it out on us. He would end me. I wouldn't be able to see Diane again. I just wanted to make it out. Make it out in one piece so I could go over to the park and see Diane. That was all I needed.

We reached the top floor and Ty knocked. We entered when Kevin told us to.

Kevin stayed on his seat, but he looked at us boldly, and began to speak right when Ty opened the door.

"Where's the other two? I sent five."

"We lost Malcolm," Ty said. "Mateo's in the hospital as a John Doe."

"And the money?"

"They attacked us, sir. When we.."

Kevin slammed the table, cutting Ty off. "Isn't that what the clubs are for?" he yelled.

"They fought back and had a knife," Ty replied.

"Get out!" Kevin yelled. "Now!"

We quickly scurried out the door, Ty being the last one out. I worried Kevin would stop me, hold me back to talk to me, but thankfully he didn't.

Ty quickly descended the stairs and Josh followed behind, leaving as though they were disappointed in themselves. I saw it as a breath of relief. This was it. I was never going to do this again.

I exited the townhouse, feeling glad that Kevin didn't assault us. He only yelled. I could take that.

I immediately went across the street, and began to walk towards the bridge. Diane was all I needed. She could be that light I needed right now. To help me escape this all. My fears would all go away. I felt petrified. But I knew that she could somehow free me.

The sights that I had seen under the bridge flashed in front of me as I walked across the park. The man in the middle getting up after being beat, to go pick up the knife. Malcolm, getting pummeled, directly in front of me. The man charging at me, punching me, before being thrown to the side by Ty. Fuck. All in the dark of a tunnel. Events occuring that no one would ever discover. Who knew what would happen to Malcolm. Would they spare him? Or would he just die, no one ever finding out. This was fucked up.

I found myself walking at a brisk pace. Soon, I could see the light in the horizon. Though I knew that the walk across the massive park should have taken at least 10 minutes, I felt myself moving faster than I had ever gone before. Diane was what I needed. I needed to hold her in my arms, know that I had someone. In such a dark time, I never realized just how powerful one person could be. Just one person could somehow make up for all of the rest. Everything could be forgotten.

I saw the stone bridge, and I saw Diane standing on top of it. I wanted to yell to her but I was just too weak too tired. I began to jog, heading towards her. I saw her turn her head and see me, as she headed down the bridge and began to briskly walk towards me.

Author's note: to heighten the effect of this scene, listen to "We Might Be Dead by Tomorrow by Soko on repeat until the end of this chapter

We didn't talk until we were close to each other. She came up and hugged me, holding me tight.

"Marcus, I thought you were dead," she whispered. I heard trembling in her voice as she held me close. "Don't talk, don't talk," she said quietly as she took her arms off me and grabbed my hand, pulling my towards the bridge. I followed her as we went under the bridge, as she sat down, pulling me down to sit too. "Marcus, just." She didn't finish her sentence before she reached over and started kissing me. I reached my hands over around her back, pulling her closer in to me. She kissed me on my lips, around my lips, as I simultaneously moved my head down and began to kiss her neck. She pushed my head back to make room, as she took off the jacket she had on. She pulled off her sweater, revealing a white bra underneath. She bent back towards me and began to continue kissing me, reaching her hands down and grabbing the bottom of my sweater, pulling it up over my head, leaving just my shirt. It was cold, but I didn't feel it. She crawled over, on top of me, as I bent down on my back. I began to feel her pulling her pants down, while her lips were still pressed against mine, lying over me, her bra pushing against my chest. I felt her pants slip off from my legs, as she pushed them back away from us. With her face directly up and close against me, I felt her pulling at my pants. I reached my hands towards the sides and began to push them down, helping her in the motion, as I raised my back to give the pants room to come off. She slid them off, pulled my boxers down and crawled up even closer to me before reaching down and sitting over my erection. I was now flat on the ground as she began sliding up and down, breathing heavily, continuing to plant my mouth with kisses. Her hands were around the back of my neck, and I felt her bra slide up and down my chest as she moved, holding me close, her glimmering blonde hair behind her, draped over her side.

As I felt her lips on mine, in this moment, it was like I forgot everything. I was in love, and with that love, it was like a seeping

187

wave through my body that flushed out all the pain, all the sorrow. In this moment, all I had was her and all I needed was her. Diane, in front of me, was my world. We could all die, everything could fall apart, but as long as I had her, everything would be ok. I was connected to her, connected by some superior force of love that could shatter any ties, break any boundaries, erase any hardship, destroy any barrier I had ever felt. I'd give up everything to have this, to have her, forever.. This was all I needed, all I ever wanted. In a world of eternal darkness, this was the only light I would never need.

A cocoon of lovers, holding each other, with nothing in the world, but everything in each other.

And when we finished, we just held each other, as we lay on our backs and stared at the dark underside of the bridge.

70

I realized that if there was anyone to talk to, it was Jack. I could easily speak with him, and I realized that we never truly did have a conversation. When I came back to him with the drugs I would just hand the bag to him and he would open the back door, let me in, and leave immediately. And if I was going to leave Kevin, I had to tell Jack too.

I waited for him in the afternoon, before he came to plant the money. I saw him walk into the square behind the market, as I sat with my back against the door of the market.

"Hey, Jack!" I called out.

"Oh hey Marcus. Why are you here now?" he replied.

"I want to ask you about something. Do you have time?"

"Yea sure, my shift doesn't start until 15 minutes," he said, as he began to walk towards me. I stood up, leaning against the wall.

"So, what's up? By the way, thanks again for everything. It's been a lot easier."

"Yea, no worries. So anyways, what's up?"

"Um," I said, thinking about how I would phrase what I was going to say. "I'm gonna have to stop doing this for you."

Jack paused for a moment. "Why?"

"I just can't deal with Kevin. Like, I guess I forgot to tell you before. I needed somewhere to sleep the other nights, so I agreed to do work for him, in exchange for a place to stay. The first job wasn't bad. It was just a delivery. But I just finished the second, and I just can't handle it."

"Shit man, what happened?"

"He sent me with some other guys to go pick up drugs and money that a group was stealing from him. We got there and a fight started. One of our guys got stabbed, and another was put unconscious and left behind."

"Oh fuck."

"It just fucked me up. I can't do this. This isn't for me."

"What did Kevin say after?"

"He was real pissed. He didn't say much. But it was like he didn't care that we lost two guys and he was more concerned that we didn't get the drugs and money. How did he even get here anyways?"

"What do you mean?"

"Like he seems to have so much control. How does he have everything?" I continued.

"I don't know the full story," Jack said. "I haven't been doing this for too long and I only got to him through another contact. But I heard from others that Kevin is just brutal. Like he has people who rely on him and because of that, they'll do anything for him."

He took a pause.

"Apparently before, Kevin had another boss. But slowly, Kevin rose through the ranks, and at a certain point, he was so feared yet respected among the dealers and workers that he didn't need the boss anymore. Kevin killed him. Just murdered him. He kept the network afterwards as well. And also, I don't know if this is true, but I've heard rumblings that Kevin's a snitch."

"What?" I asked, confused.

"Apparently he turns in his rivals to the cops. No one knows for sure though. But no one would dare question him. But supposedly, he turns in people so that he secretly gets immunity. The cops are fine with it because it gives them a steady stream of criminals to charge."

I was speechless.

"But don't take my word for it, man. I've only heard rumours."

I couldn't believe it. People like Kevin were the filth of the world. The absolute trash.

"But hey, how about this. Instead of you going today, I'll go. I'll talk to Kevin after I'm off work, and I'll let you in here anyway. Tomorrow morning, I'll come over and tell you what's up."

"Really? You'll do that?"

"Yea, I think he's chill with me. I bring in a lot of cash for him. I'll ask him what's up and I'll tell him about those jobs."

I figured that this wouldn't hurt. Worst case, if Jack came back with something negative, my situation won't change. If Kevin wanted to get rid of me, I could leave, just like how I had planned.

"Yea, sure. Thanks so much," I said.

"No worries. See you tonight then."

"Sounds good," I replied.

He left me to go back into the store from the back to begin his shift.

I felt relieved somehow. There was still a burning tension within me, but somehow, not having to get involved with Kevin felt better. Part of me hoped Jack would just come back and tell me that Kevin didn't want to see me again if I didn't want to work with him. I could leave in peace, knowing that he wanted nothing to do with me.

That night, I managed to pick up a leftover taco set from the old stakeout. After deciding not to go see Diane because I was too tired, I took a nap on the streets, until I went back to the market and Jack let me in.

71

As usual, I woke up to the opening of the lights in the back room of the store, signalling that someone had opened the store and it was time for me to leave. I got up from the hard floor, that only felt harder after having the chance to sleep in a bed in the townhouse Kevin gave me. But soon, that would be over.

I opened the door to walk out into the square behind the market, expecting an empty area, only inhabited by a thin layer of overnight snow.
As I walked out I saw someone standing in the square, someone I hoped I wouldn't see again.

Kevin was standing there, waiting for me. He was alone. Fuck, I thought to myself. Jack must have told him and Kevin must have decided to take things into his own hands. I slowly walked up to him, as I felt my heart beat faster and faster.

"I don't think you were expecting me, Mr. Smith," he said.

"No, sir," I replied softly, feeling intimidated by his presence. He wore a long black jacket that went down to his knees. He had his hair gelled up towards the middle.

"Let's go for a walk kid," he said as he began to walk towards the exit of the square. I began following him, as we walked out on the street.

"Jack told me about everything," he said. "You're not cut out for this job."

I looked down, unsure of what to say. I knew that I wasn't but I didn't want to tell him directly.

"Here's what I'm offering. I've got to settle some debts with another group. I need someone who others don't know about, since the delivery is important. But it's just a delivery."

I felt my face turn more red, as I tried to swallow the idea of doing another job for Kevin.

"At the start, I'll give you $600. You do the delivery and come back, you get another $400. And then we say goodbye and we never see each other again.'

I looked at him, surprised at the offer.

"You're a good kid, Marcus. Just not in this world. So are you good with it?"

I could say no and run away. Or I could just do this one last time. One final time. It sounded too good. But perhaps I was a rare worker who didn't do drugs. Maybe Kevin had so much money that $1000 was nothing for him. I could take the $1000 and start anew. With $1000, that was enough for some community college even at a cheaper place. I could go to some other town, maybe somewhere in Jersey. No one would know anything. I was smart enough for college, and I knew that I could get a job as long as I was a community college student. Maybe I could even help out Diane. I could stay in contact with her somehow. Maybe create something better for both of us.

"Are you serious about the money?" I asked.

"What about this. You go to the back of the black townhouse and the guy will give you $600. You can count it. If you show up and you don't want to do it, you say no and you just leave. Does that work?"

I nodded.

"Ok, Marcus. I knew I could count on you. Tonight, 10 pm. Come to the back, and someone will give you instructions."

He continued walking down the street away from me. I had just one more run.

72

By 9 pm, I was sitting outside the townhouses, waiting for Diane. I had to tell her what was going on. Once again, like usual, the street was busy. People stood around smoking and every once in a while, someone walked by and went into the brothel. I noticed just how few people really went into Kevin's black townhouse. I tried to keep count, and over what must have been at least half an hour, there were only two.

The first one was a white man with a medium build. He wore a grey winter hat and a grey sweater over brown pants. He didn't spend much time inside. He walked through the door, came out moments later, and simply walked away, going down the same direction of the street that I travelled on. Maybe Kevin was checking up on him and he was giving some sort of update for some other illicit operation that Kevin ran. Maybe he was an undercover cop conspiring with Kevin. Who knew. He could get away with anything.

The second was a much taller black man who wore considerably less. He wore just a black hoodie over grey sweatpants. He spent much longer inside. He walked in, and it must have been 10 minutes before he walked out again. But when he walked out he looked visibly shrugged. Maybe I was wrong, but it was like he had his soul wretched out. He walked slowly and went back behind the fence. Moments later, he came out with a bag similar to the ones I picked up before that stored weed. I wondered what happened to him. Did he fail a mission too? Or maybe he was the undercover cop. Who knew.

73

Diane eventually showed up, wearing black boots, light blue jeans, and a green sweater.

"Marcus, I wasn't expecting you," she said somewhat enthusiastically as she walked up to me. I stood up to meet her as she gave me a kiss. I knew that we were in public and there were people around, but somehow, I didn't care.

I wrapped my arms around her in a tight hug, with my head right next to hers, over her right shoulder. I knew I was holding her tighter than normal, but I couldn't let go or loosen my arms.

"Marcus, is something wrong?" she asked quietly.

"No," I replied, holding her tightly.

"Here, let's go talk in the park."

We walked across the street, entering the park. She quickly walked towards the nearest bench and sat down as I joined her.

"This is going to be it," I said.

"What do you mean?"

"This is going to be my last job for Kevin."

"I thought you didn't want to anymore. Don't do it if you don't want to."

"It's just a delivery. He said that he'll give me $1000. I can start new. I can start fresh."

"Are you sure it's real?"

"He told me he would give me $600 before the job and give me the rest after. I'll count it to make sure."

"That's good to hear. Hey, you better buy me some cookies afterwards," she said with a chuckle.

"For sure," I replied.

We sat still for a moment, looking across at the townhouses. They looked bland and grim.

"Wow, things have changed," she said

"Yea," I replied.

"Like remember the first time we saw each other? You were here with Chris. I thought you were another one of those teenage snobs. The ones who think they're living the good life by fucking a hooker. Thank god you aren't one of those."

"Yea. I'm pretty sure I was even scared of you. I remember you sitting there as I came out."

"Well, hope I'm not so scary now."

I chuckled. "But hey, I'm glad we met again in the market," I said. "Oh, and also, I was thinking, maybe with the $1000 I could even go somewhere, enrol in some community college or something. Find a job. It might take some time, but I'll come back and help you. We'll both make it out of here-"

"Marcus, don't worry about me."

"But really, I could-"

"No, I'll be fine. Really. I'm glad this is happening to you though," she said, as she put her hands on mine and smiled.

I took a deep breath. I really did want to bring her out of here. Bring her with me. But there was no sense in trying. This was Diane. Fiercely independent, and stronger than I would ever be.

"Don't worry about me," she said, as she bent in and kissed me again.

"Thanks for being there Diane," I said softly.

"You too," she replied, kissing me again.

We sat still for a moment, our heads turned towards each other, her hands still gripping mine.

"Anyways, I've got to go now. Got some appointments," she said as she stood up.

"Ok, have fun," I said jokingly.

She turned to me and gave me a friendly smirk.

"But good luck, Marcus. And hey, come see me afterwards. Just come to the apartment. I'll stay up and I'll keep the lights on," she said as she began walking away.

"Ok, sure."

"See ya later, Marcus," she said, turning her head back as she walked away.

"Bye Diane."

I wish I had said more to her.

74

I walked through the gates to the back of the black townhouse. This was the last time. I felt less nervous than last time, but part of me still worried the money would be fake. That there would be some excuse and I wouldn't really get the money. I walked to the back, where I saw a man holding a brown box. Upon getting closer, I saw that in his other hand, gripped by his side, was a brown envelope, that I figured must contain the money. He waited until I was up and close to him before speaking.

"Are you Mr. Smith?" he said. He was an older man, perhaps in his mid 30s. Much older than the others I had dealt with, but still seemingly younger than Kevin. He wore a grey New York Giants hoodie over similarly coloured sweatpants. The hoodie looked old, with the Giants logo on the front seemingly worn out. He was white with short hair and a round face, and around 6 feet in height.

"Yea," I replied, quietly, still feeling somewhat scared. Seeing the envelope helped ease my nerves but on the inside, I was still worried about what as going to happen.

"Kevin told me you could count this. Go ahead, take your time."

He handed me the envelope. The top flap wasn't sealed, so I pushed the flap back and looked inside. There were several bills that I pulled out after reaching my hand down. As I did, I constantly looked upwards to make sure that the man wasn't going to attack me. I grabbed all the bills with my right hand and looked at them. They were all 100s. I spread them out in my hand like a hand of cards, and counted. There were six, like Kevin had promised. I put the bills back in and pushed the flap of the envelope under the other side.

"Is it good?" he asked.

I nodded.

"Ok, here's the job," he said. "You do it and come back, we give you another $400. This is real important, you've got to follow through. You're fast and we think we can trust you."

I wondered if this man was some sort of senior member. He used "we" as if he was an instrumental part of the organization. BUt I questioned the speed. I couldn't drive and wouldn't any car be significantly faster?

"We need to settle some debts with a Triad gang in New York. So we have this delivery for them. It's an important package and it would be devastating if it ended up in the wrong hands."

He handed the box to me. It was fairly heavy, light enough that I could still walk while holding it, but heavy enough that I needed to hands.

"You're going to go out on that street and walk across the park. From there, once you hit the other side, you're going to turn right. After that, walk straight. It's a long walk. Keep going until you hit the end of the street. There'll be a street running horizontally. Turn left then, and walk down that street, going along the forest, until you see the white dry cleaning sign. It says "Dragon Dry Cleaners." There should be men outside who will know what to do once they see you. Do you understand?"

"Yes," I said. I had spent time thinking about the prospect of going across the park again, but the directions were simple enough that I felt like I remembered it all.

"You have to succeed," he said. "We're counting on it. Do it, come back, get your money, and you're free."

I wondered how this man knew so much. Typically, the people who delivered behind Kevin's townhouse spoke little and seemed to know little. It was like this mission was particularly special and elaborate and Kevin needed someone who was closer in rank to him. I still wondered why I couldn't take a vehicle though. Perhaps it was the element of stealth. Maybe all the vehicles they had were marked.

I nodded before turning and leaving. The box was once again a cardboard box. I could feel individual heavy objects shaking inside, so I figured that whatever was in the package wasn't packaged tightly like the fake wooden books were before. I wondered what it could be. Guns? Some sort of tool? Perhaps that was why they needed me to transport it stealthily, especially on my last mission. If I got a marker on me, it wouldn't matter later on, since I would never do any work again for them.

I looked forward to going across the park. I figured that if I was going to leave after finishing this mission, I was likely never going to come back to this area again, so this might be my last time going across.

I stepped onto the sidewalk, lugging the box in my arms. I looked around, hoping to see Diane again, but she wasn't outside. I figured that I could just do this trip as quickly as possible, and I could see her later. The walk across the park felt much more similar to the first one I had. There wasn't much of a rush and I was relatively at peace. It was a slow walk, as the box was heavy enough to prevent me from jogging or running. I looked around me in the dark night sky. Once again in the vast and open mark, I could make out details as I got close to them. Benches, the abandoned playground, and in the distance, the dense shroud of towering darkness that was made up of trees. I wondered how long the walk would be. The walk across the park was already long, and the man didn't say anything about this distance. He only mentioned the later one, meaning that it must be even longer.

I stopped by the bridge when I got there. Somehow, I didn't want to step over the bridge without Diane beside me. It would just feel incomplete.

Eventually I reached the other side and stepped on the sidewalk. Across from me, there was noise and lights. The stores and buildings were newer and there was less garbage lying around. People walked in groups, talking, as noises could be heard from the patios of restaurants. It wasn't the richest neighbourhood, but it was up there. It had been forever since I had been in an area like this, and now I knew why I wanted to avoid it. People stared at me as I turned right on the street and began walking down. A homeless man, wearing dirty clothes, carrying a large box. I kept my eye on the envelope of cash that I had on top of the box I was carrying. I knew that the 600 dollars wouldn't mean much to the people here, but I was still worried. It had been a long time since I had been on a street -that was this busy.

Cars filled up the street, as all sorts of different sedans, vans, and taxis drove by. Above were towering apartment buildings that weren't like the ones I saw before. These shot up in the sky, and instead of being made of brown bricks, they were often white and made up of bricks of different styles. Lights shone out of windows, illuminating the sky as well as the surroundings. The area felt alive and devoid of anything draining its energy. Including homeless people.

It was clear why no one would bother journeying across the park from this side. Why would anyone want to leave this area? This was heaven. Why would anyone want to even catch a glimpse of hell?

The walk was long. The streets were lively, and the crowds of people walking around made every area of the walk feel the same. Bright signs, loud noises, and plenty of cars. That only made the walk feel longer and only made the package feel heavier. But though the lights and the life initially felt foreign, the excitement almost transferred to me. Somehow being in this atmosphere gave me hope. It made me feel like I could get out of where I was. Like I could reach this world. Like the vast park that separated the two universes perhaps wasn't so big anyway.

I pictured what my life would be in this world. Living in a high-rise apartment and having a stable job. Perhaps I would spend most of my weekdays working, but on the weekends, I could do whatever I wanted. And I pictured Diane beside me. We wouldn't have to talk on the ledge of a fire escape. We could try out the different restaurants and perhaps explore all the other entertainment destinations that the city offered.

I wouldn't have to worry about whether or not a garbage dump had enough food. I wouldn't have to worry about getting back to a market in time to sleep in the storage room in the back, defecating into a bucket that I would empty into a sewer the next morning.

I suddenly felt like all of this was possible. That I could change my life. I would take this money and I would start anew.

75

It must have been half an hour later when I finally reached the end of the street. The nightlife had dimmed down, as the end of the street got less busy. The darkness now surrounded me, as I was alone, carrying the box. It reminded me hauntingly of my first journey downtown after I left home.

The street I as on ended at a junction with another street, just like the man had said. But what I wasn't expecting was the vast forest. The other street ran against a dense forest. I couldn't see much, but looking at the wall of trees on the other side of the T-shaped intersection, I couldn't see anything on the other side. The trees were fairly dense. There was enough space to walk between trees but in that space, a few meters back, was always another tree.

I turned left and began to walk down the sidewalk. Realizing that the store was likely close, I set the box down and opened the envelope again. Just to be safe, I took the money out and put it in my pocket. My pockets were deep, so the money likely wouldn't fall out.

This area was now quiet. It must have been almost 11 pm by now and the walk I had gone on made me tired. The box felt heavier and heavier, and every few minutes, I put the box down to rest for a bit.

The stores on the corners were mostly convenience stores and small take-out food areas. Most of the stores directly to the left of me, across the street from the trees were closed down for the night. It was dead silent and cold, and I began to feel somewhat scared.

I picked up my pace, hoping to get to my destination faster so I could turn around and return. The journey back worried me as I had to walk a long distance in the colder temperature, and I wondered what I would do afterwards. Would Kevin let me use the townhouse? Would I even want it. I pushed these thoughts aside. After this delivery, I was free.

I eventually reached the dry cleaning store as I saw several men smoking in front, dressed in hoodies. It was right on a corner on the opposite side of the road that led into the T-shaped intersection. The sign had blue block letters on top of a white background.

I readied myself to talk to the men, but before I could prepare myself, they began to approach me, menacingly.

"Are you the one!" the man yelled, in a thick Chinese accent.

Before I could answer, he ran up to me and punched me across the face, as I dropped the box.I groaned as I fell backwards and onto the ground. I was too dazed to ask anything, before he kicked me in the stomach, as I rolled over on to my back. My ribs felt like they were cracked and I felt like I was going to puke.

I looked up as I saw the men around the box, opening it, as they spoke in Chinese.

This must have been a trap. I had to escape.

I quickly pushed myself up in the opposite direction, trying to sprint away. I could run anywhere. Anywhere but here and I would be fine. But only moments later, I heard a yell and suddenly, I felt a force hit me behind, as one of the men tackled me to the ground. My nose and chin instantly hit the hard concrete of the sidewalk, as my nose went numb. This couldn't be it, I thought to myself, wincing with pain. The man was holding me against my back pinning me down on the ground. I tried to turn my head to look behind me but I couldn't. I groaned as I tried to push back against him and resist his force, ubt it was futile and he easily outmuscled me.

I heard a voice come in, the same voice at the beginning. "Where is the money!" he yelled in his thick accent. I resisted, keeping his mouth shut. "Where is the fucking money!" he repeated, as the man who was pinning me from the back gave me an elbow in the middle of my back that caused a sharp pain that drained my strength. My entire body felt numb, as I realized there was no escape. They had me, and I couldn't get away.

"Where is it!" he continued, as I stayed silent. I was now whimpering with pain. I began to feel another send of hands go over me, feeling for the cash. They started out under my sweater, as I tried to turn by body to avoid the hands to now vail, as the other man was still pushing me down from behind. The felt under my sweater for a few moments, before placing his hand on my left leg, and then into my left pocket. No, no, no. No. This couldn't now. I began to scream, begging for mercy. "Please! No! I don't know what's going on! Please don't! No!" I couldn't do anything when his hands slid out of my left pocket and went over to the right. And when his hand came out of that, I could feel the bills brush against my leg as they left my pocket, coming out with his hand. I should have hidden it, I should have given it to Diane, I should have left them in the playground in the park. Fuck me, I was an idiot. "No, please, that's all I have!" I cried out, begging for anything. The men were silent for a moment, before they spoke to each other in Chinese.

One of the men continued to hold me down as I heard another begin to speak english. But it wasn't to me or any of the other men.

"We have the money and the guns," he said.

There was a slight pause.

"Ok we will do that. Thank you don."

I shuddered. It must have been a phone call with Kevin. He had arranged this. He had sent me here to get robbed. This was his payment to the gang. But please, they did what they needed to. I wanted them to spare me. Spare the crippled life I had left.

"Get up!" the same man yelled, as the man holding me down pulled my arms backwards. I tried to stay on the ground, whimpering in pain, broken on the inside, betrayed, destroyed. My life was crap. There was no way I was getting anywhere, even if I survived this. I was a mess, I was an idiot, and I was doomed. I didn't feel it before but I wanted it to end. I wanted to die.

"Get up!" he yelled as the man behind me pulled my arms back, while another pulled my shoulders up so I was on my knees. And with my arms pulled back, one of the men kicked me in my lower back, sending another shockwave through my body as I screamed, as my shoulders felt the tension of his arms that were still pulling me back. My body was locked between the force of the kick and the pulling of my arms.

Another kick and another scream.

By the third one I was numb. I was finished.

One of the men came back around me, facing me from the front. I could barely open my eyes now. He punched me across the face, as my head swung to the side, as my back was still locked into place by another man's arms. I felt my nose start to bleed.

He dropped me and I fell down, barely making an attempt to resist the fall with my hands. They had some more chatter in Chinese, before I felt two sets of hands pull me up by the shoulders. They turned my body around, on to my back, as I felt the arms now reach under my armpits, my blood dripping over my mouth and down my chin.

They began to drag me. I tried to open my eyes to see where I was going. It was away from the street. Towards the trees. My legs stayed on the ground and I felt a mild burning as they pulled me across the pavement. But I couldn't feel much.

I could feel myself blackening out. Soon my tailbone hit a hard bump which must have been the curb. They pulled me over the bump. I felt leaves and twigs graze my legs as they continued to pull me.

Then they let go and pushed me over. I began to fall. Rolling down some sort of hill. I was rolling down as I felt several sharp points jab into my body. And at one point, my legs hit some sort of truck that changed my direction. But it was nothing and the thud at the bottom was nothing, as my head spun and I let my eyes shut.

FIN

Is this the last page to the story?

Or is it the first.

Maybe it's somewhere in the middle.

The passing through a doorway that immediately leads to another one

Or was it a glass door?

A glass door that broke

was shattered

And stomped on all over the ground.

They say diamonds are made under pressure.

But doesn't everything eventually break?

Perhaps even a broken diamond

is worth infinitely more than what it was made of.

.

SPRING

76
I woke up lying down on the ground. My body ached and my head spun. Where was Diane? I let my eyes shut and I rested again.

77
I could sense smoke over my nose as I woke up.

Where was I? Over me I could see dark leaves. My back was cold, but it wasn't wet.

Diane?

78
I didn't want to get up. I wanted to just lie there. Forever. Diane was gone. My pockets were probably empty. I wanted to lie there. My life was over.

79
I tried shutting my eyes but I couldn't close my eyes.

"Are you up?" I heard a low voice say.

I was probably hallucinating. I close my eyes again.

80
I felt a hand push my side and rock my body.

"Are you awake?" the same voice asked.

I wish I wasn't.

81
There was no point of just lying. This guy wasn't going to leave. I pushed behind me, pushing my back upwards so that my body was upright.

There was a smoke, and I could feel the heat from a fire.

From the side that I was pushed, I could see a man. He was sitting on a rock that was on top of the dark and dead ground, in front of a small flame.. There were no fallen leaves. Instead it was a scattered layering of snow. Most of the snow must have been caught by the branches of the trees, leaving scattered areas of snow on the ground.

I sat still, observing the man. He sat in front of the fire, looking at it. He wore what seemed to be a brown fur coat over similarly coloured pants. He wore a winter hat too, a red toque with a fluffy ball at the top. It didn't fit the rest of his outfit.

He had light brown skin. He was probably around 30 years old. After looking more carefully, I saw that he had long hair. It came out of the back of his toque, tied in a ponytail that went straight down his back.

He noticed me looking and turned to talk.

"Come by the fire. It'll warm you."

I slowly got up and walked over. My back still ached but it wasn't too bad.

"Won't the fire burn the forest?" I asked. This couldn't be real. This couldn't. I had to be dead. It was about time.

"Not if you make it correctly. If you shield the sparks from anything that might catch fire, it'll be safe. It's a small fire, anyway."

"How long was I out?" I asked, as I squatted down opposite from him. The fire was small, perhaps with a diameter of at most, 30 centimeters.

"I'm not sure," he said. "When I found you, you were face down, on your front. It's been around 20 hours since then."

I looked up at the sky. It must have been around noon. The sky was bright, but all hints of dawn and the sunrise were gone.

"What happened to you?" he asked.

What did happen? I couldn't tell. Where was I? Why was I alive? Was this real?

82
"Diane?"

I knew it was her. The way she walked across that dark hallway, it couldn't be anyone else. The long blonde hair. The leather boots.

"Diane?"

She didn't hear me. She walked down the hallway as I pressed my hand against the wall, leaning over to try to get a glimpse of her face. But my hand didn't stop on the wall. It went right through and so did my body after that. My feet didn't feel anything either. They were hovering off of the ground. Was I dead? A ghost? I put my hand up to the right side of my neck. There was a pulse. My heart was beating. Where was I?

I looked at Diane. But this time, there was something beyond her. Fire. A blazing fire behind her that she was about to walk in. The flames came up from the ground and reached waist height. There were also balls of fire that shot up before simmering back down.

"No!" I yelled, as she continued to walk in.

"Diane stop!"

She placed her foot into the flames and soon they began to engulf her body, going up from her legs to her torso before reaching her neck.

She turned her head and I saw tears in her eyes.

"Why'd you leave me Marcus?" she asked quietly, with a whimper, before the flame burned her away and she was gone.

83

"I need to get back. I need to get back. This can't be it," I said, as I stood up and started to look around, trying to find out which direction I had to go in. I had to get back to Diane. We were just starting something special. She needed me and I needed her. I couldn't do anything without her. I couldn't.

She was probably waiting by the townhouse for me to come back. And what would she do when I didn't? She was stronger than I was. She would go ask Kevin. She would fight her way there. What would they do to her?

I had to get back. I had to. But the man put his hands on my shoulders, urging me to sit down and calm down.

"Hey, you need to calm down," he said. But I couldn't. I couldn't.

"Sit down and relax," he said, pushing my shoulders down, trying to get me to sit down on the rock beside the fire. "What happened?"

"I have to get back to her. I have to. She's going to get killed." I said, in a panic.

"Who's she? And what happened to you?"

I felt panicked, stressed, uncertain. I could feel myself breathing heavily.

"Woah woah woah, calm down," he said. "Just tell me."

He had a reassuring look in his eyes but I knew not to trust anyone now.

"I ended up homeless after some drama in my town. And then I met this girl named Diane, but I caught up doing some other jobs. Then the boss got rid of me. He fucked me over. He sent me with some money for a delivery and he made me think the money was for me. But it was just a trap and they beat me up and took the money. I'm going to kill him. He's going to kill the girl. I have to get to him first."

"Hey, I don't think you're thinking straight," he said calmly. "If you go back now, you have nothing. He'll get you. You don't have any options. Where would you go afterwards?"

"I don't know, I'll find something. I'll find some other gang. Work with them. I'll get weapons. I'll find a way."

"Is it really worth it? One bullet and you'll die. Is your life worth trying to end another man's?"

I didn't want to listen to him. It was worth it. Worth it for Diane.

"And if you get involved in another gang, couldn't they do the same thing to you?"

"No, fuck this," I said, standing up. "I've had enough of this. I'm going to do something about it. I'm going to end him."

"Hey, you need to break from your past. Just because you've made bad choices in the past doesn't mean you should make even worse ones trying to fix those. Every decision is a clean one. Every moment is a new moment in time. You need to make the smart decision now."

"And what is the smart decision?" I asked.

He thought about it for a second. There was no smart decision for me. If I just left, I would kill myself for not helping Diane. If I went back, I would probably get killed.

"Come with me," he said. "I'm taking a journey to Phoenix, Arizona. Back to the Navajo nation. I wouldn't mind a companion."

That was ridiculous. There was no way.

"It'll be a fresh start. You could start completely new. Learn along the way too."

"What, would I learn how to make fires" I scoffed.

"You could start over in a new place. Get a job. Whatever you imagined your life to be in the past can come true. You just need to try something you haven't done before."

"Why are you doing this anyway? If you're walking, won't it take years?"

"It will. But I'll be honest, I'm on a path of redemption too. This was a spiritual journey. I went to Maine. Now I'm going back. I'm on a journey to redeem myself and rediscover myself."

"What about food and water?"

"Don't worry, I'm not broke," he said with a chuckle. "I've got plenty of money on me. More than enough. Sure, we won't be eating at Michelin star establishments, but it's more than enough for bread and water."

"Why such a long trip?"

"Because sometimes, you need a leap of faith to truly make a difference."

A leap of faith. Maybe Diane was alive and well.

84

"So are you coming or not?" he asked me. "It isn't an easy trip, but I don't mind taking someone else along. I think it could be worth it for you."

"I don't know," I said. We were walking by now, heading over a hill. He had packed everything he needed in a giant bag on his back that went from his knees to above his head. The giant bag had a sleeping bag attached, a change of clothes, tools, and more that I couldn't see inside the bag. In his right hand he carried a the handle of a pot with cups inside of it and in his left hand was a large tree branch that he was now using as a walking stick.

"I guess I'm still not sure about the point of doing it," I said. The man seemed friendly enough that I could open up to him just a bit. He didn't seem like the type that would rob me or anything. "Like I see how going back would get me killed. But why can't I just go and work my way up somewhere else in New York? Why go all the way to Phoenix? That place is thousands of miles from anywhere I've ever been."

"I guess I didn't tell you enough," he said. "I told you that this journey is about freedom and rediscovery. But I guess that isn't all. By the way, before I start, what's your name? My name is Niyol."

"I'm Marcus," I replied.

"Marcus, here's what happened," he continued. He had a low and soothing voice. By now, we were going up a large hill. It wasn't hard to climb, because there weren't any leaves or other debris that one could slip on. It was only occasional patches of snow, as most of it was melted. It wasn't snowing now, but over the last few nights, there had been drizzles of snow.

"Have you ever been lost somewhere in a place you were familiar with?"

That was all too familiar.

"Yea."

"Basically that was me. Here's the thing. I lived on our Navajo reserve all our lives. We're all modernized and everything and everything was great. I worked as an artist. I was a craftsman. I guess that's where all my skills came from. I had a girlfriend and everything."

He paused for a second, almost as if he was building suspense, encouraging me to guess where he was going.

"But I was struggling with tobacco. I was addicted. I couldn't let off on it. I'm not sure if you've ever had the feeling before, but it was just something I couldn't leave. The reserve was fairly large but I was always in a familiar place. And everything just urged me to use it. I would constantly justify myself. I would do something, and tell myself that I could just smoke one cigarette. But one cigarette was all I needed to continue the addiction. It was almost two years."

He took another big breath. By now we were walking on a flat plain. I didn't know where we were going, but we walked slow and it couldn't have been far from where he had found me.

"I tried blaming it on others. I really did. It took over a year for me to realize that the problem was always me. It wasn't the strangers who offered it to me when they didn't know I had an addiction. It wasn't the failed attempts by my counsellors. It was me. And I had to take a leap of faith to isolate myself. To focus on me. To give myself some goal to follow, some challenge to follow so I could commit to something new and escape from my past. And so I decided to go with something crazy. I told myself I was going to reach Maine and back. It's been just over 2 years now. 2 years of travel. And I haven't touched tobacco in 2 years."

I stopped for a moment again, looking forward into the distance, at the gaps between the trees in front of us.

"When you commit yourself to something big, you never know where that'll take you. My mother always told me that any person is at their best when they have nothing to lose. And for me, I was at rock bottom."

I stayed silent, taking in and processing his story. If I said no and went back, what would I do anyways? If I went on this journey and I didn't like it I could always turn back. But if I just left him and went on my own right now, what would I even do? The idea of travelling with him had sounded absurd, but now it was almost a possibility to me. What did I have to lose anymore?

"What would I do once I got there?" I asked. "I don't want to end up homeless in a new city I've never been to. What's the difference between going there and just being homeless here?"

"I might be able to work something out for you. I'll get you a job. Sure, there's more people in New York, but from the looks of it, it seems like you don't really know anyone who can help. I'll get you something in Phoenix."

I wanted to work out the logistics to ease myself. Perhaps I was forcing satisfaction upon myself, trying to look for good news so that the journey would seem like a good idea.

"Where would we stay?"

"I'm pretty good with making tents or other shelter. But we'd go get you a sleeping bag. And I've got plenty of toilet paper," he said with a chuckle.

He had stopped walking when I asked him where we would stay. He was now looking at me. I worried he was fed up with my questions but perhaps he wasn't. Maybe he just wanted to see if I would settle with a decision.

"So are you in?" he asked.

I nodded.

85
We passed by a town outside of downtown New York where there was a hunting goods store. We had travelled for over an hour in the woods and finally, we stepped back onto a road in a town. I didn't know where we were or the direction we were going in.

"How do you know which way to go?" I asked.

"Well generally, you can just follow the major highways. You can go parallel to them and you'll be fine. But I mostly use a compass. Occasionally you always end up somewhere where there's a tourism center and in there, there's always maps. I know I don't always take the most efficient path, of course, but in such a long trip, as long as you're always going in the right direction, you'll be fine. Here, let's go get you that sleeping bag."

We walked into a lone hunting goods store. The buildings were all fairly separated. It was similar to how things were in Ridgefield. The store was its own building, perhaps just wider than an average house. It was in a rectangular shape, with a brown door in the middle of the white front of the store. There weren't many people walking around and there were occasional cars that passed by.

I realized this was my first time being in a town since leaving Ridgefield. The spaced out buildings felt haunting and fresh at the same time. Perhaps this journey would go well. Perhaps I could start anew.

Inside the store was rows of different tools. We went towards the back where the gear was, and saw a sleeping bag. He immediately went to it and picked it up off the shelf after looking at the price tag.

I followed him over to the lone cashier at the checkout counter near the exit of the store.

Niyol placed the sleeping bag on the counter. The worker scanned it, before saying that it costed 29 dollars.

Niyol took his large bag off his back. He dug inside from the top. The opening of the back was closed by pulling a stretchy string around its circular opening. He dug down before pulling out a small brown leather wallet. He opened it from the fold down the middle before pulling out several bills and giving them to the cashier. He then put the wallet back inside the bag, stuffing it downwards to place it where he had gotten it before. I wondered how much money he had if it was enough for a trip that had already gone on for 2 years. But perhaps he didn't even need that much. If he could make a fire in the winter, who knew what else he could do in the wilderness?

He handed me the sleeping bag, before stopping for a moment. "Wait you're gonna need more," he said. I stood there with the sleeping bag as he went to the back of the store to pick up more things. He came back with a large bag similar to the one he had as well as several other miscellaneous items. I could see string as well as a small first aid kit. He put all the items on the counter again before taking out more money. Afterwards, he put all the items in the bag and handed it to me.

"Wow, thanks," I said, genuinely surprised.

"You're gonna need quite a lot of stuff. Here, let's go."

We left the store and began to walk down the street in the town. I was legitimately beginning a journey over a thousand miles with a man who I barely knew. But somehow, this felt like the most refreshing thing I had ever done in my life. Diane was gone. She was gone and I missed her. But maybe somehow this trip could help me in some way. Any way would be fine.

86
"Are you there?" I heard a familiar voice say from outside the door.

I was lying down on the bed inside the beige townhouse. I could tell it was dark out from the lack of sunlight anywhere around.

I went up to the door and opened it, as Diane came through. I held her in my arms as we began to walk backwards, kissing each other.

I sat down on the bed with her legs wrapped around me as she began to undress.

"Marcus, we don't have much time," she whispered, in between our kisses.

I felt her around her waist, moving my arms upwards as her top began to come off. She reached down and began pulling down on my, taking them off.

Suddenly, the pressure on my legs began to decrease. The force I felt from her weight began to disappear. She was fading away and my arms began to move through her, through the air.

"No, Marcus," She whimpered as she disappeared. "What have you done? You killed me."

And she was gone and I sat there on my bed, staring at the wall.

87

"No I can't do this!" I screamed, waking up in my sleeping bag in the middle of the night. "No, no, no, this isn't real. I have to get back, I have to get back."

"Hold on, calm down," I heard Niyol say as he grabbed my shoulders, trying to calm me down.

"Diane's gone, Diane's gone," I whimpered.

"Hey, hey, calm down. Just sit, sit."

He pushed me down so I wouldn't be able to jump up or run away. He was stronger than I expected. With one gentle hand on my shoulders, it felt like he had me locked in place. In the dark night, the already tall man felt even bigger, even stronger, and my fears only felt worse.

"I'm never going to see her again," I said. I felt calmer now, with his hand on my shoulder, but I didn't feel any less worried.

"What happened with her?" he asked.

I paused for a second, not knowing how to phrase myself.

"I just had something special with her. Like it was so real. We were there for each other when we were alone. It's just... I don't …."

I couldn't think of what to say, how to describe the loss I felt without Diane.

"It's never easy," he said. "I wish I could just tell you to move on but I know that just doesn't happen. If anything, you can only hope that she's fine. Hope that she turns out ok."

"But I wish I could be there. See that she's alright. If anything, I hope she stopped caring about me. If she forgot about me, she wouldn't do anything that could harm her."

"I know that people say this a lot, but I really believe that time will heal everything," he said. "You'll only look back at your time with her with fond memories. You loved her when you could have, and that's all you could have done."

"It's just that I wish that didn't end. I wish I could be with her forever. That she could come with us or something."

"I understand. And there's no way out of it. Everything ends and we can't do anything about it. If anything, you can only look back and just be glad that you had her."

I still wanted her. I still did.

"Yea, I guess so," I said.

I took a deep breath and went back to my sleeping bag. It wasn't too cold, so we were sleeping out in the open.

"Try going back to sleep," he said. "I'll be here if you need anything."

"Ok," I said, as I lay back down.

I missed her.

88

Halfway through the day, we had reached an area that was beside a body of water. After travelling through the down, we had reached a forested area again. And after following our continuous Southwest trajectory, we reached an open area beside the water. THere wasn't a beach. Instead, there were rocks near the water. Some large and jagged, but many small and round. THey weren't comfortable to stand on, but they didn't hurt too badly.

We had spent the last day eating bread and drinking water. Niyol had gotten me a canteen to put water in, and he had several loaves of bread in his bag. I worried that we had a lack of nutrients, but in the wooded area, he had found several trees with fruits that after some observation, he deemed to be edible. They tasted ripe and somewhat bitter, but they were still refreshing, as I had gone for months without having fresh food.

The water was also a nice sight to see. The closest thing I had gotten to seeing nature before was the vast unoccupied park opposite the townhouses. Seeing the glimmer of the sun over the water felt nice. Though there was snow along the rocks, especially in the crevices between them, the water wasn't frozen at all. I didn't ask many questions about where we were going, trusting Niyol and his compass. But I wondered why we had come down to the rocks.

"Wouldn't it be faster to just stay in the woods?" I asked. "The rocks are harder to walk on."

"Have you ever gone fishing?" he asked.

"A few times. But we don't have any rods."

"Not yet," he said.

He settled on a spot along the beach were the ground extended towards the water, going roughly 50 or so meters outwards. We walked towards the front of the peak and Niyol set down his bag and I followed. He took the walking stick he had and from his bag, he pulled out a knife. He began to cut away at the stick, explaining that he was making a grove to attach string to make a fishing rod.

He asked me to hand him string, which I took out of my bag. He tied the string around the top of the stick where he had cut a groove. Then, he measured out a length of string perhaps around 3 or 4 arm lengths long and cut it there. He handed me the stick, and he went into his bag and took out a tin. In it, I could see soil with worms and inside the soil were hooks. He took a worm and put it on a hook, pulling his sleeve up from his sweater as he dug his hand into the tin. I saw a green tattoo of what looked like an arrow on his forearm.

He took hold of the string, as the stick was still in my hand, and he attached the thook to the string, tying several knots. Then, he told me to give him the rod, and he cast the line into the water.

The entire process took less than two minutes, at most. He seemed to be a complete master at the craft.

"Wow," was all I could say.

"I should've gotten another stick. But no worries, I'll have one for you next time," he said.

We stood there silently for a moment before he spoke again.

"Here, come help me out with this," he said, as he set the rod down. He walked back away from the water and reached a big rock. Together, we lifted it, bringing it to the edge of the water so we could sit on it. It took several stops for us to bring it there, setting the rock down after taking a few steps each time. But eventually, it got there and we were able to sit on it, with his fishing line in the water.

"How are we going to cook it later?" I asked.

"I'll start a fire. We'll set up a makeshift stove and we'll fry the fish."

I nodded. It sounded complex, but I figured that Niyol could do just about anything.

Moments later, his body suddenly got still, as he pulled up on the stick. "Got one already!" he shouted joyfully, as he pulled the stick up, revealing a fish around the hook. It was a small fish, perhaps just under the length of a forearm.

"Go and fill the pot with water," he said, as I took the pot that was set behind us and went out to the water. The water was cold and it tingled my hand. I brought it back, and Niyol had already taken the fish off the hook. He placed it into the pot, which I put down on the ground.

"Wow, that was fast," I said.

"Yea, sometimes you just luck out," he said. "Feels great though. Sometimes I go for hours without getting anything."

"Here, why don't you do it this time," he said, handing me the rod. "The worm's still on the hook, so that's one less job for you."

I nodded, taking the rod. I cast it out into the water and sat down.

"So, Marcus. How's it been these two days?" he asked.

"It's not bad," I said. "I spent lots of time leaving in a dark storage room before. Just being out in the open was nice. With the trees and everything."

"Yea, it's always nice," he said. "Two years, and the nature and the journey still feel as fresh as it did the first time."

I nodded.

"By the way," I said, "what does your tattoo mean?"

I was curious. The arrow on his forearm was quite big, starting from his wrist and going halfway down his forearm.

"It represents Time's Arrow," he said.

I looked at him with confusion.

"It's just a constant reminder to myself that time never stops. Everything only travels in one direction. The past is the past, and you can never change that. And because of that, all our choices have consequences. Every moment we live through, we only get to go through that moment once. It's what gives our life meaning. We can't change our past decisions, but every moment is a new one, and every moment can be savoured."

Wow, I thought to myself. I thought about everything with Diane. Even everything with Angie, everything with my parents. None of that would change. Never. But at least I had Diane. He was right.

"And you only have so many moments because the arrow eventually just falls to the ground. But it's your choice what you do with those moments. It's both our biggest blessing and our biggest curse. No matter what, Time's Arrow marches on, and we can do nothing but live in its wake."

I nodded, looking back out at the water. I felt brighter, It was like losing Diane had temporarily gone away from my mind. I felt free, sitting on this rock, with a fishing rod in my hand.

Time's Arrow, I thought to myself.

"What if we could go back though?" I wondered out loud, with curiosity. "Couldn't we just relive those good moments? LIke is it really a blessing?"

"I feel like we think that," he said. "We wish we could relive those moments. But if we could truly go back in time, why would our decisions matter if we could just redo them later. Why love, why help others, why care about anything? If we could go back in time, anything we did wouldn't mean anything because it could just be changed. That's why I think it's a blessing. Once the story's written, it can't be changed, but at least you had the chance to write it in the first place."

"That's true," I replied. "I guess I never thought about it that way."

"I think it just puts stuff in perspective," he replied. "I just like keeping that on me as a reminder."

We sat there on the rock for several moments, watching the slow waves come in and hit the shore. Eventually, I managed to catch another fish that was of a similar size to the one Niyol had caught. He helped me take the fish off the hook and we put it on the pot that we carried over to the back of the rocks, and with us, as we continued walking down in the woods.

89

The way he made a fire was even more impressive than his ability to make a fishing rod.

He started by going around, looking for rocks. He found several dry ones, examining them and scraping them with his knife to see if they were suitable for use. He moved swiftly and picking up a rock, he almost instantly could tell with a decisive swiftness. After gathering several rocks, he brought them into a clear area. "Here, put them in a circle. I'm going to go grab some sticks."

I began to arrange the stones in a circle. I guessed how big the circle would be based on the number of stones there were. There were perhaps twenty and I began to arrange them in a circle.

I tried to notice similarities between the rocks to figure out why he chose them. They ranged in size and colour as well as shape. Some were larger and bumpier than others, while others had more spherical shapes. I couldn't see what was special about. Maybe Niyol saw something that I didn't. Or maybe it was the other way around. Perhaps they weren't special at all.

After the rocks were in a circle, I squatted down with my bag by my side, waiting for him to come back. Eventually he did, with sticks and twigs in his hand.

"That looks good," he said. "Here, take these."

He tossed me the sticks he had. They varied in length as well as thickness. Some of them still felt somewhat wet from the light snow. I wondered what would happen if the snow had been heavy. What would we do?

As I looked at the sticks in my hands, I didn't realize that Niyol had begun preparing the fire. I looked at him, seeing a lit paper in his hand. A full sheet of paper. A third of it was on fire, and he was holding that down near but not touching the ground, within the circle of stones.

"What's that for?" I asked.

"It helps to dry the ground. It isn't perfect. But a sheet of paper can be used several times. And it's more efficient than just using the lighter. Here, come over with the sticks."

I walked over and he looked into my hand and took out the thickest stick. Then the second thickest. He continued, arranging the sticks in a cone shape, going in circles, with the thinner sticks covering the thicker ones from the outside. Finally, when there was one stick left, he took the sheet of paper, which he had blown out but was still hot and smoking, and rubbed the stick against the paper. It brought off the ashy parts of the sheet of paper, leaving the white. It also heated the stick and melted any remaining snow that may have been on it. He reached into his pocket and pulled out his lighter which he had used before, and after holding the flame against the end of the stick for a few moments, a small and faint flame began to show. He was methodical in his movements yet still fast. From an outsider, it may have looked as if he was in a great rush. But up close, it was clear that he was in total control.

He took several leaves out of his pocket and placed them between the sticks as well as inside of them. Then, sticking the stick with the flame into the leaves with his right hand, he took his left hand with the lighter, and simultaneously held the lighter flame next to one of the leaves between the twigs. He held it there for several moments as I watched on, as I heard several snaps and cracks from the twigs.

"Hey, Marcus, why don't you go get something to sit on?" he told me.

I nodded my head and turned around, going into the woods. We were in a clear area between trees, and as a whole, this area of the forest contained trees that were thin and decently sparse. I didn't have to walk long before I saw a part of half of a tree trunk, lying on the ground. I picked it up and brought it back into the open area. I set it down and turned back around to go find another piece. Several more meters, and part of a trunk was there, on the ground. Perhaps someone had cut it before. But regardless, it worked well for us. I brought it back and set it next to the fire. There was a small flame now and Niyol stood beside it, looking at it. "That should be enough for a boil," he said. "I think we'll boil the fish instead."

I went over and brought the other piece over and placed it at around a 90 degree angle from the first piece. I had the entire trunk part placed vertically like a stool, while the half-trunk was set on the ground with the flat part facing upwards. "Have a seat," he said, gesturing for me to sit down. "Up to you which one," he continued.

I sat down on the lower half-trunk, wanting to leave the better spot for him.

"Try to go find a long stick," he said. "One that's long enough to go across the fire. You go that way and I'll go this way."

He gestured in opposite directions as we went out. It wasn't hard to find and soon we met each other back at the fire.. He took the stick I gave him, walked over to his bag and took out a knife, and cut down one of the ends of the stick, making it sharp enough to stick into the ground. He stick it in diagonally to the ground, so that the stick hovered over the fire. Under the stick and between the ground where the stick was in the ground, he took the shorter and thicker stick that he had found and stuck it under, preventing the original stick from falling down. He then took the knife and hiselled away at the top of the stick until there was a groove long and deep enough to insert the thin handle of the pot, with the fish and water inside.

He stood back and took a deep breath, sitting down on the makeshift stool that I had brought over.

"That was pretty cool," I said, as I sat down too.

"Yea. When you get used to making them, it becomes far easier."

"Do you make one every night?"

"During these seasons, yea, I try to. It's just helpful in general. Fire is one of nature's greatest blessings. It can heat, it can cook, and it can also be a light."

I nodded in agreement.

"But don't worry, I think you'll adapt. You seem like a quick learner."

"Was it hard for you to adapt? I feel like even small details that we take for granted are a pain in the wild. Stuff like going to the washroom and finding shelter."

"Well I guess I like to think of everything in a positive way," he said. "I really think that whether or not something is good or bad ultimately comes down to a decision you make. Like if it rains and you think of it as a bad experience where you'll get wet, then you won't like the rain and the storm will be miserable. But if you think of it as a source of water, or a way to clean yourself if you're days away from any town, then you'll see the rainstorm as something good."

"But isn't it natural? Like depending on what situation you're in, won't it always be good or bad?"

"I used to think so, but I feel like it isn't true. I think your perception of a situation really is something that you intentionally tell yourself. You might not think so, but if you keep telling yourself, I feel like you eventually believe it. So if you keep telling yourself positive things, you'll eventually see that situation to be positive."

"Maybe you try hard to get something, some job but you don't," he continued. "You could live your life wallowing in sadness and disappointment, or you can tell yourself there's other chances and that you'll find a way. Perhaps that job you wanted was the best. Perhaps objectively, there won't be anything better. But if you tell yourself that whatever plan b you followed was great too, won't you still end up satisfied and in a good mood?"

"But aren't you lying to yourself?"

"Maybe you are. But I don't like to think of it that way. At first, it may seem like it. But by the end, when you look back at what could have been negative and you only see a positive experience, was it really a lie? If you've truly convinced yourself and it's done you a good thing, isn't that a favour for yourself? I think there's an opportunity in everything. You just need to convince yourself that it's there."

"But let's say it is a lie," he went on. "If it's a lie that you believe in, helps you, and doesn't harm anyone else, is it bad at all?"

He appeared thoughtful. I thought about the way he worded things. He was masterful and what he said might be true. Perhaps this was a good opportunity for me. I had learned so much already. And sure, making a fire in the woods might not always be relevant for me, but perhaps I could use those skills in some other way. Maybe this really was positive.

"Well, I think the fish might be ready now. Come, let's eat."

We at the fish, spitting bones out into the fire. It tasted fresh, almost too fresh. But it was fish and it had been ages since I had it.

Afterwards, I lay in my sleeping bag, thinking about my experiences and what he said. Could what happened at James' house truly be seen as a positive? Could Kevin? Perhaps he could find a way. Perhaps Niyol could go through all of that unscathed, maybe come out a better man.

But I couldn't yet.

90

For the next few days, we continued walking in the woods walking during the day and making a fire at night. I had found myself a good walking stick by the third day and I followed close behind him, as we went through an area that had more hills. I could see why he used the walking stick. It made the bag on my back feel much lighter and manageable, as it seemed to take pressure off my legs, as I could use the stick to help push upwards against a hill.

"Hey Marcus, you like sports?" he asked me as were walking up the hill.

"I played Little League. Occassionally I'd go see a Mets game. I don't know why, but our neighbourhood always went for the Mets. We didn't hate the Yanks or anything, the Nationals were always our biggest rival. But yea, it was mostly just baseball."

"Who were your favourite players?" he asked. "I don't completely follow baseball but I know a decent amount I think."

"David Wright was my favourite. To be honest, for a while, he was the only good guy we had. What about you?"

"I never got to see a game, but we often played with each other in the reserve. If I had to pick a team though, I loved watching the Phillies."

"I hate them," I said with a chuckle. "Always beating us. By the way, are we going to pass by Philly?"

"No. We do go through Columbus though. And eventually, St. Louis. We'll mostly just follow the I-40."

"How long's this forest going to be?" I asked. It had been well over a day and I wondered when we would reach a town or city again.

"I'm not sure," he said. "Probably a few days. In the eastern parts of the country it's never too long before reaching a city. In the Midwest though, I had a stretch of weeks without seeing another human. And when you did, it was a lone house on a prarie inhabited by a single family that grew their food and got their water on their own, meaning that there weren't really any markets or anything."

"What's your reserve like?"

He looked to think for a moment.

"We've got everything covered in it. It's really big. Real big. Not quite New York City, but it's big enough for everything we need. Homes, markets, schools. Some people like me worked in the reserve as an artist in one of the art workshops we had. But others also worked around the reserve. In the last few years, a good chunk have also moved out to Albuquerque or Phoenix. They still come visit the reserve. I've got several close friends working in Phoenix."

I figured that was how he was going to hook me up with a job.

"What do they do in Phoenix?" I asked, curious as to what was possible.

"All sorts of normal stuff. One buddy of mine is a computer tech guy. Some work in retail, some in customer service. But it's a big city and there's lots of opportunitites. But it's still close enough to home."

"Oh, ok," I responded.

"Did you have a job?" he asked.

"No. I spent most of my time studying. There weren't too many opportunities in our town, either. The economy wasn't going that well, so lots of adults were working in places like the supermarket where we typically would've gone."

"Oh, that's unfortunate," he said. "But yea, eventually we'll actually go through Columbus and St. Louis. If you want we can take some time to check things out."

"That would be cool," I responded. "I've never been there."

"Even better then. It's always nice to travel to different places. To see different cultures. Even though we're all in the same country, compare somewhere like San Francisco and somewhere like New Orleans and it'll seem like they're two different worlds."

"Have you been to other countries?" I asked. "I only ever did close road trips."

"Yea, a whole bunch. I went on a trip through Asia once. It was when I was around twenty. So something like 10 or 15 years ago.

I went to Cambodia, China, Vietnam, and a few others. It really opens your eyes."

"What was it like?"

"Well they're a lot less developed. It makes us think about what we take for granted. Eating something like a boiled egg can be a delicacy for them. It's like the stuff we have every day is what they dream of having."

"Oh wow," I said.

"Even our worst things can be great to them. Like food we might think is bad may be something they'll never get."

Thinking about that really made this journey seem okay. It had only been several days, and the experience of nature really was something fresh and new. I was glad I had taken it. And perhaps, in the future, I would just look back at this like a big trip.

"Hey, how are you holding up, buddy," he asked.

"It still hurts," I said, figuring that he was referencing Diane. "Like she was some huge part of my life that's still gone. I still worry about her. I think about these horrible situations she might be in."

"I want her to be her somehow, but I guess I've accepted that I can't do anything about it. It still hurts though. I guess there just isn't as much of a panic anymore."

He nodded silently with compassion. I wondered if he had experienced something like heartbreak or losing someone he loved. But I didn't want to ask.

"So anyways," I said, trying to change the subject so I could take my mind off Diane. "What else do you know how to do, aside from fishing and starting a fire?"

"I typically figure things out as I go. But I know how to tie a harness for climbing. And if there's good wood, I can set up something like a grill. There's more, but I just can't think of it right now."

We kept walking through the forest, until after several more days, we reached a small town where there was a laundromat for us to use. I hadn't cleaned m clothes in a long time and with what I was wearing being the only clothes I had, I had to wash everything one by one so I wouldn't be standing naked in public. But it was fresh and I felt great. My legs ached slightly from all the walking, but Niyol gave me a massage that instantly helped by the next day. Journeying with him was chill and calm, and everything went better than I thought it would go. But I just still couldn't take my mind off Diane. Part of me still longed for her to be with me now. Part of me still needed her.

91

We missed the snow when we travelled through the next town. Travelling through another small town with a laundromat that we could use, seeing the dry and cracked roads made me wonder if winter had fully passed. I had never really kept track of the date ever since I left Ridgefield. But after asking a local from the town, I found out it was already March.

Part of me felt like time had gone by quickly. But another part felt as if I had been away from home for much longer than 4 months. I missed Diane, but I felt hopeful, and with every coming day, I looked forward to the warmer temperatures and an easier journey.

But we hadn't evaded the last snowfall of the year yet, and it hit us when we went back into the woods. According to a local in the town we had passed by, we were 300 or so kilometers away from Pittsburgh. Niyol told me that the wooded areas would be ending soon, and eventually the terrain would turn into plain. The timing was perfect; as we lost our cover from the snow, the weather was getting warmer, making it easier to travel.

92

The light snow began in the evening, as we were just about to set up the fire. By now, I was capable of gathering all the sticks while Niyol gathered the rocks, making the process faster. There were times when Niyol struggled to start the fire, but this time, even when the snow began to fall, the bundle of twigs and leaves lit up almost instantly.

We had bought some beat from a grocery store that we put in between slices of bread. I wondered just how much money Niyol had. He had enough for everything we needed, but he still spent it frugally, as if he knew that if he spent too much, we would run out.

After we ate, we grabbed some extra rocks to contain the fire which we needed throughout the night. We stacked up a half-meter tall wall of rocks around the fire to prevent the spread, even though it was unlikely with the snowfall.

Finally, we set up our sleeping bags beside the fire, with my feet right next to his head as we were around the fire. I wanted to keep my boots on inside the sleeping bag but they wouldn't fit. I knew it was really cold. Though we didn't feel it because of the fire, I just hoped I could get through the night some way or another and go on to face the sunnier days ahead.

It was difficult sleeping. I worried about how cold my body was and every time I closed my eyes, I felt myself panic and worry, dreaming about my old situation inside the townhouse. *It's going to get better,* I tried to tell myself, remembering what Niyol had told me. *This is just a phase. It isn't even that bad.*

Eventually, I managed to feel my eyes close for long enough that I began to feel like I was falling asleep. And my eyes stayed closed, as the snow continued to fall.

93

I woke up in the middle of the night. I didn't know what time it was. I got up slightly, pushing my back up to look at what was around. I coughed. I coughed several times, feeling a slight shortness of breath. No, this couldn't be, I thought, as I coughed again. The fire was now out, the twigs and leaves all black. I could smell a faint scent of the burnt matter, but perhaps I was imagining it in the middle of the night.

I lay back down and closed my eyes again, coughing a few times. No, this couldn't be.

I hoped it was a dream and when I woke up, it would be gone. I closed my eyes again and went back to sleep.

94

Niyol woke me up in the morning, tapping me on the shoulder. I opened my eyes and let out a few short coughs. Fuck, it's real, I thought to myself. My body was drowned in sweat. I could feel my undershirt and underwear wet and stick to my skin. I pushed myself upwards, bringing my hand to my mouth to cover several more coughs. My nose felt stuffy, and I felt mucus in my throat, that I turned and spit on to the ground.

Niyol was on the other side of where the fire was. He was now coming back with some of our equipment, which he had put under a tree for cover. His bag was on his back, and he was carrying mine over.

"Thanks," I said, as he dropped my bag beside me.

"No problem," he said.

I coughed a few times, once again covering my mouth with my hand.

"Are you sick?" he asked.

"I'm not sure," I said, coughing. "I think so."

"Ok here, you stay in your bag. And here, drink some water."

He grabbed my water bottle from my bag and handed it to me.

"I'm going to start a new fire. I'll go and grab some sticks. You need something warm," he said, as he turned around and began walking.

He didn't need to do this for me.

"No, it's fine," I called to him. "I'll be fine."

The truth was that I was worried about myself. It was probably just an ordinary cold, but I worried it could be something worse. But I didn't want him to go through too much for me.

"Just stay there," he called back as he walked away.

I coughed a few more times, as I thought about Niyol. We had probably only known each other for a bit over a month by now. But things felt natural and he really was helpful to me. He felt wise but also complete and pure, the type of person who anyone could benefit from knowing. The type who just looked out for each other. I wondered what he was like before with the tobacco. I couldn't imagine a tobacco addict acting the way he did now with his wisdom and calmness. Maybe it was the trip that changed him, turned him into this great human being.

I looked above me. Through the foliage, the sky was still mostly visible. The snow had stopped falling, even though there was a moderate layer on the ground. The fire would definitely be harder to start. I wondered if it was even possible. But if anyone could do it, it was Niyol.

He came back a while later, with more sticks than he had ever used before. His hands were full of them, and he had even more squeezed between his arm and his torso as he walked over. He came up to the stones and dropped all of the sticks into the ring where the previous fire had been. Because of the fire from the night before, the area within the stones was more clear of snow than the rest of the ground. It was definitely still too wet for a fire though. Niyol went back to his bag and took out a sheet of paper. He went through a sheet of paper around every three days and in the last down, he had picked up some more to use. He lit the paper up again like normal. But this time, he moved the lighter around the paper so that more of it would catch on fire. The sheet slowly ignited, and I could partly feel the heat of the bright flame. He once again held it down to the ground, close to the thin layer of snow.

"This might take a while," he said with a chuckle.

"No worries," I replied.

The burning sheet gave me warmth again that felt real this time, compared to the heat of my sweat under my clothes. The sheet hovered over the ground, the flames moving up and down and side to side. His gaze was fixed on the flame as he watched the ground around it. It felt long and I didn't want him to keep spending his time helping me. But I felt grateful. The flame was a redeeming one, one that perhaps signalled healing and recovery over destruction. Maybe some things that seemed to burn didn't always do that. Maybe some burning was necessary to pave the way for eventual healing. The burning of a field of grace in order to grow a forest of trees.

Eventually, he deemed the area ready. He grabbed the sticks and brought them over. I got up to help, but he motioned for me to sit down, telling me that this wasn't the time for me to do any work. He set the sticks up in the usual cone. As there were more sticks, the cone was slightly wider at the base, but it was more noticeable that the cone was taller in height. While each area of a previous fire had cone stick on top of another, the sticks were layered 4 or 5 sticks thick across the cone that he made.

He went back to the bag, going to grab another sheet of paper to start the fire, as the previous one that been burned away melting the snow on the ground. He came back with the sheet of paper in his hand but I could also see him holding a knife, along with his canteen of water. Perhaps the knife was to cut paper. But that wasn't ideal. Maybe it was to cut the sticks. I wanted to ask, but I figured that I would find out in a moment.

He came over and knelt by the sticks. In his hand was a lighter that he put on the ground.

"We're going to need some fuel to make a good fire," he said.

He took the knife and with his left hand holding the lighter in place, he smashed open the bottom of the see-through lighter with a quick crack of the knife. He picked it up and drizzles the lighter fluid over the sticks in the pile. Next, he took his canteen of water, opened it with his hand that was holding the knife, and rinsed his hands in the water, cleaning them. He reached into his pocket and pulled out another lighter. He had placed the sheet of paper on the ground, but he picked it up again, set it on fire, and pushed it into the sticks.

The fire began to spread quickly as the sticks caught on fire. With the extra rows of sticks, the fire also rise higher than any other one. I could begin to feel its flame. Niyol turned around again, going back to where his bag was. This time, he came back with the pot. He stopped short of the fire and emptied the rest of his canteen into it. He walked over and put the pot directly on top of the fire.

It was brilliant. The extra sticks not only caused a stronger fire, but caused enough stability that the pot, weighed down by the water, could form a indent within the sticks that kept the pot in place as the water heated up.

I'll be right back," he said to me, as he turned once again to leave. "I'm going to go get some leaves."

The pot had taken away some of the warmth of the fire, but I could still feel the heat and it felt good. Niyol was a genius. I wondered if he had done something like this before, or if it was something he had just figured out. The fluid of the lighter allowed him to make a fire even when there was still snow around, and the extra sticks he used made it possible for him to boil water without having to set up an extra contraption. It was like I was still learning new things from him every day, even after months of travelling together.

Eventually, he came back, with his hands clasped together in front of him. He walked over to the pot, and I saw him release what we had collected into the pot of water. It was boiling now.

"Spruce tea will heal you. It's great for coughs and sore throats, and it helps your immune system. You'll feel better soon," he told me.

I nodded, understanding now what this was for.

"It's incredible what nature can do," he continued. "Sometimes the best medicines are right around us."

He turned to look at the pot again, observing the water inside.

"How do you know what to use?" I asked.

"It's something I learned when I was young. Nature is always there for you, as long as you know how to use things right. There's so much that's possible, and you eventually just learn what to use in each situation.

He looked over again.

"Here, it should be ready," he said, as he stood up. He reached into his pocket and pulled out a brown cloth, and using the cloth, he carefully reached his fingers over to the pot and pulled the handle upwards, before pulling the pot up. He carried it over several meters, outside of the stone circle, and set the pot in the snow. The fire was now much small now and the twigs and sticks were burnt and cracked.

He squatted there for several moments, waiting for the pot to cool down.

"Here, can you come over a sec," he said to me, as I got out of my sleeping back, put on my boots, and walked over. Luckily, I had put the boots next to the fire so the outside stayed warm. The soles were still somewhat cold, but it wasn't too bad.

"Can you hold the canteen in place?" he asked me, as he moved to the side so it would be easier for him to hold the pot. I opened the lid of the canteen and held it in the snow. My hands were cold, but I knew they would be warmed soon.

He used the same cloth as before, and with his left hand on the colder handle, he used the cloth with his right hand to grab the back brim of the pot. He slowly poured the tea inside the canteen. It was a yellow-ish colour, and there were still small spruce leaves that went into the canteen.

He stopped pouring as the canteen filled up.

"It should be cool enough now. It tastes bitter. And the leaves are completely edible."

I stood up and held the canteen up to my mouth, drinking it. The tea did taste bitter, and I felt small bits of the leaves go into my mouth, as I chewed them into small pieces to swallow. It didn't taste like other teas. It was pungent with a unique taste, one that was bitter but also had a tasteless, grass-like backdrop. Slowly, I finished the canteen.

"Here, finish it all. It'll help," he said, as I bent back down to hold the canteen in the ground as he filled it up again.

I drank it again. I was getting used to the flavour, and the warm tea felt soothing and relaxing. The flavour of the tea was also something fresh, as we had only drank water when out in the woods.

When I finished the entire pot and we packed up our belongings to continue the journey, I still had a light cough. But I felt confident that with the tea Niyol made, I was going to get better soon. And more than ever, I knew that the trip would turn out well.

95

I got fully healed only two days after first noticing my cold. Niyol made me tea every night for three days, and eventually, after several more weeks passing through the woods as well as small towns with tiny populations, we reached a slightly larger one, one that had rows of houses and strip malls that larger than those in Ridgefield, but still much smaller than what there was in New York.

There hadn't been any snow since the night I got sick. The frosty winter skies were now replaced by the clouds of spring. It must have been April by now, but it didn't feel like it, as the sights and skies in the woods seemed to make any changes in climate difficult to notice.

After going to the laundromat we found instantly, and replenishing our stock of water and food in the local grocery store, we went into a tourist information area to figure out where we were. A sign said that we were in Newark, Ohio, but we didn't know exactly where that was. We must have been past Pittsburgh by now, and though we had generally followed the compass in the west direction, we didn't know which way to proceed to reach Columbus.

We walked into the information center. It featured several displays with brochures and up in front of us, there was a worker behind a desk who called to us when we entered the building.

"Hi," I said to her, as I walked up towards the desk. "How far are we from Columbus?" I asked.

"40 miles," she said. "Are you two walking?" she asked, seeing our large bags.

"Yea," I replied.

"Just follow highway 62. You'll get into Columbus from the top right."

"Ok, thank you. How do we get there?"

"Here," she said, as she took out a map and a pen. "Follow this road we're on until this intersection. Fro there, head down here, and you should see the highway."

I looked at the marked map which showed a simple path for us to take.

"Ok, thanks," I said again, as she pushed the map towards me for me to take. I picked it up and went back to the door of the building, where Niyol was waiting. He pushed open the door and we walked outside, making a left turn, as indicated on our map.

"It's only 40 miles," I said. "We're closer than I thought we'd be."

"Yea, that shouldn't take long," he said. "We're on good pace too. I think we might be able to get to the nation going through just one more winter. But we'll be down south by then so we won't have to go through snow."

"This trip's been pretty good," I said. "It's been a good break from everything before. Like here I am, with nothing, but it feels so much better."

"It's because we always have the wrong idea of what happiness is. We think it comes from buying things and satisfying our ideas, but it really isn't. You can live in the woods your entire life, and be happier than anyone who lives in a paradise where they can get anything."

"How? In a paradise you wouldn't have to worry about anything?" I imagined a paradise where all my stresses were gone. How could I be unhappy?

"You might feel good at first. But soon, you'd run out of things to do and it would become pointless. If you could have anything you wanted, why would you even get up in the morning? Eventually I think you would become bored and your life would become mundane."

"How do you make yourself happy then?"

"From doing what you love. From committing yourself to something you care about, and following through with it, struggles and all. I think happiness really comes from the journey. The end result is worth celebrating, but how long does that celebration really last?"

"Yea, that makes sense. But what if you don't have anything to pursue? What if you finish the thing you want to do?"

"You find something worth fighting for. Something that gives you purpose. I think happiness is really sustained by finding new things to go after, and truly putting your heart into them. Sometimes we get so caught up in chasing the ladder of success that we forget to turn around and enjoy the view."

"But won't you be forcing yourself to like something you don't?" I asked.

"At the start it might seem like that. But when you look back at the end, once you've accomplished your goal, you'll realize that although you may have started out disliking whatever you're doing, you've grown to love it. And that love is real."

We were within sight of the highway now. It ran by the town, and next to the highway were all sorts of motels that were probably cheaper than anyoptions that existed within the city.

"I never realized that," I replied. "Like I never thought about it that way before."

I had a drive now, I had a goal, and I had a path that I knew would take me there.

"It's really why I went on this trip. Like I thought that the tobacco could keep me sustained, and I would feel great every time I used it. But as a whole, I felt miserable. I needed something to commit to. And this was probably my best decision ever."

We were now walking on a residential street that ran parallel to the highway. It wasn't completely insight, but in the gaps between buildings I could see it. Soon, we were going to reach Columbus, a major stop on a journey that had already spanned hundred of miles.

"What about loss?" I asked him. "What if something is just so bad that you can't help yourself feel better."

"Then you just hang in there. Time marches on, things change, and wounds heal."

It had been forever since I had felt this satisfied with myself. Perhaps this was my best decision too.

96

We stood on the street that we were on, looking towards the towering buildings in the distance, as we reached Columbus.

The 62 ended up taking us on a clear route to the edge of the city border. From there, we followed a street that took us from the suburban outskirts into a denser area that marked the beginning of the city.

We were still on the outside of the city, but in the far distance, we could see the tall buildings that marked the downtown core. The city was beautiful. Around us were countless trees, various cars, and a mix of modern and older buildings that gleamed with life. There were old stone churches mixed between new health centres, all interspersed with gas stations and restaurants. It sunlight made the trees glow, as countless cars buzzed past us, heading towards the city centre.

The first time I saw a forest after weeks of living downtown was refreshing. But this view of the offices and cars felt just as fresh. We had only been through small towns for the last couple of months, and just seeing the tall buildings in the horizon seemed to fill the slight void of loneliness that came with travelling in a pair.

The city was nothing like New York. The sidewalks weren't crowded with people, and there wasn't an overwhelming sprawl that came out of the city. The outskirts, that we were walking along, didn't seem to be infected by the toxicity of a really high population. It was like this place was safe from the rot that a dense city brought.

We reached an intersection where ramps let to highways that travelled in all sorts of different directions. The sign on the right signalled a route to Cincinnati, while another one displayed Pittsburgh, which we had passed while coming here. Here the road widened with more lanes, but across the road, the city continued as before, with only the skyscrapers in the back looking taller and taller as we got closer.

"The skyscrapers are nice to look at," I said to Niyol.

"Yeah. Especially for me. I never really saw big cities that often when I was growing up. Seeing different ones was especially great."

Somehow, Columbus felt like a major destination. It was nowhere near where we wanted to eventually get, but something about this city already felt like an accomplishment to me.

97

We spent the day going around the city. We went through the gardens, conservatories, and parks the city had, while also touring the museums and offices situated in Columbus. The entire city was far more fresh than New York, and it almost felt like the two cities were from different countries. Everything in Columbus was open and there were trees planted everywhere. In New York, the only trees there existed in abandoned pieces of ground, and on sidewalks, supported by stilts and slowly withering away.

I wondered what Phoenix would be like. I knew it was warm and that Arizona was almost a desert, but how were things spread out? Was the nature allowed to grow inside city areas or was it all gone, covered by massive buildings? I just hoped there was space. After this journey, there was no way I would ever be able to live in such a dense and compact area.

Some people gave us weird looks, but for the first time in the last few months, while walking through a garden, I realized that the people glaring at me didn't necessarily look down on me. I always imagined that after a mother and a child saw me homeless, the mother would tell the child about how I was garbage, and how I was a failure. But the people staring at us now perhaps looked at us with curiosity. We were outsiders, but we weren't below anyone in status.

When it got dark, we needed a place to settle down. There wasn't an information center we could find, so we went into a convenience store to look for someone we could talk to. We walked into the store, and we picked up several drinks so we wouldn't feel bad asking the worker for help. Niyol took a green tea, while I settled with some apple juice. Niyol began to speak as the man working began to scan our items.

"Hey, do you know any open parks we can stay in?" he asked.

"Um," the man murmured, as he continued to go about his job. He put our items in a bag and put it on the counter.

"Most parks are watched and they won't let people in. But there's one on the far side of town that's really open. It's called the Willow park. By the way, your total is 5.93."

Niyol handed him the money.

"How do we get there?" I asked.

He took the money, put it in the cash register, and took out our change.

"Easiest path is to go down the street we're on until 6th street. Then go West from there, all the way until you reach the park."

Niyol took the change, put it in his bag, thanked the man, and we left. It wasn't too dark out, perhaps 8 or 9 o'clock. We followed his directions, until we reached the large park as the sky got dark.

98

The man we saw under the tree was certainly someone I didn't know, but he looked incredibly familiar. We reached the park from the sidewalk we were on, and we walked down a small slope that led into the park. The nearby lights from the city provided some light, but I still couldn't see completely clearly. The park was vast, but there were several tall trees growing in spaced out locations, eliminating the barren feel that resonated from the abandoned park across the townhouses in New York. It partly reminded me of Diane, and the part of the New York park that was on the other side of the townhouses, were the bridge was.

I still missed her.

The man wore something similar to me. It was an old and dirty brown sweater and brown pants, with muddy black boots underneath. He had a dirty beard that was several inches thick, and he wore a dark green beanie that went over medium-length hair. He looked like he hadn't showered in weeks. He was like every other homeless person I had seen.

I realized that I didn't even really see him as a unique individual. When you're homeless, you're homeless. And that's the only label you'll ever get. Your name, your ethnicity, your life story become irrelevant. You're just known as homeless.

Part of me wanted to walk by him and forget that he existed. But another part of me wanted to stop and ask him what happened, perhaps even help him. Luckily, I didn't have to make the decision. Maybe it was because of my story that I told him. Or maybe it was just how he was as a person. But upon seeing him, Niyol immediately walked up to him, as I followed.

"Are you hungry?" he asked, bending down.

"Do you have money or what?" the homeless man asked.

Niyol began to reach into his bag. Part of me almost didn't want him to give him any money. There were better homeless people, and based on this one's tone and voice, he was probably an alcoholic or drug abuser.

Instead, Niyol pulled out a slice of bread, and gave it to the man. Then, he stood up and began to walk away, as the man started to nibble on it. I followed him.

"Why'd you give the bread?" I asked.

"If you give them money, you don't know how they'll use it. You might just be fuelling an addiction that keeps them homeless. But water, food, those can and will help anyone."

"Do you always help homeless people?" I asked.

"If I have something I can help them with I will."

"Why? Like most people just avoid them."

"I think we just forget about perspective We forget about the fact that everyone's human. Every homeless person was born to two parents, grew up in some way, and is living their life just like you are. We never truly put ourselves in other people's' shoes."

He thought about it for a moment, and the continued.

"I really realized it when I was driving. I noticed that I'd sometimes get mad at people for doing wrong things. But then sometimes, I'd be in a situation where I'd resort to driving wrong in some way. And when people would honk at me, I'd feel like they were unreasonable. But when I was the one honking, I always thought I was justified. It's really just a perspective thing. I try to help others whenever I can."

Maybe that was why he even offered to take me along. He saw the life that I had lived. He saw a kid who had parents, who grew up, and was lost, stuck in a world without purpose. Without him, who knew where I would be. I might be dead.

The idea scared me more than ever. If he hadn't thought about where I had come from, I would be dead. I would have ran back, maybe going after Kevin. I would have been shot and killed. But instead, I was now in a beautiful city, and I was filled with hope, while accompanied by the wisest man I had ever met.

We continued to walk along, until we found an area with several trees, where there was enough shade that we could lie down and camp for the night. My bag felt especially heavy after carrying it through tourist areas. It was a relief setting it down. He told me we couldn't start a fire today. But it was warm enough that we didn't need to. We set out our sleeping bags and took out the food we bought, and we ate it, before talking for a bit, and going to sleep.

99

I didn't know if I had been awake the whole time, or if it was the sound of the twigs that awoke me. I lay there, unsure if it was someone else's feet, or if it was just Niyol getting up to take a piss.

My sleeping bag was comfortable and the area was warm, so I didn't want to fully get up. I turned my head to look at where Niyol was, and I saw his body in his sleeping bag, sound asleep. The twigs had come from the other side of me, and the snapping continued, as I got up to look to the side. I saw a shadow approaching, but before I could react, I felt a powerful weight descend up ome, as two hands went around my throat, pinning me against the back of my sleeping bag, with my legs still in the dark.

I couldn't see much in the dark, but I saw a bald man on top of me, perhaps forty years old. He began to speak.

"Listen, real quick," he whispered. I realized I was frozen. I thought about doing something, I thought about striking him but I didn't, as i was in shock, listening to what he was saying.

"You're going to give me all your money," he continued to whisper. "You're going to get up and give me all your money, or else I'm going to kill you."

He let go of my throat and took several steps back, still staying close enough that he could pounce at me any second. Niyol and I had our bags between us, intentionally positioned there so that they couldn't be stolen without waking one of us up. Perhaps the man had planned to take our bags in the first place, and he only demanded the money from me upon waking me up.

I pushed my back up, thinking about what to do. I could try to find Niyol's money. But if I gave it to him, we wouldn't be able to finish the trip. That wasn't an option. I could wake Niyol up, maybe. The two of us might be able to bring him down. Or I could take one of our walking sticks to attack the man.

I was glancing over at our bags when I saw Niyol turn over and open his eyes. Suddenly, like a wild cheetah, he sprang out of the sleeping bag, and at the bald man.

The man swung a punch at Niyol as Niyol was charging at him. Niyol stopped before him, parried the punch with his left arm, before swiftly reaching at the man's right shoulder with his right hand. Niyol kicked his right foot around the man's right leg, and quickly, he pulled him to the ground.

He held the arm of the bald man as he was on the ground, pulling it straight, with his right food in front of the man's body, allowing Niyol to put pressure on the man's arm if he needed to.

"Go away," Niyol said, calmly. "Stop doing this to people. It's only time before someone kills you in the act." He let go of the arm, and gave the man a small kick to signal to him the leave. The man jumped up and scurried away, turning his head back several times to make sure Niyol wasn't chasing him.

Niyol came back over, walking by me.

"Are you okay?" he asked.

"Yeah," I said. "How did you do that?"

"I've done Judo my entire life. It's all about de-escalating conflict and bringing people down. There was no way I was actually going to harm him in any way. But if he took our money we would've been ruined."

I nodded.

"Well, I'm pretty tired," he said, as he went back into his sleeping bag and went to sleep.

I lay back in my bag and started at the night sky. I was partly still in shock at what had happened. I didn't know if it was because of the attack, or because of Niyol's quick and effective response. I had never seen that side of him. The side that would be willing to protect himself when necessary.

Part of me felt somewhat uncomfortable. But I also felt safer. I knew that Niyol had my back in more ways than one.

I closed my eyes and went to sleep.

100

We walked down the sidewalk of another road, as I turned my head back to take one last look at the skyline of Columbus.

"I'm going to miss this," I said to Niyol. "What's next?"

"A lot of walking. A lot of plains and small towns. Mostly nothing. But in a few months, Indy. And after that, St. Louis."

"It's gonna be a few months though, right?"

"Yeah," he replied. "But no snow. It's all easy travels from now on."

As I turned my head back around to face the direction, I tried to remember in my head the image of a city, as it was the last one I would see in a while.

We continued walking down the road, hundreds of miles away from the slums of my old home of New York, but still hundreds of miles away from where we wanted to be, facing a journey that was still very much uncertain..

But I knew we were going to be alright.

With Niyol, I was going to be just fine.

SUMMER

101

The sign said that we were 40 miles away, but it felt like so much less.

Just several hundred meters after the "Welcome to Arizona" sign, we saw a much smaller one, that similar to the other one, stood on the right side of a lone road in the middle of the desert. In the background we could see brown hills and canyon-like mounds of brown dirt. There were cacti every now and then, seemingly dried out until the point of death, but they probably could survive. That was what they were built for.

We had come into Arizona from New Mexico. There wasn't any snow, and we were able to pass the last winter without experiencing anything cold. It was probably around May right now, meaning that the journey as a whole had taken a year and a half. The lack of snow brought up another problem though. In the woods along the Eastern United States a bottle of water might have been able to last half a day. But now, it was like I finished a bottle every two hours. I had already discarded all the unnecessary baggage that was used against the rain. But that space i my bag was now filled with water, which was heavier than everything I had before. Particularly in the long stretch in New Mexico before reaching Albuquerque, we were loading up on water whenever we could, in any store that we saw. And when walking through the desert, instead of carrying a walking stick for navigating hills, my hands were carrying bags filled with water bottles.

The journey had been long, but now I was excited. I was going to start a new life, and we were less than a hundred miles away from that dream becoming a reality. I thought about where I had come from. I was broken. Lost. Devastated from losing Diane. But now, even though I realized that I would always wish she had somehow come with me, I had come to understand that she was in the past. I would always look back at my relationship with her with fond memories. Things didn't work out in the end, and that was life. But I had learned how to find happiness within myself, and towards the end of the journey, as the distance to Phoenix got smaller and smaller, I only got more excited to reach our destination.

"Hey, are you excited?" I called out to Niyol. Any shyness I had or any skepticism I had about him was completely gone now. We were good friends, and I think we saw each other as equals far more now.

"I don't know how it's going to be like now," he said somberly. I had expected more excitement from him. But so often I forgot that he had set out on the journey far before I had even ended up homeless. He had travelled more than twice the distance than I had.

Who knew what life was going to be for him now. His old life was probably all gone. In the last few years, technology had probably taken over. He was changed for the better, but what if his community had changed for the worse?

I thought about how Ridgefield was now. How were my parents like? Was my dad still a drunken bastard? Did my mom still stick around, hoping that someday he would change? Maybe they cleaned the graffiti off the walls that lined the playgrounds. Maybe the old houses were renovated. Maybe they were even torn down by now. Tearing it down was probably for the better anyway.

We walked silently along the road, my last question seemingly worrying him. He looked pensive and nervous. But it was natural. How would people react upon seeing a former tobacco addict return, fully clean and changed?

102

By the late afternoon, as we could feel the sun setting, we reached a small town that was just several miles away from the reserve. Niyol told me that he didn't want to go back to the reserve at night, and that it would be best if we returned in the morning or early afternoon. With more than enough money left, Niyol said that it was best that we went to a hotel for the night. We hadn't slept on a bid in over a year. Though we showered occasionally in community centers, anything that felt like a home felt like a foreign luxury. I almost didn't mind the sleeping bed anymore. But when I leapt on to my hotel bed like a little child, the feeling of pulling the sheets out from underneath the mattress was glorious.

The hotel was a small one. It had two floors, with all the rooms on the second floor being connected via a patio-like hallway that oversaw the parking lot. It was right beside a department store that sold all sorts of tools, including drills, wood, rope, and glue. Niyo wanted to gone inside to see if there was anything useful, but we didn't see anything that might have been of use to us. In our room was a small chandelier in the centre of the room that only came down perhaps half a meter from the ceiling. There were two moderately sized beds, along with a closet and a bathroom. It was comfortable, and after my shower, even though we had walked in warm weather for moments, it felt like my body had never reached temperatures as warm as what I felt after exiting the shower.

Afterwards, we flipped on the TV, watching what seemed to be part of a crime drama. Niyol didn't look the same as before. He had always stood tall and he had always been confident in what he was doing. But he looked dropped over, as he sat on the edge of the bend, his head pointing downwards. His demeanour didn't feel as energetic or excited as mine. Perhaps he was just anxious about seeing his old friends again after leaving them as a different person.

"Are you nervous?" I asked him.

"No," he said quietly. "I'll be fine."

He didn't sound okay.

"Also, when you were in the shower, I went through the call book and I found the company and the guy I had in mind. Told him everything. Can you work as a customer service agent?"

I had been so caught up in moving to a new city that I had forgotten that Niyol would get me a job.

"Yea, for sure," I replied enthusiastically.

He didn't have a response like I would have expected.

"What's wrong?" I asked again.

"Have you ever done something wrong and just hoped people would forgive you?"

I thought about it for a second.

"Yeah, there were a few times when I broke some rules as a kid. Broke some stuff. It all turned out okay."

"No, I mean really bad."

I was confused. I had never heard anything like this from him. I knew about the addiction, but he had always spoken openly about it.

"What is it?"

"Don't worry about it," he said. "Anyways, I'm going to get some sleep. I'm dead tired."

He came over and turned the TV off, before going back into his bed and under the sheets. It wasn't even that late yet, with the clock showing that it was quarter to ten. But I figured that with Niyol tucked away, it wouldn't hurt if I got some extra sleep as well, so I went around the room and turned off the lights, before lying down on my bd and pulling the blanket over myself.

103

I had trouble sleeping because I wasn't too tired yet. But after only moments after lying in the bed staring at the ceiling, I began to hear Niyol rolling around in his covers. At first, it began quietly, as I looked over to see him go from one side of the bed to the other. But then it became more aggressive, his bed sheets being tangled up around him. His quick and frantic rolls were mixed in with groans. I thought it would end soon, and I hoped it was just some temporary discomfort.

Feeling a need to pee, I got up to go use the washroom. I looked over at the clock. It was now 10:45. Niyol didn't start rolling around right away, but it still must have been at least half an hour since he started. I walked into the washroom, closing the door silently behind me. The washroom had a shower over a bathtub to the left, covered by a white curtain. On the right of the entrance was a marble sink with a large mirror that went from one of the wall to the other.

I looked at myself. My forehead had moderate acne, and I had noticeable facial hair above my lip. I figured that I should shave before heading for the job. But this was me. Me, after an 18 month journey across the country. I thought about what I looked like before. I couldn't even remember. It must have been different. But every big change is made up of small changes. Small changes along a long journey that eventually completely altered who I was as a person. And a large portion of it was thanks to Niyol.

After I pissed, intentionally trying to hit the edge of the toilet bowl to avoid making a loud noise that would wake Niyol up. I finished, washed my hands, and opened the washroom door again, closing the lights as I quietly stepped out. I walked back to my bed, before seeing that Niyol was sitting down on the edge of the bed again, in silence.

I didn't know if I should call to him or not, but as I got closer, he spoke first.

"Can you promise to remember?" he asked.

"Remember what?" I replied, confused.

"Remember me."

"Of course. But we'll stay in touch, even if I go to the city. But of course I'll remember you. You saved my life."

He nodded. "Thanks," he said quietly, with a whimper.

"Really, is there something wrong?" I asked. I began to worry that there was an issue beyond his fear of returning home.

"No, no, it's fine. I was just wondering. Anyways," he trailed off, as he got back into bed and I followed. I slept well through the rest of the night, though I worried about Niyol. I wondered how much more he would toss and turn in the night. Something was consuming him.

104

As we left the hotel, it felt like part of the satisfaction I should have had was missing because of how Niyol was. We walked out silently, with Niyol following a map we had previously gotten. I walked close behind him, and after some time, he spoke in his previous voice.

"So, that was a great night's sleep, right?" he said.

I knew it wasn't for him. He didn't get much sleep at all. I knew that there was something wrong. But Niyol didn't want it to affect me.

"Yea it was nice," I replied. "It's been forever since I had a bed."

"You'll get used to having one soon," he said, showing a smile.

"So, what's the job going to be?" I asked, trying to start a casual conversation.

'It's in Phoenix. It's with a good friend of mind. I told him how you would be a quick learner and a disciplined worker, but that you also have a good and open personality. It's working as a customer service agent at a phone company. Are you fine with that?"

"I don't know much about phones though," I replied. "But I think I can pick up."

"Yeah, he told me there'll be training."

"Ok."

I was going to get a job. It was ages ago but I still remembered being rejected from the store in Ridgefield. Here I was, ready to get a job. I knew that I was going to work my ass off once I got it. I couldn't let myself lose anything now.

We became silent afterwards. I could tell Niyol was really troubled. He didn't want it to show nor did he necessarily know that I had seen him twisting and turning in his bed last night. I was worried, but I hoped that at the reserve, if he felt awkward, I could help him out and go around and perhaps help him reconnect with others. If people questioned his sobriety, I would advocate for him. I would do anything for the man.

We continued to walk, mostly in silence. From Niyol's tenseness, it was like I could feel his heart beating faster and faster as we got closer and closer to the Navajo reserve. From him, I could see how I felt coming home in Ridgefield to my father. But I knew what I was going to face. What was Niyol afraid of facing?

105

The entrance to the massive Navajo reserve was incredibly modest. It was made up of three road lanes in each direction that passed by a wooden entrance building, with a booth at each of the six lanes, with a worker inside who would open the gate to let you through. Those who wanted to walk in would follow the same path, simply walking on the road that was made for cars.

On the right, there was a large brown sign with huge white writing, with every letter being spelt in capital letters. It said NAVAJO NATION, with the word ARIZONA written in the bottom right, in smaller letters than the rest.

The area outside of the six lanes and the brown building that went on top of the lanes like a bridge was covered in fencing. It was fairly high, perhaps two times my height, with wires running along the top. It looked vast, and I could see many buildings when I looked down the lanes of the road. The lanes converged into a two lane road, and I could see several buildings slowly populate the sides of the road, until the buildings got more and more dense the further they got from the entrance to the reserve. Eventually those buildings must have led to an entire town, one with houses, services, and stores.

"Is this the only entrance?" I asked Niyol.

"No," he replied. "There's many. But this is one of the bigger ones. This is also the one I left from."

I understood why he choose this one. It was probably for a sense of closure. So that he could finish his journey where he started it.

"Are you ready?" I asked, as we stood there. I was looking all over the place, seeing what it was like. But I wondered what he was thinking about.

He took a deep breath.

"What's wrong?" I asked, as he stood there beside me, perhaps 100 meters away from the entrance.

"It's just...," he said. He let another breath out. His face looked red. He took a look at me, and then began walking down, towards the entrance. I figured that I would wait where he was. He could go and sort things out with whoever worked there, and then we could go in together. It seemed like the place charged money for tickets for tourists, and Niyol would have to explain that I was with him for us to pass through. I wondered if the people remembered him. I doubt the employees at the gate did. In such a large reserve, who knew how many people each person knew?

He walked up to one of the gates on the right side, the side where there were arrows on the car lanes pointing in the forward direction towards the reserve. He slowly went up to the counter in the booth, where I saw him begin speaking to the person who was working there. I couldn't hear what they were saying, but I saw him lean on the counter as he spoke. He looked more relaxed than before, and I figured that upon seeing someone from the reserve, he was going to settle back into how he was before.

They continued to speak for a while and it looked like everything was going good. But after some back and forth exchange, Niyol suddenly staggered back, putting his hands over his head, as if he was shocked by disbelief. He then bend forward and down, his hands on his knees, bent over. His hands went back to his face as he clutched it again. He bent back over the counter, his hands moving in frantic gestures, as if he was pleading with the person there.

What was wrong? I could understand Niyol being nervous. But frantic and desperate? I thought about the possibilities, as I felt my own body shudder as well. If Niyol couldn't get in there, what would we do? Maybe he said something wrong. Something that offended the person there. Perhaps their customs had changed over the years that Niyol was gone. But that couldn't make that much of a difference. Maybe the reserve was completely different now. But wouldn't they still let Niyol get in?

He was now walking back towards me. He walked slowly and he looked defeated, with his shoulders hunched over as he slowly shifted his feet up. His head was pointed down and as he walked, he suddenly swung his arm downwards angrily, giving out a short scream. When he got closer to me, I began to hear sniffling, and I realized that there were tears in his eyes. His face was completely red, and I could see the wet streaks that ran down each of his cheeks.

I was shocked.

"What happened?" I asked, going up to him.

"Forget about," he said quietly, as he walked by me, going back down the path that we came from.

I quickly went after him, walking beside him and grabbing his shoulder.

"What the just happened?" "Why couldn't you go in?" I begged him, as he continued walking forwards at a faster pace after shrugging his shoulder to get my hand off.

"What's going on?" I continued. "What's been happening the last few days?"

This wasn't characteristical to Niyol. He was always stoic, always unbothered, and he always faced his problems instead of turning away from it. I wondered what he said before. About remembering him. About forgiving him after doing something wrong. Was this it? Was this all a lie? Had he been lying to me, and was this whole Navajo nation thing a scam?

"You knew about this, didn't you?" I asked, grabbing his arm again. He immediately threw my arm away, this time using more force than before. But he stayed silent, even with my persistence.

I stayed close to him, continuously asking about what happened. I asked him what was going on. I asked if the worker there had something wrong. But with every further question I asked, and every continued moment of silence he gave me, I began to feel more and more like I was the victim in this. That this whole journey was a lie. Maybe he had nothing to do with the Navajo Nation. He was just leaving me out here. Like Mr. Thomas did. Like Chris did. Like Kevin did.

"You need to fucking tell me," I said, louder than before. Suddenly he turned to me and with one arm, gave me a shove as I fell to the ground.

"Leave me alone!" he yelled to me, as I sat back with my arms behind me. He continued walking forwards, back along the path that we came, going faster than before. He left me sitting on the dusty ground with hot red sand around my hands. I wanted to chase after him, even tackle him. But that would be no use. It wouldn't help anything. What was it that he always told me? Stay calm at any time?

I cooled myself down and began to think of the possibilities. He could be feigning all of this. Perhaps this would all be a trick. But he went through years of helping me. He spent countless dollars on me. If this was a trick, what could he be getting out of it? By leaving me here alone, how would that benefit me in any way? He could have abandoned me at any time along the trip.

It couldn't be his fault. It had to be something with the reserve. Some problem that he saw coming before and was worried about. Was it a cultural change? Did something major happen at the reserve? Was it a loved one? That seemed possible. Maybe he found out through some source that someone he cared about died. And he got that confirmed at the reserve. But why did he seem angry? Why was he frantic when talking with the person working there? It didn't add up. I had no idea what happened.

I got up and dusted myself off. If I went and chased down Niyol, who was almost out of sight by now after walking fairly fast, he might act the same way. He probably would. I wouldn't get any answers. But I could go back to the reserve. I could talk to the worker there. They would know what happened.

106

I walked slowly back to where the reserve was. Niyol had scurried away so frantically that I didn't realize how much distance I had covered chasing him until he pushed me down. The area was all sandy, with the exception of a two-lane road that ran down the middle of nowhere. I had to walk a noticeable distance before turning on another road that led into the reserve.

It was hot and it felt like the sun was baking me. It was perhaps around noon now, when it was always the warmest, and I really wanted water. But I didn't take any with me, and my bag was still in the hotel room, which we had booked for two nights so I had a place to settle before going off the job. I instinctively reached behind me as if to take a bottle of water out of my bag. I knew it wasn't there. But I still reached, hoping there was something I could latch onto.

The ground was warm, and though I couldn't directly feel the heat through my shoes, it was like I could feel the heat from the ground radiate up to my shins. Each step felt longer and longer and with each second that passed, I felt more worn down and tired. The beaming of the sun never stopped and I just wanted to be somewhere indoors.

Eventually, I made the turn and I saw the sign again on the right side of the road. I proceeded forwards, picking up the pace slightly, so that I could reach the gate of the reserve faster. I walked down the same lane Niyol had taken, the third one from the right, and went up to the booth to see a native man, perhaps twenty-something years old. His skin was of a similar dark brown shade to Niyol, but his hair was short and black. He was still older than me but younger than Niyol. He wore a brown vest on top of a green sweater, as he stood inside the booth with a computer in front of him.

"How may I help you?" he asked.

"Hi, my friend just came by, and I was wondering what happened? He came out…"

"You're with him?" he interrupted.

"Yea, we travelled together," I replied. "How come he couldn't come in?"

"You don't know?" he asked. The man had a medium-pitched voice and he had a look of surprise on his face. He didn't seem hostile in anyway, but he looked like he had just seen an alien.

"Was it the tobacco? But he's clean now. He's completely clean. That's what the trip was for. He really helped me, and trust me, he's clean," I urged, insisting that Niyol was perfectly fine now.

"He didn't leave because of tobacco," he said. "It was because of what he looked at."

"But he's clean in every way," I continued, partially ignoring what he had said. "He really is…"

"No, you don't understand. He never told you," he said quietly, and seemingly with remorse.

I stopped speaking and looked at him, confused.

"It was child pornography. He had it on his computer. Everyone here knows about it and he was basically an outcast.."

"No, no, no," I blurted out, in denial of what he was saying. "That didn't happen, that didn't happen. It was tobacco, he was addicted, …"

"No, it did happen-"

"No!" I yelled, hitting myself on the thighs. "That didn't happen. It didn't-"

"Hey, hey, hey," he said, waving his arms to calm me down. "I was in high school. It was really big. His girlfriend found it saved. Yeah, he was a great guy. I knew him personally. But he was kicked out and no one will take him."

Everything began to piece together in my head but I refused to accept it. His worry for what was going to happen. His begging for forgiveness. He didn't know if everyone would forget. He left because of it. It wasn't his own decision to take the journey; he had no choice. He was kicked out. He was a criminal. An outcast. A phony.

"No…" I whimpered one more time, holding my hands to my face as I shook my head.

"I'm sorry," the man said.

I turned around and left, walking slowly, as I put my head down. It couldn't be true. I refused to believe it. But I knew that it was.

Who was Niyol? Really? I had spent all this time with a disgusting pedophile like him? Fuck. Fuck this. He deserved to be kicked out. Who gave a crap where he was going now. I wasn't going to chase after him or anything. He could go off on his own. A liar. A cheat.

I walked back up the path that took me here. I was furious. My vision of Niyol was crumbling. I wanted to hate him. He was disgusting. He lied to me. This was all a huge lie. He tricked me. He screwed me over. He took me on this bullshit trip, with a bullshit reason, and it was all because he had no other choice. He was trash. Greater trash that I ever was. He took me on the trip that took me here. Here, where he wasn't even welcome. And he spent all that money to fool me. The hotel room, the food, everything. He was like Chris. Or Kevin. Or my father.

I didn't even care about myself. He deserved this. I could just be here forever. I would be fine. But he was trash. Really? He never told me? I wondered how I would feel about him. Would I take his help differently?

I wanted to do something to him. Do something horrible. He deserved a punishment. He was a liar. A cheater. He was just one of the others. Nothing was different. Nothing changed. It was all a lie. People were filth. Everything was stupid, hopeless, wasteful, and just not worth it. His smiles, his laughs were all tainted now. I couldn't go back to that hotel room. Everything was trash. It was all fake. And in that hotel room was nothing. Nothing. There was nothing.

Except a big book, that had the phone number for the job I was going to get.

That had to be real. He did it for me. That was legitimate. His call to the worker, his searching through for the number. He set me up with something fresh. He taught me how to fish. He showed me how to make a fire. Niyol bought things for me, and made me tea when I was sick. What was it that he said? That perspective matters? That everyone goes through a childhood, goes through a life? He went through an entire life A good life. And his life was crippled because of one mistake. I never heard it from him but I knew that he would do anything to change that. He had so much to give the world. He did all those things for me. Maybe he wasn't horrible. Maybe he was doing everything he could to try to make up for it. Perhaps he was trying to make the best out of the situation like he had said before, trying to always tell himself that there was hope, that it wouldn't be bad.

I wanted to hate him. But I couldn't.

I couldn't hate him.

Because behind a horrible crime was a man who truly helped me. A man who would always do anything he could to help others. A man who picked me up as I was passed out in the woods and brought me on a trip that gave me a new beginning. A man that taught me more than anyone ever did before. A man who cared not only about himself, but also for me. To give me a new opportunity.

Did all the good that he did get wiped out by this? No. It still happened. Everything he did still happened. He still saved me.

I couldn't just leave him. Now it was him who needed me.

107

I didn't even make it back to the hotel before I heard frantic shouting that came closer and closer to me. Walking on the road leading to the hotel that was now in sight, a white man in a dress shirt ran up to me, waving his arms frantically.

"You need to go now! Find him!"

"Woah, woah, woah," I said. I thought he was coming to the wrong person. I had never seen him before. "Who are you?"

"You're friend, I think he's going to do something! I work in the store. I didn't realize it. But he looked angry and he bought a lot of rope!"

"Oh fuck!" I yelled as I turned and began to sprint to the hotel, following an initial urge that preceded the piecing together of what he had said. I ran, going to the hotel, jumping through the plants in the parking lot. I paused as I was in the middle of the lot, gauging what the quickest path was. To the left of me, I saw the lobby and I ran in, pushing my way past a group of people who were pulling open the door. "Sorry!" I yelled instinctively, as I looked around, and saw a sign that had a picture showing the stairs were to the right. I went down the right side of the hall, sprinting towards the end, swinging my arms as I almost slipped on the smooth carpet that lined the floor. I ran and suddenly stuttered my feet to stop myself in front of the door, before pulling open the heavy metal door, leading to a series of metal stairs. I raced up them, going up two steps at a time, and turning 3 corners, before reaching the door of the second floor and pulling open. I sprinted down the hallway, running down to the room we were in. The room numbers went down until it hit 211, the room we stayed in.

I reached into my pocket to grab the key. It wasn't there. I went into the other pocket. I had forgotten it in the room. I began to furiously bang on the door.

"Niyol!" I yelled. "Stop!" "Let me in!"

I paused my banging for a moment to try to see if I could hear anything. After several seconds of silence, I continued my banging. "Niyol don't do it! It's all okay! Don't! I'll help you! You have me!"

Still, there was nothing. "Fuck," I muttered, as I turned around and ran back to the stairs. I had to go get a key myself.

I wanted my mind to stay clear but it just wouldn't. He was gone. No. He couldn't. He couldn't just leave me. I sprinted down the hall, feeling my feet slip on the carpet as I went stumbling, catching myself on the wall. This couldn't happen. No. Everything had gone so well. There was a way out of this. Stay calm, I told myself. Stay calm. Everything was going to be fine. Niyol might just be in the washroom. Perhaps he was just showering. Maybe he was taking a dump. Maybe he wasn't even in the hotel room. Perhaps he just went for a walk somewhere to clear his mind. He was out there. I would get back into the room, and moments later, he would get back. The rope was for our trip. Yea, it was our trip. It was so we could climb something. Maybe we could build a swing. That's what it was for.

I stumbled down the stairs, rushing back down the hallway I had gone down when I had just entered the hotel. I couldn't have spent more than 2 minutes inside the hotel, but it already felt like forever. It was too long. Too long and I couldn't save him. I ran over to the front desk , and went straight to a woman who was working there.

"I need a card. A key card. Room 211."

"Sorry, sir, could I have some ID?"

"No. I don't have any. I need it. Please. Now!" I wanted to calm myself down. But I couldn't.

"Sorry, our polic-"

"No, no, no, you don't understand. I think my roommate's going to do something. Please. I'll bring the key back."

She took a deep breath and pulled out a card and stuck it in her computer.

"Bring it right back," she said quietly, as she stuck her hand out and gave the card to me.

"Thanks," I called out, as I took the card and sprinted back down the hallway. I went back to the stairs, running faster than I had ever gone before, and I pulled the door open, and began to sprint up the stairs. I was breathing heavily now after the sprints, but I couldn't feel it. I felt almost dizzy, going up the stairs two steps at a time again. This couldn't be it. This couldn't. I felt my heart start to beat faster and I started to feel uncomfortable and nauseous. I reached the floor and pulled open the door, running down the hall and getting back to room 211.

I took a deep breath and took the key and stuck it into the slot in the door.

It beeped red.

I took the card out and flipped over, before sticking it back in.

It beeped green.

I pulled on the handle and pushed open the door.

Niyol's limp body hung from the ceiling.

108
It dangled back and forth. That was the worst part.

I stood, frozen. I was empty.

I shook my head quickly, coming back to my senses. I ran up to his body. His eyes were closed. His long hair dangled down the side of her neck.

"No, no, no" I muttered, coming out of my initial shock. "Niyol, Niyol," I called as I put my hands on his torso. He had to be alive. He had to be. "Niyol!" I yelled. "Don't do this! Don't do this!"

I held my hand up to his throat, looking for a pulse. "Niyol!" I yelled, gripping his face. "Niyol!" I felt around his neck until I reached the back. His neck was broken. I could push his skin in much further than I should have been able to. It was like his bone was just gone.

I crumpled on to the ground, as I began bawling. One stupid fucking thing. One stupid fucking thing from five years ago. This was fucking bullshit. Fuck. Fuck. Niyol didn't deserve this. Chris did. Kevin did. Not Niyol.

As my tears went down my face, I still didn't believe he was dead. He would wake up just about now. He would open his eyes. He would begin breathing and then, he would comfort me. He would tell me that loss was part of life. He would tell me that in a finite life, one should look back with fondness. Instead of grief on a past loved one. But he was the one I lost. It was him.

I bent my head back up to take another glimpse at his body which I now couldn't bear looking it. He hung there, lifeless. Like he was a nobody. Like the greatest man I ever knew was just any other maniac, killing himself after realizing he couldn't escape the past. He was just gone. That was it.

I bawled. I kept my eyes on the ground, now in a kneeling position, letting the tears seep through my hands and into the carpeted ground. With every tear I felt, I hoped I would wake up from a nightmare. WIth every sniffle, I wished that none of this was real. I just couldn't accept it.

When my eyes finally dried, I stood up again. His body was still there. Perhaps I actually thought it would disappear. It didn't. I walked over to sit on the bed to gather my thoughts. As I looked on to the top of the sheets, I saw a brown piece of paper. A note.

I picked it up. It was addressed to me. It was written on a slip from the hotel. I realized it was my first time seeing his writing. I blanked out looking at it though. The writing was right in front of me but I didn't bother making out what the letters spelt. I began to make out certain words on the sheet, though I tried to intentionally keep my gaze blurry and unfocused. "Hope," he wrote at one point. "Pain." I gave in and began reading.

Marcus,

I'm sorry about what happened. I'm sorry about lying to you. I wish I had told you. It was the biggest regret I had along the way.

I hope you can at least keep the good part of me alive in your memory. I'll never be able to escape my past and I know that no one will ever forget what I did. I'm sure that by the time you're reading this, you'll know what happened.

But it's your choice how you take it. I guess it's like I always said. But I never thought it would appear like this. You can choose how to perceive this. But if what I did can't be forgiven, I understand. I probably deserve it.

I want you to know that for me, the worst part of it all wasn't that I had to face the consequences of what I did. I had already come to terms with that. I feared that you would have to endure the consequences. Consequences that had nothing to do with your actions. I had lied to you. I had tricked you. And it was killing me inside.

That being said though, I know that you're going to make it back. In the drawer beside the bed, you'll find the rest of my money. There isn't much. But take it, and take the 12A bus to Phoenix. Once you're there, head to 249 Haverstein Avenue. Look for Jake. He'll understand. He knows everything.

I'm sorry I failed you Marcus. But be strong. And understand that the world will always be the way you see it. Stay positive. If there isn't a way make a way. I will always believe in you.

It wasn't signed. Like he couldn't bear putting down his name.

"God dammit!" I yelled out. Why? Why him? He would have gotten through. After all he did for me, I was going to be there for him. I would take another trip back to New York for him. I would do anything.

I didn't care that he had lied. Because even with the lie, even with his flaws, he was still the best human being I had ever met. Why was it like this? Why him? He would have made it. Why'd he leave? Why?

I was almost furious now. I didn't know if it was at him, at myself, or perhaps at the world. I should have done something. I knew something was wrong. I could have told him I'd do anything. Anything for the man who saved me. But it was also the rest of them. Niyol could have helped everyone. He would make any place better. Why didn't he get a second chance?

I wanted to tear up the letter. Instead, I folded it and put it into my pocket. I felt miserable. I felt empty. I was broken.

There was so much that I could have done. But I didn't do any of it.

I sat down on the ground. It had been years since I had been alone. Now I was again.

109

I had to leave when the police came. I went outside and told them what happened. They took me to the station. Ran some tests. But I couldn't bear looking at Niyol's body again. I left my bag and the rest of my equipment in the hotel room, leaving with only the money Niyol had left me and the note he gave me. It was all I needed now.

The police helped me out with the bus lines. Soon, I was at the station, waiting for the bus to come. There was an older woman next to me. The road I was one would take me almost directly to Phoenix and to the office where I would be working. Soon, the blue bus came and I went and stepped into it. I deposited the money needed for a fare before walking down a few steps and sitting near where the driver and the entrance had been. I didn't realize that I was still wearing my baggy clothes. They were clean now, but in the hot Arizona weather, the people on the bus gave me stares. It was fairly empty, with perhaps one person sitting every two rows.

I tried to look outside the window behind me in order to take my mind off of things. There was just too much to think about. I felt like I was past the stage of denial but I was still very much in shock. It was like the whole journey was a dream, and I would soon wake up in New York. Maybe I would even wake up in Ridgefield. But no. I knew I could tell myself those things but it wouldn't change. I was here, on my way to Phoenix.

I hadn't even bothered thinking about the job until now. It was customer service for a phone company. What did that even mean? What would I be doing? I hoped Jake would understand. I was unsure about things but I knew that Niyol had worked it out. He always did.

"Hey, how long is this ride going to be to get to Phoenix?" I asked out loud, to the bus driver.

"40 minutes," he replied quietly and sternly.

Part of me wanted to demand for the driver to stop the bus so I could jump out. I didn't know what I would do if I did. I just wanted to lose myself out there. Run across the desert plains towards nowhere.

This is going to be better, I told myself. Hang in there. Just like Niyol said. It was peculiar how it was always his losses I thought about. Him losing his family and friends. I never thought he would be the one I would lose.

Suddenly, my silence was interrupted by a loud honk that followed a stop. It startled me and I got up to see what happened through the front windshield. The traffic was jammed. We were at a part on the road where the lane next to us merged into ours, and I saw a small blue sedan that was trying to get onto our lane, between the bus and the car in front of us. The bus driver honked again, furiously.

"Why are you merging now!" he yelled, with only the bus passengers being able to hear his voice. He was making frantic gestures through the window on the bus door to the right at the sedan. "God dammit!" he yelled again. Other cars were honking too, in an absolute ruckus.

The sedan was trying to get through in front of the bus but the bus driver wouldn't let the car pass. Once the green light far in front of us went on, if the bus driver paused for a moment before driving, the sedan would have enough space to drive into our lane and along the road.

"Stupid!" the bus driver yelled again, directing his anger at whoever was driving the sedan. I had enough. It was just unnecessary.

I got up and went over to the driver.

"Hey, calm down," I said to him.

"That stupid bitch is trying to get in," he said, quietly so the bus couldn't hear his profanity.

"Think about it from her perspective. It might just be a mistake. A one time thing. Imagine you were there-"

"I'd never be there," he said, angrily. "It's a rule. You're not supposed to cut like that."

"But hey. Jam her once we go and both of you end up pissed. Just let her go. She might just be feeling horrible right now. Let her go, and everyone ends up happy. Who cares if she isn't supposed to cut. It might just be a mistake."

He gave a sigh. "Fine," he muttered, as I went back and sat on the seat. I watched him, gauging his reaction when the light would change. Up ahead, the light turned green and the cars in front of us began to drive. He paused before he hit the gas pedal, as the woman in the sedan drove in front of us into our lane. Then, he followed, right behind her sedan.

I sat back in my seat, feeling as if that interaction somehow made me feel better. I knew it was what Niyol would have done.

110

Eventually, the electronic display read Haverstein street, and looking around me only to see that I really had no belongings other than the money and the note inside my pocket, I got off the bus once it stopped.

It must have been the late afternoon by now. But the sun was still high and it was still bright outside. I had completely lost track of time throughout the day. It had felt like it had been ages, but I had only found Niyol dead around noon today.

I got off and looked around me. We had already passed through the downtown area of Phoenix and we were now in a suburban area on the other side. I walked down the road we were perpendicular to. Everything was more spread out now. But up in front and to the right of me, across from the intersection I had gotten off at, I could see a brown building that spanned a large width. This was Haverstein street for sure.

I kept walking until I was standing right in front of it. In big silver letters, I saw the numbers of the address I was looking for. It was here.

The building was large in width but it wasn't too tall. It was rectangular and one storey tale, except for a part above the central entrance that extended up.It also extended forward, making the each side behind the centre by a bit. It was a rectangular prism shape that displayed the company name in silver letters on the front.

ARIZONA CONNECT, it said.

The building was mostly symmetrical, its brown cinder-coloured bricks extending equally in both directions. The double glass door in the front had a blue tint and the company name was clear on the door, creating negative space over the tinted background.

Around the building was sparse grass. The the right of the building, a moderately sized distance away, was a fast food joint. The buildings in this area were mostly isolated and not connected to each. But as far as I remembered, it wasn't too far from downtown Phoenix.

On the sides of the entrance in the front, there were small shrubs planted in the ground below the windows that gave a uniform look to each side of the building.

What if Jake was against Niyol? WHat if Jake felt that Niyol deserved being kicked out? I was worried. But I knew Niyol that Niyol knew what to do. This would work out just fine.

I opened the doors and walked through. I suddenly felt a comforting breeze of air from the air conditioning. I stepped forwards and opened another set of glass doors, before being greeted by a secretary behind a brown semi-circular desk that had a white marble top.

There was a brown-haired woman who was around 30 years old. She had her hair tied back in her bun, and due to the height of the desk in front of her, I could only make out the top half of her face and her hair.

"Hi, how may I help you?" she called out.

"Hi, can I see Jake?"

"I'll ring him out for you. Are you Marcus?" she asked.

I felt a sigh of relief knowing that my arrival was expected.

"Yes."

I heard a small beep.

"Jake, Marcus is here for you," she said into a machine.

"He'll be out in a second," she said to me.

I nodded my head before looking around. The room I was in was small and the area behind her semi-circular desk took up a large portion of it. Behind her, the company name was once again etched into a glass oval that was placed on the wall. The ceiling was fairly high and comfortable. On the left and right sides of the room were glass walls that featured a glass door in the middle that presumably led into a larger room. I could see the blurs of people behind the glass wall and I could hear faint talking. To the right of her, there was another door that was black with a square window in the upper middle of it. Perhaps that was the manager's office, or possibly someone else's. The entire area was very clean though, and it felt like a haven from the hot sun outside. The building felt fresh and new. It felt like a place where I wanted to be.

The door on the right opened, and a man in a suit walked out. He was of a similar skin tone to Niyol. He wore a royal blue suit with a black tie. He was short, but he had his black hair slicked back with gel. He had strongly defined cheekbones.

"Hi, I'm Jake, I'm the manager here," he said, reaching his hand out for me to shake.

"Marcus," I replied.

"Here, let's go in here for a bit."

He led me to the black door, pulling it open. I followed him in. Inside was an unoccupied desk with paperwork all over it. The room wasn't too big and there was a large whiteboard on the wall.

"Hey, I'm glad you could make it. I know it's hard," he said to me. "But I'm going to do anything I can to help you."

I nodded.

"Niyol told me about you. And I know Niyol's a man of his word. I know you haven't got that much experience but I trust that you'll learn quickly."

Something struck me the way he talked about him. It was like Niyol was still alive. I thought about him, calling Jake and telling him about me, perhaps knowing that he would end his own life. I pictured him beside the phone in the hotel room, with a rope by his side, doing whatever he could to help me and make sure I ended up okay. I could feel myself turning read and breathing heavily.

"Did you hear about it?" I said with a whimper.

He nodded. "I wasn't at the phone. I heard the message. He told me you were coming today or tomorrow. And then he-"

Jake began to crack too.

"He just said goodbye. I wish I was there."

I could see tears in his eyes.

"It was only this morning. I tried calling back. It's bullshit. We grew up together. He was the greatest man I ever knew. I just can't believe they did this to him."

By now, I was crying too, as the tears on his face began to drip down faster. He stepped towards me and embraced me in a hug as I could feel myself sniffling. I cried and cried. I could feel my tears dripping down my cheek and landing on his shoulder on his blazer.

I cried. I felt memories flash before me. Sitting by the water and fishing. Making a fire for the first time. The time he made me tea when i got sick. There was just so much.

I cried. I thought about where I was before. I had been beat up while working for a criminal. I was alone and lost. Now here I was, a new person, and it was all thanks to Niyol.

I cried. He was my only friend. My only one. The reason I still marched on. I had to do this for him. I couldn't let his work go to vain.

We let go of each other as he stepped back.

His eyes were now red and he was sniffling.

"We grew up together. I thought the day he got kicked out would be the worst day of my life. But I guess it's not. It's bullshit what they did to him. He was the greatest man I ever knew."

"Yea," I said softly.

"It's going to be alright," he said, quickly and with heavy breaths, as if he was determined to do whatever he said.. "You're going to be fine. I'll set you up with everything for now. Niyol told me you'd be worth it and I'd do anything for him.I didn't see him for years. But you? I can't even imagine how you're feeling."

He reached over to the text and pulled out a tissue and wiped his eyes. He pulled another one out and handed it to me, which I used to dry my eyes.

"Here, forget about work for today. You've been through enough. We'll start the orientation tomorrow. I'm sure you'll do fine. I'll show you the room I've got for you in my house for now."

He walked towards the door. "Here, let's go," he said, as I followed him out the door.

Somehow, just knowing that he cared about Niyol too made me relieved. I had just met him, but having someone who saw Niyol as the amazing man he was just made me feel safer.

He brought me to his car, and we drove off, as the sky began to dim.

111

The bedroom he gave me was far more spacious than I could have imagined. It was a moderately sized home in a residential area. It had a white exterior. Jake showed me into the bedroom, which was very big and had a large queen-sized bed that had a green and pink flower pattern on the blanket.

"Is this really for me?" I asked.

"Yeah. It's only temporary though. I'm in the process of finalizing the rent of an apartment. I'll cover the cost for you for a month."

It made sense that he would put me in my own place. It would be far too awkward staying her with him.

"Really?" I asked, still surprised at how much he was doing. It was incredible how far he'd be willing to go.

"Anything for Niyol. And I trust that you'll do well at your job."

I sat down, looking around the room.

"Do you want anything to eat?" he asked.

"No, I think I'm good." I felt somewhat hungry, but I was more tired than anything.

"Here, I'll go get you something to wear."

He went out the door and soon after, he came back with a pair of white pajamas he tossed to me.

"Thanks so much," I said to him. "What time do I need to go tomorrow?"

"I'll wake you up," he said to me. "Night."

"Night" I replied.

Thanks, Niyol, I thought to myself as I lay back into the bed.

112
Jake woke me up at around 7 am. There was a digital clock in the bed. I woke up in a pool of sweat, almost forgetting where I was. He opened the door and when I heard his voice, I began to piece everything back together, realizing where I was.

He also came in and tossed some clothes on to the bed before he went out of my room again. I looked over. It was a light blue dress shirt as well as brown khaki pants.

"I hope they fit," he said. "Try them on."

I got up out of bed. My skin felt wet under the fairly tight pajamas. I took them off and put the dress shirt on, buttoning it up. It had been years since I had worn something like this. The shirt felt tight and slightly uncomfortable. But I still felt blessed being able to have it. I pulled the pants on, which fit much better and I stepped out of the bedroom.

Jake was already sitting at a table eating cereal. Across from him was another bowl. I wasn't sure if it was for me or if it was for someone else.

"Is that for me?" I asked.

"Yea," he replied. "I only live with my fiancee and she's in Boston for a business trip."

I sat down, munching down on the cereal. It was sweet and crunchy and the cold milk tasted great and hydrating. After we finished, he collected the bowl and utensils and put them into the sink. Then, I followed him outside as we got into his car again. It was a small white sedan. It had a sports look to it and it had a shiny clean exterior. We got in and began to drive back down the road we had gone on yesterday.

The air felt cooler with the windows rolled down. His radio quitely played some soft music. It was a country song, one that I didn't recognize.

Jake must have noticed that I was looking at the radio. "You want me to change it?" he asked.

"Nah, it's fine," I said, not wanting to bother him.

"Don't worry about it. Here, what do you want? Rock? I'll play my disk. You ever heard the Queen is Dead?"

"No," I said.

"It's a good one. Pretty old rock though."

He reached above him and pulled out a disc that he put into his audio system. The system buzzed for a moment, making a humming noise as the disc was being read. Then, there was a click, as the pounding of several drums came in. And then a synthesizer beat.

It sounded awfully familiar.

Then the voice came in. An unmistakable low voice that gave a nostalgic crooning of the lyrics. It was the same song Diane had played me.

"There is a light that never goes out?" I asked him.

"Yeah," he said, surprised. "How'd you know it?"

"I had a friend before. This was one of her favourites."

I sat back, listening to the tune of the verses, before the powerful chorus came in. it was powerful, and I felt my mind being filled with memories of everything that happened before. Meeting Diane for the first time. Our rooftop conversation that night. Even the last moments we had together. The last goodbye I said to her.

But it felt different. It wasn't gloomy anymore. THere was no regret. It wasn't a dark part of my life I wished I had never endured. Instead it was bright, it was joyous, it was gleeful. Diane was a light in my life. And now I knew she would never go out.

I almost forgot about the wind that was reaching my right shoulder from the opened window. It now felt relaxing and I felt at peace. The smiles Diane gave me, the moments we had together. They were all something special that I had the chance to hide. Sure, everything ends. But so often it never even happens.

The song eventually came to an end as the next track on the album began to play. We must have almost been there by now, as I had lost track of time as the song played.

"What will I be doing for the job?" I asked Jake.

"I think for the first year or so I'll have you as an assistant. Helping a group of 6 customer service reps. It'll mostly be note taking and file storing. But after that, we'll see."

"Ok, sounds good," I said, glad it was something that didn't seem to challenging.

"Here we are," he said, we we pulled into the same building we had met in yesterday. He got out swiftly and went to the door, pulling it open for me to walk in. I followed him in, as he greeted the secretary at the front and led me into the room on the left of the secretary's desk.

It was very large and was made up of rows of booths. People had headsets on and some were speaking into them. There were around four or five rows of desks, and behind the desks, on the far side of the room towards the back, were several whiteboards and meeting desks in glass meeting rooms. I counted three meeting rooms in total. Around the room there were also water dispensers and office equipment, including printer and photocopy machines. The area felt vibrant. There was a good mix of people of native, white, asian, and black descent and there was also a mix of men and women. People were dressed nice but not too formal. Most men just wore a dress shirt and women wore varied tops with skirts.

"Hey, Jake," called a man as we walked by him. We were walking along the row of desks where people had headsets on and the man was standing on a corner, drinking a cup of water.

"Is this the new guy?" he asked.

"Yeah," Jake replied. "Marcus, meet Dave. He's our director of operations. Dave, Marcus."

He reached out his hand and I shook it. He was a tall, buff black man with a strong grip. He looked like he was in his forties. He had a pink dress shirt on with several pens in his chest pocket. Dave looked friendly and he looked like he was glad to meet me. It felt welcoming me and helped ease any more worries I had.

Jake led me into one of the glass meeting rooms and pulled out a big leather chair for me to sit in.

"Just one sec, I'm gonna go grab the people you'll be working with."

I watched him go out back into the large room. He went along the rows of desks, tapping people on the shoulder and saying a few words to them before they got up and followed him. He went around the desks, eventually gathering six people before coming back into the room.

"All of you, I want you to meet Marcus," he said. "Marcus will be starting out as an assistant. We'll take him through everything today and after that, if you need anything you go to him."

They all greeted me individually. They were all working as customer service representatives for the company, which was a telephone and internet service provider. They ranged in age. One man, named Josh, seemed like he was only in his twenties. Another woman, Linda, was much older, perhaps in her fifties. She was shorter, and her blond hair had streaks of grey that ran through them. They all seemed jubilant though, and I didn't feel any scorn at all. It was like they all already knew who I was. Though I had never seen the people before, it felt more like a reunion than a first meeting.

Then, they took me through an orientation. They showed me how to work the printer and photocopier, which I caught onto quickly. Then, they showed me how to log calls, first taking notes on a clipboard after a worker waved me over. The clipboards were all kept on a rack by the shelf and whenever I needed one, I could just go grab one. I would flip to a new sheet if there wasn't one on the clipboard directly, and I would write down the phone number the call came from, the reason for the call, and any notes that the representative had taken. After that, I would take the clipboard over to a computer on the far side of the row of desks. I used a general login to open the computer and used a tracking system to input data. The system was unfamiliar to me at first. But they were helpful and after some persistence, I was comfortable knowing where to click and where to go to perform whatever task was necessary. When no one in the group I was assisting needed help from me, I had free reign to go around the room. They encouraged me to check if everything was maintained. Everyone's goal was to refill coffee makers and water fountains right when they were finished, but often, someone had an immediate call and was unavailable. I didn't mind performing the tasks. I learned new things and it kept me active throughout the day.

Eventually, the clock hit 12 pm and everyone began to pull out their lunches. I looked on confused for a moment, as I sat next to Becky, another representative whom I was helping.

"Does everyone bring their own lunch?" I asked, unsure of what was happening.

"Yeah," she said, as she pulled out a salad. "Did you want my apple?" she asked, holding out her apple to me.

I declined it, feeling bad for taking stuff from someone I had just met. However, just moments later, Jake walked over to me and handed me a sandwich wrapped in tin foil.

"I hope you like beef," he said. I chuckled. "Yea, for sure," I replied. He smiled and walked away again.

I opened it up. The roast beef smelled good. I took a bite, tasting the bread, the beef, as well as a sweet-tasting sauce. It was savoury and nice and even though it was just a sandwich, I was glad that Jake had made it for me.

"So where are you from?" Becky asked me.

"It's a long story," I replied. "I was in New York. Then I ended up homeless, and after a few years, I managed to get here?"

"You were homeless?" she asked with shock, holding her hand up to her mouth to prevent herself from spitting anything else.

"Yeah. It was just a few months though."

"Wow, how was it?"

"Pretty bad. Like all the stuff you hear about happens and there's more beyond that. There just isn't much access to anything. Water, shelter, food is all hard to come by."

"But you made it, eh?" she said with a smile.

"Yeah, I did," I replied. I sure did make it.

It felt so weird now meeting people on the outside of it. The people I had met over the last few years all knew about my homelessness. It was either from my clothes, or the backpack, or the walking stick. But now, wearing the dress shirt Jake gave me, all of that was tucked behind me, in the past. I had a fresh start, one that my past didn't affect.

We finished up our food and I finished gathering the data from the call that Becky had just made. Afterwards, I recorded the data in a computer and by the later afternoon, the shifts of those I was working with ended, and so did mine, as the night time workers came in.

Jake left too, as I followed him back to his car.

"Do you feel comfortable?" he asked me as we stood beside his sedan.

"Yeah," I replied. "It feels good."

My mind felt clear and I felt excited. Niyol's death still lingered but the people here were nice and my job was pretty engaging.

"That's good," he replied. "Real good."

113

I had the weekend off, and so did Jake. After working for three days, I felt like I was completely settled in. There wasn't a moment when I didn't think about Niyol. But Jake was a good person too. He wasn't as wise and pragmatic as Niyol, but he helped me greatly while also working very hard for his job.

I woke up Saturday morning and once again, Jake had cereal ready. We had eaten the same thing for breakfast for the past few days but I didn't mind it. It had been forever since I had cereal and maybe I was just making up for all that I had missed.

"How'd you sleep man?" Jake asked me. He was dressed in green pajamas, a different sight from the suit that I typically saw on him as he ate his breakfast.

"Good. I'm getting used to everything."

"That's good. Hey, what do you say, do you wanna head out somewhere? There's somewhere I actually wanna take you to see."

"Sure," I replied. I didn't have much to do. I figured he was probably taking me to some tourist destination and it really wouldn't hurt to go out and see more of my new home.

We finished up our breakfast. I went back into my room and changed. The other day, we had gone out to get myself a wardrobe. It was more than I needed. I had two dress shirts, two pairs of dress pants, as well as shorts and sweaters to wear outside of work. I put on a pair of shirts and a white t-shirt. It was always hot outside and with the temperature only getting warmer and warmer as we approached the heart of summer, I knew that it would always be warm outside.

I followed him outside, as he grabbed a pair of reflective blue sunglasses. His hair wasn't as gelled today but it was still combed back. He worse a white tee shirt too but it was on top of loose green sweatpants. We hopped into the car again and he turned his radio on to a rock station.

"Where are we going?" I asked him.

"You'll see soon."

We drove in a different direction from where we typically went to get to the office building. Things looked the same though, from this side. Buildings were spread out just like the other side and the building styles vary from brick structures to newer white and silver areas that housed medical centers and research facilities.

Just moments later, when the first song that played wasn't over yet, Jake made a turn into a park area. There was a large area with grass and trees and I could see benches with people walking around.

"Here?" I asked.

"Yeah."

He shut the car down and walked out as I followed him. He went towards the grass and into the park. It was bright and green, with large stones of various colours placed around the park. There were white and silver ones, red ones, and brown ones. They also ranged in size, with some being knee-high decoratives while others were tall enough for anyone to sit on.

It was vibrant. It had a different feel than the one in Columbus. This one was warmer and didn't have a cityscape behind it. It was also more spread out, as the trees were far less dense.

Jake continued walking through the park. We kept walking along the grass, passing through trees and eventually, a playground. I was confused. Perhaps we only came to the park to walk through to go somewhere else. Maybe Jake was just walking around, breathing in the fresh air before we would leave. In the distance, I began to see a large metal cage that signalled a baseball field.We walked closer, towards the field, and finally, after several minutes of walking through the large park, Jake stopped next to the field.

"This is where I last saw Niyol several years ago," Jake said.

"Did he come by before he left?" I asked.

"Yeah. By then I had heard the news. I was still working here back then. I didn't know what to make of it. But he came by at night to talk to me. At first I was skeptical. I didn't want to do anything with him."

Jake paused for a second.

"But then we played some baseball. Man, Niyol was good. I'm not sure if he ever told you about it."

I thought about it for a second.

"I remember him bringing something like that up. But he never talked about what he did."

"He was a monster. He could really hit the ball. We played catch for a bit before I threw some balls at him. He had a really big hit on one of them. The ball went sailing."

Jake gave a chuckle.

"He had the funniest swing too. It had a huge arc. But it worked."

I pictured them playing right in front of me on the field. Jake throwing the ball to Niyol. Niyol taking swings at it. I pictured them laughing, filled with smiles, trying not to worry about what was happening to them in the world.

"It was like everything was alright that night. I forgot everything. When we played, it was the same Niyol I had known before. He was never a criminal or anything bad. A good person who got killed because of a single mistake."

"Did he come by to play often?"

"Not too much. That's what made that night so special. I remember it as if it was yesterday. ANd then when we got tired, I asked him if he wanted to come over for dinner. He refused. Then we just said goodbye as I got into my car and drove away. I always thought I'd see him again afterwards. At least once. But I guess all I have is the memory now."

Jake didn't look particularly miserable. He almost seemed fond of the past, fond of the opportunity he had to be with Niyol. He was looking down and smiling, as I imagined him going through his memory of playing with Niyol.

"There's something else too," Jake said, after a noticeable pause.

"What is it?" I asked, after he didn't say anything for a few seconds.

"That apartment. It'll be ready by Monday night."

"Really?" I asked, surprised with joy.

He nodded with a smile.

"Thanks," I said, letting out a huge grin. Wow, I thought to myself. Now I was going to have my own permanent place to live.

We stood there for a few more minutes, staring at the baseball field. Thanks, Niyol, I thought to myself. Thank you for everything.

114

The apartment was small, but it was larger than what I would ever need. It was located in the suburbs in an area of low-rise buildings, around 5 minutes from Jake's house and 10 minutes from . It was on the top floor of the five-storey building, right along the edge of one of the buildings.

Jake had told me that he would cover the rent for the first month and that after that it was up to me. He had taken me up here and handed me the keys after walking in, but now he was gone, having left to go back to his own home.

The entrance led directly to the kitchen which was connect to a lounge that had a sofa bed. On the left was the washroom and right to the back of the room was a closet. I walked over to the sofa. It was brown and soft, and feeling tired, I took off my dress shirt and threw it onto the couch. I took my backpack with my belongings and opened it up on the couch, changing into a pair of pajamas. When I was finished, I raised my head, only to notice a different colour than what I had seen before.

To the right side of me, and directly behind the couch, was a window through which orange light gleamed.

I walked over to the glow of the light.

The sun wasn't blinding. I could see through the window, and in the distance, I could see two large round peaks of stone that the sun was setting in between. It wasn't blinding at all. In fact, it was magnificent. The glow of the sun illuminated all that was caught in the light while darkening all the rest. The mountains left a sliver, a crack of space that allowed the sunlight to spread out until it reached my window.

I took a deep breath, keeping my eyes fixated on the setting sun.

Here I was, standing in my own apartment. One that was for me and only me. It wasn't on loan from a crime lord, nor was it a one night stay in the midst of a long trip. I was here, with a job, in a city that I could really call my home.

It was only a few years ago that I was alone, in the streets. Lost, without a cause. I always imagined that a few years was a lot of time. A few years meant the difference between being born and being able to talk and play with other kids. A few years was the difference between starting off high school as an indecisive teen to becoming a young adult with a future and a vision in mind.

But none of those years were as life-changing as these.

But still, it felt like just yesterday when I was going through a dumpster looking for leftover tacos. When I was running errands and bringing dirty money between criminals. When I was hiking through the eastern US, with my feet aching and my back hurting.

What was it that Niyol had said? That time was an arrow that kept marching on?

It sure did. Everything that I went through, it mattered.

The love I felt with Diane. The lessons I learned from Niyol.

But there was also the bad.

Being tricked by Kevin and getting beat up by the other gang. Seeing Niyol's body hanging from the roof of the hotel room.

Could things have turned out better if I hadn't done anything wrong in Ridgefield? For sure.

But this was my life and this was the path I was given. I could dwell on the imaginary, wondering where I would be if things didn't go wrong. I could wish for a future where I was with my family, pursuing my dream career, living in the city that I grew up in.

Or I could live with the journey I had taken and I could relish. I would remember the connection I had with Diane. I would remember the new experiences I had along the way to Phoenix. I could show up to my new job every day with a smile, doing my best to get whatever I needed to do done. And I could live with the blessing that I had the chance to meet the greatest man I would ever know.

Because at the end of all this, I knew that it didn't matter how my life actually was. It was how I took it.

I knew that no matter what, the future was going to be bright.

I was a new person, with a new perspective on the world.

And I knew that I was ready to savour every moment in the future.

I was reborn.

EPILOGUE

115

I walked down the downwards escalator at the airport, eager to get to the ground floor as fast as I could. My arm still itched a bit from the new tattoo I had gotten, but I knew it would be worth it. My arrow was a different colour than Niyol's and it had a different style. It was smaller and blue, with the feather at the end being sharper and the arrow tip having more of an arrowhead shape.

I had worked at the same job for three years until I had saved up enough for a trip our east. Here I was, having landed in New York in the heart of August, ready to go back and see where I had come from. I was now the assistant operations manager, still under Dave. Jake had been promoted to work in a corporate office, but we were still good friends and we often had dinner together.

I went and hailed a taxi as I stopped outside, reaching my hand out to signal for the man to stop. I told him that I wanted to go to Ridgefield, as I got into the taxi and he began to drive off.

New York felt like it was the exact same even though It had been around ten years since I had been here. There were billboards lining the highway that clustered the skyspace. It was really different to the downtown areas of Phoenix, but even New York had a certain beauty to it. It was clustered, but everything was so connected. It made you feel like you belonged.

As we were driving, I noticed one billboard in particular. It had a familiarity to it. The face on it along with the name.

FRANCIS TONG.

I soon recognized the face. He looked really similar to when we were in high school. His jaw was long and his cheekbones were defined, and he had his hair gelled to the side the way he always did it.

Wow. He sure did make it big. He was a consulting executive and his billboard advertised his firm.

But I wasn't surprised. Sure, he had certain qualities that weren't the most likable. He didn't rub everyone the right way. But he worked hard and he was driven. And here he was, with a massive billboard beside the highway.

Wow, I thought again.

We continued driving down the highway. It was a long ride and the traffic was bad as usual but eventually, the buildings got less dense as we reached the sign that said Ridgefield.

From here, I directed him on where to go. The town was so small that upon reaching the center, there were only several paths possible, and I remembered which one led to my old home. But when we came close to the entrance of the street, I told the cab driver to stp, I paid him the fare, and I got out to ewalk.

It was scary how little changed. On the street that i lived on, I could almost picture my younger self standing there, in the same surroundings that were present today. The trees still draped over each side and the houses still looked old. Some of the graffitti that lined the white concrete walls in certain areas was now gone, having likely been painted over.

My old house jumped out at me. I had forgotten the house number, but upon seeing the porch in front of the entrance, I knew I was home.

I walked up to the door and knocked.

I heard some steps come to the door, and the door opened, with my mother standing there.

Her hair was now grey and she worse a pink sweater.

"Hi Mom," I said, with a smile.

"Marcus?" she asked.

I nodded.

"Oh my god!" she yelled, putting her hand over her mouth.

"Marcus I thought- I thought-I thought you were dead!"

I chuckled. "Not yet," I said quietly.

"Oh my!" she yelled again, reaching her arms out to hug me. She began to cry now, sobbing loudly. "I'm sorry, I'm sorry. It's all my fault. I should have known. I should have known that my boy was going to be okay. I'm so sorry. I'm so-"

"Mom, don't worry," I said, letting go of her. 'It's my fault. I was an idiot. I did things I shouldn't have done. I put you through so much."

She smiled, almost with gratification, like she was glad that I could finally own up to a mistake I had made.

"Come inside," she said, leading me in.

"Where's dad?" I asked, as I walked in.

"He's gone. I haven't heard from him in six years. You were right. He was unfixable. I tried rehab again. But I had enough. I couldn't deal with it anymore. I sent him away. He never came back."

"You did the right thing," I said, thinking back to all the times he would walk around drunk, yelling at my mother and beating me.

"It was too late. I should -"

"It's never too late," I said to her.

She smiled again, with each smile appearing wider than the previous one.

"Here, I'll make you some food Marcus. What do you want? I can do anything. Oh and I want to know what happened. Where have you been? You look tanned."

"Actually, mom, if you don't mind, could I come back here tonight for dinner? I want to go see some other things."

"No worries, sweetheart."

I walked outside, heading back to the center of Ridgefield. I felt a joy inside of me that I had never felt before. Family would always be family and though we spent years far apart from each other, I still wanted nothing but happiness for my mother.

The transit system was simple enough that I managed to make it to New York easily. After locating the area I remembered coming from, I asked around the street for a green market. Some people were clueless as to what I was saying but one man finally pointed me in the right direction. The market was still there and the sign was still the same, and from there, I knew exactly how to get to Diane's old apartment.

I walked down the street as the buildings once again got older and older. The five-story buildings turned into three-story buildings, before those structures became the brown buildings with fire escapes. I remembered the pattern in front of Diane's building. It was a ladder to the right that was several meters off the ground. But I didn't have to take the fire escape this time.

I walked into the entrance of the apartment building and took the stairs to the top floor. When I got there, I thought about where I had come from to figure out which direction I had to go in to reach the apartment in the top right corner of the building from the outside. I went to the door where I remembered her living, and I knocked.

I wanted to see her but I didn't know how I would react.

Instead, an older woman opened the door. SHe was perhaps sixty and she had short and curly grey hair.

"How may I help you sir?" she asked.

"Hi, do you know about the girls who used to live in this unit? I wanted to get in touch with one of them."

"I remember there being girls in here before I moved in six years ago. But it's been six years and I don't really know anything. Sorry."

"Thanks," I said, as she closed the door.

Perhaps there were no trails left to Diane. But I could only hope she was doing well. I could only wish that she was living somewhere better, even though she never actively wanted to change her situation. But I believed she could eventually do it. She could live in a nicer area, working at a different job. And I hoped she was in love with someone who loved her. I wanted that for her. She deserved it.

I knew there was one last place I had to see before I went back to my mother's house.

I walked down from Diane's house, following the road that I had gone down from the market. I kept walking, with my head tilted to the right, continuously eyeing the buildings on the horizon, looking for different colours. The apartment buildings turned into houses, but the stretch of houses seemed to carry on.

Eventually, I saw a different colour in the horizon. But it seemed to have a glimmer. I kept walking, picking up my pace until I reached it.

The townhouses were still there.

But in front of it was a large chain fence. The fence extended across the townhouses, and there were parts of the roof that were gone, and some of the townhouses were already halfway torn down.

A bright yellow sign was on the fence.

Demolition.

I kept walking along the fence, until I reached one house that looked awfully familiar. The black paint was still there and I could still see the fence door on the side of the house.

It didn't look nearly as menacing now, with the fence in front of it, with the house being set to be torn down.

I wondered how Kevin's empire ended. Maybe someone from within took him down. Maybe it was another gang. Perhaps he was still running it and had just moved somewhere.

Or maybe, like everything else, there came a time for his empire to end and for the townhouses to be demolished.

I turned around to look at what had once been the park. It was completely unrecognizable now.

There were fences lining the sidewalk, and in what used to be a vast barren area, there were construction vehicles along with piles of materials such as wood and metal.

Development in progress, it said on a sign.

I walked right up to the sign, putting my hands around the metal links in the chain and bringing my face close enough that it almost touched the fence.

I imagined how it was before. The abandoned playground. The benches. The lights on the other side. And most importantly, the beautiful stone bridge.

I wish they had kept that.

But now it must have been gone too.

I turned around and began to walk back.

Perhaps everything did have to end. The good, the bad. The joy and the pain. Everything lived its life out and would eventually disappear, never to be seen again. Kingdoms would fall, generations would end, and worlds would return to dust, only to live on in the faint glimpses lodged in the back of our memories.

Maybe that was just fine.

Maybe it was.

AUTHOR'S NOTE

I always wanted to write a book as a bucket list item. I wanted to do it so I could spent the rest of my life knowing that I had written one. But that was never enough motivation and I never actually started writing.

That really changed when I read the Wikipedia biography of Game of Thrones co-creator David Benioff. I read that he began his first novel on his own time. I realized that I had all the tools to do the same. I had a laptop to type with and I had an idea for a story. All I needed to do was commit to it. I chose to begin, and I wanted to test myself to see if I could actually do it

I began the project on September 16, 2017 and I finished on April 12, 2018. I wrote 91150 words, resulting in an average of approximately 436 words a day.

It really was an incredible journey. My senior year of high school was definitely the most turbulent, with grades and university applications to worry about. But throughout the process, I had Phoenix has a constant source of what almost felt like relief. It was my escape from the rest of life. I learned so much about writing and I can't wait to begin new projects in the future.

tl;dr: If you wanna do something just do it

94013481R00186

Made in the USA
Columbia, SC
25 April 2018